MW01611594

SHATTERED

By Donna Ball

Copyright 2012 by Donna Ball Inc.

All rights reserved. No part of this book may be reproduced in any form without the express written permission of the author.
www.DonnaBall.net

Published by Blue Merle Publishing
Drawer H
Mountain City Georgia 30562
www.bluemerlepublishing.com

ISBN-13:978-0977329687
ISBN-10: 0977329682

This is a work of fiction. All characters, events, organizations and places in this book are either a product of the author's imagination or used fictitiously and no effort should be made to construe them as real. Any resemblance to any actual people, events or locations is purely coincidental.

A slightly different version of this book was published under the title *Just Before Dawn* by Penguin Books. This edition has been updated for modern tastes and revised to suit the author's preferences.

Cover art by www.Bigstock.com

Chapter One

It was past midnight when the phone rang. Carol Dennison, still groggy from the muscle relaxants she had taken earlier, was jarred awake by an adrenaline surge that shattered her nerves and pounded in her chest. Two days ago she had slipped on a stepladder and aggravated an old back injury, and the sudden movement of sitting up sent a spasm of pain through her left quadrant from hip to shoulder. The numbers of her bedside clock were a blurry glow as she groped for the phone, knocking over a tissue box and a framed photograph: 12:18. Only drunks and emergencies called after midnight. It was always bad news after midnight.

She snatched the phone up in the middle of the third ring, half sitting, squinting in the dimness, trying to sound awake. "Hello?"

Silence. Carol's heart was pounding from the abrupt awakening and sheer irritation, and she started to slam the phone back into its cradle. She had the receiver an inch or so away from her ear when she thought she heard a voice on the other end. Scowling, she said again, "Hello?"

A soft breath, then a young girl's voice. "Mama?"

Carol's heart stopped beating.

The voice was high and small and shaking, as though with repressed sobs. The words came out in a rush, choked and almost indecipherable. "Mama, it's me, you've got to help me Mama, please ..."

Carol whispered, "Kelly?"

On the other end of the line there was a gasp, and silence, and a dial tone.

Carol sat there, holding the humming telephone for an unknown length of time. Only when the dial tone switched over to the raucous buzz that indicated a line left open too long did she remove the instrument from her ear. But even then, she merely placed the receiver on the bed beside her, as though the act of returning it to the cradle might in some way more permanently sever the connection that had already been broken.

She reached for the lamp, found it, and turned the switch. She picked up the photograph she had overturned and held it in her hands. It was an outdoor shot of a pretty teenage girl in a big straw hat, laughing into the camera. Long dark hair, green eyes that looked hazel in the photo, tanned skin. Kelly. Her baby.

She hugged the photograph to her chest, trying to stop the shaking, squeezing her eyes closed, pressing her lips tightly together. But it was no use. Tears seeped out, breaths turned to sobs. Carol bowed her head and wept.

One by one the lights in the upper floors of the big, multi-turreted house on the bluff switched on as Carol crossed the gallery from her bedroom, moved in front of the bank of cathedral windows that looked out over the ocean, and went down the three steps that led to another suite of rooms. The March wind hissed and grumbled in the night outside, and the roar of the surf was muted. The windows were misted with salty sea fog, and Carol could not have seen the watcher from the beach even if she had looked. And she did not look.

She turned on the final light and stepped into the tower room that had been her daughter's. Kelly had chosen it herself when they first moved in, even though it was smaller than the other room on that floor, the closet narrower, and the bathroom had only a corner shower rather than a tub. Kelly had been nine then, and she had been enchanted by the romanticism of the curving walls and bowed windows.

They had painted clouds on the ceilings and carpeted the floor in pale blue with a lavender- and-blue floral wallpaper. Her bed was canopied, and carpeted steps led up to a deep, comfortable window seat piled with cushions. Kelly used to spend hours there, reading or talking on the phone or watching for dolphins. Her father used to call her "the princess in the tower" and teased her by chanting, "Rapunzel, Rapunzel, let down your hair." When she was younger, Kelly had been delighted by that. As she grew older, her tolerance for her parents lessened in the way of teenagers everywhere, and the best she could manage in response to her father's teasing was a roll of the eyes and a disparaging look. Remembering that made Carol smile wistfully.

The room was exactly as Kelly had left it two and a half years ago. Tattered stuffed animals lined shelves beside her bed, their winsome innocence offset by the posters of Anime characters and Justin Bieber on the opposite wall. Bookshelves sagged with a collection that ranged from Golden Books to *Watership Down*. CDs and DVDs were scattered over the shelf that held her entertainment system. Her violin case was by the door, and Carol bent to touch it lightly, as she always did when she entered this room. She never opened the case, or took out the instrument, for doing so would seem to violate some unspoken rule of privacy that even now Carol could not bring herself to ignore.

On the desk adjacent to the window was a computer system which, at that time, had been state of the art. The new system had been a gift from her father—a "guilt gift", as Carol came to call them—right after the divorce, and Carol had been furious. He had bought the system without consulting her, presumably unaware that Carol had turned down Kelly's request for just such an upgrade two weeks before. Carol felt that large purchases like that should be earned, not given, and she ended up looking like a witch while her ex-husband accepted accolades from his adoring daughter. She hated it when he did that, and she told him so over and over again. They had had a big fight about it; Kelly had overheard and spent days glaring at her mother with accusing, resentful eyes.

Carol went to the desk and gazed down, remembering that fight, remembering the others, remembering the last one and the note that had ended it, propped up in front of the computer for Carol to find when she came home from work.

The last fight had been about a concert Kelly wanted to attend. Kelly was a responsible girl, mature for her age, and trustworthy in almost every respect. But the concert was in Tallahassee on a school night, involved a teenage driver, a van, and some college kids on spring break, and as far as Carol was concerned it was out of the question.

Kelly had tried to overrule her by going to her father, who was by that time living in Tallahassee and who, in the way of newly divorced fathers everywhere, would have done anything to make himself look good in his child's eyes. And if it also involved making his ex-wife look bad, so much the better. He took Kelly's side immediately and, in fact, his arguments sounded solid. He would be there in case of trouble. He could even pick Kelly up after the concert and take her home to spend the night with him. He would drive her home the next day.

But Guy was a reporter for a television news station and he did not even give his last report until eleven p.m. The nature of his work was immediate and unpredictable, and his hours were never regular. If he should get called out on a story, Kelly would be placed far down on the list of his priorities, perhaps even forgotten. Carol refused to change her position.

Guy argued with her, but finally was forced to support her decision. Kelly had accused Carol of turning her father against her. Carol accused Kelly of trying to turn both her parents against one another for her own selfish ends. Kelly screamed that she hated her and ran from the room.

In her heart Carol knew it was not the concert Kelly was furious about as much as it was the cumulative assaults—real or imaginary—on her already turbulent adolescent psyche. The divorce had been hard on her. She was having trouble in school, and everything Carol tried to do to help only alienated her further. In retrospect, she should have seen it coming.

The note said, "I'm not a child anymore and I can't let you go on treating me like one. Don't worry about me, I can take care of myself. After all, I've been doing it most of my life."

She had taken with her a cloth backpack and, as close as Carol could tell, one or two changes of clothes. Naturally, they assumed she had gone to the concert.

But Kelly did not turn up in Tallahassee, and the friends with whom she was supposed to have gone had neither seen nor heard from her. A week passed, and another, and Carol was frantic. Then she got a letter, postmarked Tallahassee. In thin, wavery handwriting it said, "I am fine. I'm going to Hollywood so you won't hear from me for awhile. I have money. Watch for me in the movies. Love, Kelly."

That was when Carol knew her daughter was in real trouble. And she had not heard another word from her for two and a half years.

Mama, you've got to help me....

The room still smelled faintly of Kelly, of childhood lilac and young woman musk, of crayons and makeup and computer paper and baby powder ... or perhaps Carol simply imagined it. Most likely she did, but she still liked to come here sometimes and breathe that scent, and feel close to the child she had lost. Tonight she needed that comfort more than she had in a very long time.

She went to the window seat and curled up there, still holding the photograph of her daughter. Outside the wind gusted and the surf tumbled, and the windows were opaque with the reflection of a cloud-blue room. Carol sat for a long time, hugging the framed photograph, feeling the chill of the windowpane through her nightgown, remembering.

It was close to three o'clock when the lights went out, one by one, as Carol once again crossed the gallery, moving before the big windows, and went back to her room. At last that lamp was extinguished, and the big house was in darkness.

Only then did the watcher move on.

Chapter Two

Did you call the police?" Laura Capstone divided the last of the coffee between two mugs and brought one to Carol's desk. She cupped the other mug—the one with the #1 REALTOR 2010 emblazoned on it—between her hands and sat on the edge of Carol's desk, a worried frown on her face.

The offices of Beachside Realty were located in a bright coral clapboard building at the corner of Pacific and Main. If you came to St. Theresa-by-the-Sea you saw it; it had become something of a landmark for tourists and residents alike. "Turn right at the orange-colored building" and "Go past the coral real-estate building" were common phrases in any set of directions—even those given by other realtors. Laura Capstone and Carol Dennison had been partners in Beachside Realty for almost fifteen years, and most of the dramas, mundanities, and fantasies of their lives had been played out within the walls of that bright coral building.

Laura had been there when Kelly was born, when Carol divorced, through that dark desperate time after Kelly disappeared. Carol had been there for Laura through three marriages, innumerable boyfriends—each one less suitable than the last—and the deaths of both parents. They had built a business together, they weathered storms together. The turbulence of their individual lives left their friendship unshaken and there were no secrets between them. Still, Carol looked uncomfortable and unsure as she related the events of the night before to Laura, and it was a moment before she answered the question.

Finally she shrugged, a little irritably. "And tell them what? They weren't interested when Kelly disappeared. What makes you think they'd listen to my report on a phone call from her?"

Laura said, "That's not entirely fair, Carol. The police did everything they could——"

"They put her on a runaway hotline!"

"That's standard procedure, they explained that to us at the time."

Carol's hands tightened on her coffee cup. "That's standard procedure for ordinary runaways."

"But they had no reason to believe she was anything else! You had two notes from her, one telling you she was leaving and another one later telling you not to look for her——"

"I told them that second note wasn't from her! It didn't even sound like her. You know it didn't. And the handwriting was all wrong."

Laura said gently, "The handwriting analyst didn't think so."

Carol drew in a sharp breath for retaliation, then caught herself with a shake of her head. This was all familiar ground and she didn't want to argue with Laura. Laura was not the enemy.

For a moment they were silent. The sun painted a bright windowpane on the bleached wood floor, and the ocean was noisy enough to be heard even through closed windows, even from their location across the street. Outside the office, a telephone gave a muffled ring, and they heard Tammy, the receptionist, pick it up. They both waited expectantly for the intercom to buzz, but apparently the caller was not in need of a broker. They looked at each other and smiled, faintly and wryly.

In another month moments such as these, in which they had time for a leisurely cup of coffee or an uninterrupted conversation, would all but disappear. But it was early in the season, and most of the calls they received this time of the year were from college students looking for a place to rent for spring break. Beachside did not rent to students, so business was slow. They had learned to savor the moments.

Carol sipped her coffee, waited another moment, then said, "Anyway, the police didn't believe me then and they certainly wouldn't believe me now."

Laura chose her words carefully. "But… you think it was Kelly? I mean, after all this time, do you really think it's—likely?"

"For God's sake, Laura, you don't think that I'd make something like that up?"

Laura threw up a hand in self-defense. "Of course not! I mean, of course, you got a phone call, I'm just wondering if…"

Carol's voice, and her expression, were cool as she supplied, "You're wondering if I heard correctly."

"Or if it was some kind of sick joke or a wrong number or—okay, yes, if you heard correctly. I mean you've been zonked out on pain killers for the past couple of days—"

"They're muscle relaxants and they're perfectly safe."

"But why would she call, after all these years? And why would she ask for help and then hang up without telling you how to help her? You've got to admit, Carol, it all sounds a little—convenient."

"Convenient," Carol repeated blankly.

Laura's lips tightened and she looked for a moment as though she was uncertain whether to continue. Laura knew what Carol had been through when Kelly disappeared two and a half years ago; Laura had been through it with her. And there was very little she could say to help her now.

She said, with an extreme diplomacy that she did not usually find it necessary to exercise with her best friend, "It's just that the police never had even a shred of evidence that Kelly was anything more than an ordinary teenage runaway. You were the only one who was certain she had met with foul play. And this phone call— a sobbing girl calling you Mama and asking for help—it seems to prove your theory, doesn't it?"

"For God's sake, Laura do you think that's what I want?" Incredulity and agitation propelled Carol out of her chair, and she paced the few steps from her desk to the window. "Don't you think if I were going to make something up I could come up with a better fantasy than that my fourteen-year-old daughter is being held captive and can't even make a phone call for help?"

She hugged her arms so tightly that her fingers left sharp crease marks in the sleeves of her linen suit, a sign that she was holding herself together through sheer force of will. The morning sun on her pale and puffy face was not kind, testifying to a sleepless night, tears, stress or perhaps all three. Her makeup had been carelessly applied, her short blond hair finger-combed. Her eyes, squinting a little in the bright, ocean-reflected light, were grim and haunted.

"Sixteen," Laura corrected quietly.

Carol turned.

"Kelly was fourteen when she left home," Laura explained. "She would be sixteen now."

Carol's shoulders sagged; she dropped her gaze. She released a long low breath and with it she seemed to shrink like an inflatable doll slowly losing air. She lifted a hand and wearily pushed it through her hair. "God," she said, "I know that."

After a moment she gave a small apologetic shake of her head. "I'm sorry if I snapped at you. It's just that ... the truth is, I'm not sure it was her, you know? I mean, how could I be?" She looked at Laura with eyes that were troubled and unsure. "It's been two and a half years! She was crying and I was half asleep but ... I keep thinking, what if it was her? I can't get it out of my mind. What if she was on the street and she only had enough money for one phone call? What if she's been in jail or in an institution or, God, I don't know, on drugs or something and all she had was this one chance, this one little moment when she could get to a phone and remember my phone number and ..."

"Carol, don't torture yourself." Laura was swiftly beside her, embracing her shoulders with one arm. "This isn't like you."

"I know." After a moment, Carol took a long, unsteady breath, and tried to straighten her shoulders. "It's just that... it really threw me. A young girl's voice, calling me Mama, crying..."

When she trailed off, Laura said sympathetically," But it didn't sound like her at all, did it?"

Carol shook her head wordlessly.

"Oh, honey." Laura gave Carol's shoulders a sympathetic squeeze. "What an awful thing. After all you've been through, to have something like this happen just when you were finally getting over it."

Carol shook her head. "You never get over it. It's a nightmare that never ends."

She walked back to her desk and picked up the coffee mug. She gazed at the contents but made no move to drink. "You're probably right. A wrong number, a misunderstanding, a sick practical joke ... or I dreamed the whole thing. In a way, I almost hope that is what happened. It's easier than thinking she's out there somewhere, needing me——"

"Carol," Laura said firmly, "no mother ever fought harder for a child than you did when Kelly ran away. No mother ever tried harder to help her before she left. Whatever has happened since then isn't your fault, and God knows it's out of your hands. Please don't start beating up on yourself again."

After a moment, Carol managed a strained smile, and she sipped her coffee. "I suppose you're right."

Laura hesitated. "Did you tell Guy?"

With a grimace, Carol resumed her chair. "God, that's all I need."

"He's her father. If it does turn out to be anything, don't you think he has a right to know?"

Instead of answering, Carol began to shuffle through the folders on her desk. Her relationship with her ex-husband was complicated, and did not lend itself to easy replies. So much of what had gone wrong with their relationship was tied up with Kelly, and so much of what still linked them together revolved around Kelly, that it was difficult at times to know where hurt ended and need began—even now.

Their marriage had begun deteriorating long before Kelly's problems started, of course, and the fault had been with Carol as much as with Guy, though it was she who had finally and inevitably borne the responsibility of asking for the divorce. When Kelly disappeared, the hurt and anger of separation was still too fresh on both their parts for trust to survive; reckless accusations had been thrown back and forth about her motherhood and his fatherhood, blame had been cast irresponsibly, and instead of joining together in crisis for the sake of their child, they had turned against one another, working oftentimes at cross-purposes and to no avail. Months had passed before each of them, privately and alone, had learned to forgive the other—and themselves—for the things that were said and done at the peak of fear and crisis. And though now that Guy had moved back to the island, they were in many ways closer than ever, the peace they maintained was often an uneasy one. She did not want to talk to Guy about this. Not until—or unless—she had to.

She said, changing the subject, "What a week. First I lose the Kerrigan listing, then I almost missed that closing yesterday.... It's no wonder I'm having nightmares. Have you seen the folder on Porpoise Watch? I had a callback message."

Laura took the hint and let the subject drop. "Yes, they called again before you got in this morning." She took the folder from her desk and handed it to Carol. "They're coming in at ten and they sound pretty serious. They're looking to rent for the whole season, maybe buy if they like what they see. I thought if Porpoise Watch doesn't work out, you could show them Sea Dunes. We had it booked for June, but the party cancelled, so it's free for the season."

Carol gave another shake of her head as she glanced over the message slip. "I have never understood why anyone would want to spend the summer in Florida. Fortunately for us I don't have to, hmm?"

Laura grinned, relaxing a little now that Carol's mood seemed to be back on course. "You got it. Besides, this isn't Florida, it's Paradise. It helps to remember that when you're showing $3500-a-week rental property."

"I think I'll have that laminated on a key chain."

Carol's smile, though faint and not very convincing, faded altogether as she looked again at her friend. "Do you know what I think is bothering me the most? The thought that some mother's child, somewhere, was crying out for help ... and no one will ever know."

Laura wanted to say that she understood, but the truth was she didn't. Instinctively, she knew that no one could ever understand the pain that was in Carol Dennison's eyes unless she had first experienced motherhood. And Laura was ashamed of the relief she felt when the phone rang and she could put Carol's problems aside in favor of those she did understand, and could do something about.

Chapter Three

Well, I guess my official quote is that St. Theresa County welcomes all visitors—as long as they abide by the law. Unofficially ...” Sheriff John Case rocked forward in his chair, balancing his linked fingers flat on top of his desk blotter. “You could take the whole lot of the jive-talking, bare-assed, horn-honking drunks and goose march 'em right into the Gulf and me and my deputies would manage to be otherwise engaged in an important poker game at the time. I'll tell you the truth, Guy, this whole goddamn business has gotten out of hand. In my day it was a privilege to go to college, something you worked hard for and were damn proud of. Now it's just an excuse to run wild at taxpayers' expense. Things are too damn easy for kids these days, that's the whole problem. Everything is too damn easy.”

Guy grinned. “Now are you going to tell me how you won the goldfish swallowing contest and crammed sixty people into your Stutz Bearcat, Granpap?”

Case tried to frown but his own reluctant amusement won out. "Yeah, okay, so I guess I pulled a little mischief in my day, too. We all did. The trouble is..." And his grin faded. "The kind of shit we did was just that—mischief. I'll tell you the truth, Guy. I'm fifty-two-years old, and when I was twenty, I couldn't even think of the kinds of crimes kids are committing today just for fun."

"Come on, John, we're talking about spring break, not the L.A. riots. Don't you think you're overreacting a little bit?"

The sheriff's expression was impatient. "St. Theresa County averages one reported rape every three years, maybe two grand thefts and half a dozen burglaries a year, twelve or fifteen possession arrests. Between March fifteenth and April fifteenth of last year we had six rapes, two grand-theft autos, an average of three break-ins a night, and a hit and run. I'd have to break out the computer to even tell you how many D&Ds, driving under the influence, and possession of controlled substances we brought in. And we're sixty miles from Panama City. We're just getting the leftovers. I'm telling you, it's getting way, way out of hand."

Guy was jotting down notes in his cramped, all but illegible shorthand as he spoke. "How much do you estimate it costs the county to host spring break?"

"Host is a bad choice of words. Tolerate is more like it. As for my guess—it could get as high as a couple of hundred thousand dollars a week. Of course, that's just in public property damage, court costs, overtime for emergency personnel, and now the county attorney is telling us we've got to hire lifeguards for the beaches even though eighty percent of them are under private ownership. Now, that wouldn't be a lot if we were Gulf

County, but we've got limited resources here. I couldn't hire as many temporary deputies as I need even if I had the budget—they just ain't to be found, you know what I mean? Same with EMS and the fire department. And you need to talk to the Coast Guard and the Marine Patrol about how their business goes up during spring break. I tell you, it's out of control."

"So how do we control it?"

Case shrugged. "We can't. It's greed, you see. We've got four hundred and sixty motel rooms in St. Theresa County—you figure six kids to a room—and maybe two hundred rental houses open this time of the year, and you can get ten, fifteen kids easy into a one of those beach houses. There are maximum occupancy laws, but who's going to enforce them? And what about the merchants that cater to college kids? March first like clockwork and here they come, like the goddamn swallows to Capistrano—T-shirt stands, head shops, surf shops, skateboard rentals ..."

Guy smothered a grin. "I don't think they're called head shops anymore, John."

"Same difference." Case waved an impatient hand. "What it amounts to is no better than a sign over the freeway saying This Way to a Good Time. Nothing's going to change until A"—he ticked it off on the index finger of his left hand— "we pass an innkeeper's ordinance with some teeth in it and B"—second finger— "The merchants stop targeting kids and transients. In other words, roll up the welcome mat and slam the doors, just like they did in Fort Lauderdale— only do it before we turn into Fort Lauderdale."

Guy said, "March is not exactly a boom month for tourism in St. T., you know. A lot of realtors refuse to rent to spring breakers, but those who do seem to be pretty happy with the profits. And some of the merchants and restaurants reported making one third of their yearly income in March last year. So what do you think it's going to take to get them to roll up the mat?"

"When the bill for damages is more than their profit," Case replied promptly. "I just hope it doesn't come to that."

"Or maybe," suggested Guy with a smile, "we could impose a special tax on spring breakers and put it into the sheriff's department budget."

"You're joking, but that's not such a bad idea. What people don't realize is that maybe spring break only lasts a month, but the mess we're left to clean up can go on for years. Take that Conroy kid, disappeared during spring break last year. Now the parents are claiming somebody saw her here, in St. T., the day she disappeared, so I've got to assign an investigator. And that was not even in my jurisdiction. As far as I can tell, that kid's just another runaway—hell, they get dozens of them every spring break. What makes this one any different? She's going to turn up walking the streets somewhere—"

He broke off abruptly, a faint red line of embarrassment creeping up his neck as he realized what he had said and to whom he had said it. Guy kept his attention on his notes and his expression unchanged, and in a moment Case went on, a little self-consciously. "Anyway, you ask me, the worst thing that ever happened to this county was taking down the toll booth on F. W. Jackson Bridge. Not too many troublemakers will pay five dollars each way to get to the scene of the crime, if you know what I mean."

"Not too many tourists, either."

"Like I said."

Guy flipped his notebook closed, smiling. "Sounds like another article, John."

Case gestured toward Guy's notebook. "You're going to make me sound like a real son of a bitch in this one, aren't you?"

Guy reached for his jacket, which he had tossed carelessly across the arm of the chair, and absently brushed at the wrinkles as he stood. "Toughest gun east of the Mississippi," he assured him.

"Well, as long as you spell the name right." Case walked him to the door. "So how'd you get stuck doing piss-ant little stories about spring break, anyhow? Seems like I remember you from much bigger things."

"Didn't you hear? I got a promotion. I get to pick my own stories now."

"And you picked spring break?" Case gave a sad shake of his head. "I hate to tell you, my friend, but that ain't the way to becoming a prize-winning reporter."

"Yeah, well you do me a favor and be sure to give me a call the next time the Democratic party holds its national convention here."

Case grinned. "Hell, I'd probably just get your answering machine. 'Gone fishin,' it'd say."

"Yeah, you got me there."

They had reached the outer office and Guy paused, glancing around casually. Two deputies, a man and a woman, were at their computers, filling out up reports with that pained hunt-and-peck method favored by law enforcement officers everywhere. Maryanne, the dispatcher, had her earphones on and was talking to someone about a dog—lost or found, it was difficult to tell. Static and muffled voices came from her scanner as the units talked back and forth to one another, and in another part of the room a tinny-sounding radio was tuned to a country-western station. Garth Brooks.

Guy glanced toward the back wall, where a steel door separated the jail from the offices. He said, keeping his tone negligent, "So what's the story on that guy the state police brought in?"

Case's eyes narrowed with amusement and mild incredulity. "You sneaky S.O.B., you suckered me right in. You tie up a busy public official with an hour and a half of bullshit about spring break——"

"More like forty-minutes." Guy lifted a shoulder toward the jail. "So how about it? 'According to Sheriff John Case.'

"He's gone," Case said.

"Yeah, I know. Four o'clock this morning."

"So there's your story." Case turned back toward his office.

"Big-time drug pusher, huh?"

"Come on, Guy, all we did was store him. And you know how the state boys feel about locals riding on their coattails."

"So what'd the state police ever do for you?"

"Cute."

"I heard you confiscated eighty kilos."

Case grunted. "Where are you getting your information? More like a hundred eighty."

Guy gave a low whistle, scribbling in his notebook. "False bottom in the trunk, right?"

"Wheels. Jesus, what are you writing this down for? Nobody said you could have the story."

" 'According to an unnamed source ...'" Guy quoted, not looking up. "What's the street value?"

"You figure it out. You know more about this shit than I do."

"I'm flattered. What did you do with it?"

"What?"

"The coke."

"It's evidence. The state's sending a crime lab van for it."

"Meantime?"

"What do you mean, meantime?"

But his eyes betrayed him with a sliding glance toward the steel door that led to the jail, and Guy burst out laughing.

"Are you kidding me? You're holding several hundred thousand dollars worth of high-grade cocaine prisoner in the county jail? Now, that's a headline."

"Goddamn it, Guy—"

Guy put his notebook back in his pocket, still chuckling, and slipped on his coat. "Now do you see why I love working here?"

"Now you listen here, Guy—"

Case was starting to look alarmed, so Guy said, "Relax. I'm not going to say anything to impugn the integrity of your high office. You're too valuable a source." He pretended to think about that for a minute before adding, "In fact, in a county this size, you're my only source."

Case scowled at him, still disgruntled. "You better not forget it, either. That jacket looks like you slept in it."

Guy glanced down at the jacket, brushed again at the wrinkles, and said, "Damn. I've got a lunch meeting with the commissioners, too."

From her desk three feet away Deputy Marge Albrecker spoke up, her attention focused on her computer screen. "Hang it on the shower rod with the hot water going full blast for fifteen minutes. It'll look good as new."

Guy glanced at his watch. "Don't have the time or the shower."

Marge grinned at him as she got up to collect some papers from the printer. "Then don't worry about it. People expect reporters to look rumpled—it's part of their charm."

"Yeah, I guess. Kind of makes me wish I was one." Guy lifted his hand to both of them as he opened the door. "Thanks for the story, John. You know my number if you think of anything you want to add."

Case replied sourly, "Nothing you'd want to print, Ace."

Guy grinned and stepped out into the salty Florida sun. There were times, bleak, self-pitying times, when he wondered what the hell he was doing here. But on days like this—which outnumbered the bad days a good two hundred to one—he couldn't imagine why he had ever left.

If Guy Dennison's resume could be plotted on a chart, it would look like the world's longest roller-coaster ride. It began with a Wakefield, North Carolina, radio station and progressed to the Miami Herald, a giant upward curve. A sharp fall led to the position of general reporter on the Gulf Coast Sentinel and another, smaller, upward curve took him to investigative reporter on the Franklin County Summit, then a straight run to newswriter for WECV-TV in Panama City, and another giant leap to crime reporter for WLTL, Tallahassee. A sharp downward slope resulted in a job as staff writer for the Tallahassee Herald and then a small hill and a straightaway took him back to the Gulf Coast Sentinel as managing editor, which position he currently held with varying degrees of enthusiasm.

It was no secret that his lack of ambition had been a major point of stress in his marriage and no doubt a contributing factor to its ultimate failure. Carol used to accuse him—usually at high pitch and in strident tones—of going out of his way to disguise his talent lest someone offer him a decent-paying job, and sometimes he thought she wasn't far from wrong.

After the divorce, which for some reason took Guy completely by surprise, he had been seized by the need to prove Carol wrong, or perhaps by the unconscious hope that if he worked hard enough and became important enough, she would somehow love him again. Toward the end of his marriage, he had taken the television job in Panama City and refused to understand why it only exacerbated matters between Carol and himself—which anyone with any insight at all into the woman he loved could have predicted. He had left her home alone with a career and a demanding teenage daughter while he worked long hours sixty-five miles away, and he told himself he was doing it to please her. The truth was that he was escaping from something he didn't understand and couldn't control, and by the time he realized his actions were only punishing them both, it was too late. He let the tide carry him to Tallahassee because he had no place better to go, and was well on his way to becoming the most relentless television reporter in the state when he—inexplicably, most people said—left to write the news again.

Small-town newspapers were what he knew and what he liked and he no longer apologized for that. The occasional crooked councilman, the land-use debates, the small-time drug bust— those were enough excitement for him. He liked a paper where the managing editor could go out and round up stories, where county officials didn't care if he came to lunch wearing a wrinkled jacket, and where, when the mood struck him, he could turn the whole thing over to his staff and go fishing without worrying that the fate of the free world might be irretrievably affected by his absence. He liked knowing that, for as long as his career lasted, he never had to look at another gunshot wound or gangland-style execution or listen to a mother's choked, terrified voice describing the last moments of her missing child. He never, if he chose, had to even know about another missing child.

He lived on a boat. He owned a cell phone, a police scanner, and a television that picked up one station when the tides were right. When he went into a restaurant or a bar, people called him by name. Sometimes he was alone more often than he wanted to be, and he often spent more time regretting the past than he liked to admit, but he was, in general, satisfied with his life … or at least as satisfied as he ever expected to be.

The office of the Gulf Coast Sentinel was on the river side of town, a small brick building with a twisted live oak shading the crushed-shell parking lot. There was a sandwich shop on one side and a bait-and-tackle shop on the other, and half a block down, the paved road turned into a sandy track that led into the marsh. If St. T. had possessed a low-rent district, this would have been it.

The office was arranged like a beehive, with the reception/subscription desk centered in a small cool foyer that was decorated with Press Club awards and banner copies of memorable front pages. The reporters' room—three desks, six telephones, and a computer—branched off to the east, advertising to the west, Guy's office to the south, and the publisher and general manager's office to the north adjacent to the front door. Ed Jenkins, the publisher, was on the telephone and beckoned to him from behind the open door of his office as Guy came in. Guy waved to him and picked up his messages from the receptionist's desk.

Rachel, the receptionist, gave him an exasperated look as she noted the wrinkled coat he carried casually in his hand. "You know, you could save a fortune in dry cleaning if you would just hang your jacket up once in a while."

"What? You're supposed to dry clean these things?" He glanced through the message slips as Rachel took the jacket from him and, with an air of exaggerated forbearance, hung it on the coat rack next to the door. "Who is this?" He waved one message slip at her, the name of which he didn't recognize.

Rachel glanced at the message slip, puzzling for a moment, then said, "Oh, yeah. Some guy with a basement full of rats. He says he uses them to predict earthquakes."

Guy lifted an eyebrow. "In Florida?"

She shrugged. "According to him, we're due for a big one."

"So say the rats." He dropped the message slip into the trashcan by her desk. "I don't suppose Walt Marshall called, did he? We were supposed to take his new boat out this weekend."

"Not that I know of. This one fellow called two or three times, but he wouldn't leave a message."

Guy grunted and started for Ed's office. "Well, put him through if he calls."

"Who? The mystery man?"

"No, Walt. He's got a new Sea Ray and I haven't even seen it in the water yet."

"Who's that, Walt Marshall?" Ed was hanging up the phone as Guy came into his office.

"Yeah, have you seen his new boat?"

"No, but he was telling me about it last Rotary meeting. Says it can do forty knots in a high sea without even straining a gear."

Guy grunted. "That I'll have to see. We're going to try to take it out this weekend if the weather holds."

"That water's like ice."

"I don't plan to spend much time in the water." Guy sat down in a well-worn black leather chair and stretched out his legs. "Anything happen while I was gone?"

"A woman walked into the Sun Coast bank in Appalach, put a package wrapped in birthday paper on the teller counter, and demanded fifty thousand in cash. She said the package was a bomb. The teller handed over the money and the woman departed, leaving the package on the counter. In the mad rush to evacuate the bank, the package got knocked off the counter and the lid fell off. There was a slip and pair of panties from J.C. Penney inside, no bomb. The perpetrator, meanwhile, got half a block down the street when the dye bomb went off. The police picked her up in the laundromat on West Main, trying to wash the red dye out of her purse. WOMAN CAUGHT LAUNDERING MONEY. What have you got?"

"THREE THOUSAND SPRING BREAKERS DESCENDING ON ST. T. and ONE HUNDRED EIGHTY KILOS OF COKE BEING HELD PRISONER IN THE COUNTY JAIL. You get all the good stories."

"That's why they made me publisher."

"Oh, and the county commission voted to move the Barbecue Cook-Off to the weekend after Memorial Day because the mayor's wife is having surgery in Tallahassee Memorial Day weekend."

"What's she having?"

"Hysterectomy."

"Remind me to send flowers."

"You bet. Listen, it'll take me about twenty minutes to get this in the computer and then we'll start laying out the front page. What kind of art do you want to run with the headline?"

"Well, I'd like to have a picture of you and me on Walt's new boat."

Guy grinned. "Second choice."

"Excuse me, Guy?" Rachel leaned around the edge of the doorframe. "That man is on the phone again. Do you want to talk to him?"

"Who?"

"The one who keeps calling and won't leave a message."

"Does he have a name?"

"He just said to tell you he's an old friend. Do you want me to put him through?"

Guy glanced at Ed inquiringly, and Ed made an acquiescent gesture with his hand. "Take it here. I think I left the art folder with Jacobson."

He left the office and when the call buzzed through, Guy picked up the phone. "Guy Dennison."

"Well now, you're a hard man to track down."

The voice on the other end was a low, smooth drawl, generally Southern in accent, not particularly educated, and completely unfamiliar to Guy.

"Not usually." Guy sat on the edge of Ed's desk and, with absent curiosity, turned his calendar around to read the notations there. Nothing interesting. "Who is this?"

"Come on, now, Guy, you don't mean you've forgotten already. You're gonna hurt my feelings if you're not careful."

Guy said, "Listen, I'm pretty busy here, so if—"

"Let's just say you did me a service, once upon a time," said the man on the other end of the line. His voice turned harsh as he added, "And now, old buddy, it's payback time."

Guy's attention sharpened. "What are you talking about?"

He answered smoothly, "So how's that pretty little wife of yours, Guy?"

Something about the way he said that made the fine hairs on the back of Guy's neck prickle. He said, as casually as possible, "You know Carol?"

"Carol, yes." Too smooth, much too smooth. "She's a real looker, isn't she? And living up there in that great big house all by herself..."

Ed came back into the office, art folder in hand. With an abrupt motion, Guy, gestured to him to close the door, saying into the phone at the same time, "Who is this?"

The frown on Ed's face faded at the tightness of Guy's tone, and, after only a moment's hesitation, he closed the door. Guy pushed the speakerphone button and lowered the receiver gently back into the cradle.

"—really don't know, do you?" The voice, amused and contemptuous, sounded tinny as it filtered through the telephone speaker. "Hell, this is going to be more fun than I thought. Let me give you a little hint."

Ed and Guy looked at each other as the man on the other end of the telephone began to sing softly, "Mary had a little lamb, little lamb, little lamb..."

The sound was chilling in the hushed room. Guy felt it all the way down his spine.

And then the voice demanded harshly, "Do you know where your little girl is, Guy? Do you?"

Guy lunged for the telephone, snatching up the receiver in a gesture that was as futile as it was dramatic. Nothing but the cold, dry sound of the dial tone met his ear.

Guy looked at Ed slowly, his face white. It was a long time before he could speak. "Christ," he said shakily, and that was all he could manage. He sank into the desk chair and stared fixedly at the telephone until Ed came over and put a gentle hand on his shoulder. Guy looked up at him. And all he could do was repeat, softly, "Christ."

Chapter Four

T he town of St. Theresa-by-the-Sea—known affectionately as St. T. by locals—was technically one of three small islands which had once been a single unit. Little Horse Island—so called because it resembled a horse when seen from the air—was three nautical miles to the west, and had been separated from the mainland some time in prehistory due, it was thought, to undersea volcanic activity. Lighthouse Island had been created much more recently, when the channel was cut in 1972, neatly slicing off the northern tip of St. Theresa Island. The historic lighthouse, once one of the most photographed in the state, had gone with it, and was now a crumbling, if scenic, reminder of times gone by. Of the three, only St. Theresa Island was inhabited. Bordered by the Gulf on the west and south, an inlet bay on the east, and the Catchaw River on the north, it was a vista of scenic bridges, lush tropical vegetation, and expensive beaches. The nearest shopping mall was sixty five miles away, in Panama City. Tallahassee, over a hundred miles to the north, was the closest major center of commerce, and most people in St. T., like full-time residents on the other barrier islands that lined the "Forgotten Coast" of Florida's Gulf, contented themselves with making the journey to the city once or twice a month for necessities that could not be obtained locally. St. Theresa County, eighty-two-square miles of snakes and trailer parks, would have been bankrupt long ago were it not for the resort attractions of St. T. And in the resort business, profit meant real estate.

There were twelve thousand full-time residents in St. Theresa-by-the-Sea and thirteen real estate companies, each one of them fighting tooth and nail for its share of the exclusive beachfront lots, million-dollar homes, and inflated rental management fees. Beachside Realty was only a two-agent operation, but it held its own in the real estate wars, thanks in great part to the ambition and determination of Carol Dennison.

When Carol and Guy were first married, her ambition was a good thing; the only thing, sometimes, that kept three meals on the table. Guy was a cub reporter for the Miami Herald, making barely enough to support himself, much less a wife, and Carol was trying to teach elementary school in a city that was becoming increasingly violent, for a salary that was doing less and less to make ends meet. She studied for her real estate exam at night and when she made her first sale— a one-bedroom condo for $86,000—they celebrated with a nine-dollar bottle of champagne and started looking for a house.

The house they found was in St. Theresa County, where a group of savvy investors was just beginning to activate a plan for a luxury beachfront development in a little fishing village called St. Theresa-by-the-Sea. Carol and Guy both were disillusioned with Miami and were ready to try small-town life; Guy had an offer from the Gulf Coast Sentinel which almost, but not quite, matched the salary he was leaving behind and, most important, neither of them wanted to bring up a child in the city.

Carol went to work for Laura Capstone in the coral-pink building at the corner of Pacific and Main, and seven months later Kelly was born.

It never occurred to Carol to stop working. For one thing, they simply couldn't afford it. For another, she was really good at selling real estate; better, perhaps than she had ever been at anything in her life—even being a mother. She closed a half-million-dollar deal when Kelly was five days old, with the baby sleeping quietly in an infant seat on the floor of the lawyer's office. In fact, Kelly spent most of her preschool life playing on a quilt in the corner of the office, being passed from Laura to Carol, depending on which one of them had a free hand; or strapped in her car seat in the back of one of their cars while they inspected property or showed a house. Carol was helping to build a business, a community, and a future for them all. She didn't think in terms of sacrifices, not then.

They lived in eight houses before Kelly started first grade, always trading up until finally ending up in the rambling cedar three-story on a bluff overlooking the ocean where Carol still lived and in which Kelly had lived until the day Carol came home to find nothing left of her daughter except an angry note.

She had no need for the house now, of course. It was far too large for her and difficult to maintain. The taxes were murder and her money could certainly be more wisely invested elsewhere. But she couldn't leave the last home Kelly had known. Not when there was a chance her daughter might come back someday, needing her mother, or might call.

During the off season, the society of St. T. was divided into three distinct castes: the local working class, like fishermen and carpenters; the merchants, business owners and other full-time residents; and the real estate people, who were a breed apart. The bars and restaurants of the area inevitably catered to separate segments of society. Captain Jack's Seafood Shack, with its raucous music, dartboard, and pool room—also the best fried shrimp on the island, which was served on a paper plate to absorb the grease— was preferred by the working class. Bay Breezes, with its varied menu and peaceful bay views, was a favorite of families. Michael's Grille, centrally located oceanside and tastefully decorated, with its stunning views and restrained menu, was the perfect place for realtors to take their clients for lunch, and to gather after a long day's work to brag about successes and catch up on industry gossip.

Carol was by no means a regular at Michael's. If she didn't have a late appointment or a rental house to check on, dinner was generally a salad and a glass of wine, and she was happy to be in bed by nine o'clock. But Laura had insisted on dinner at Michael's tonight, no doubt because she didn't want Carol to sit at home alone and brood about the phone call from last night.

Carol was not the kind of person to sit by the phone and brood, but that phone call had opened the door to a lot of painful memories. She thought Laura was probably right: This was not a good time to be alone.

On a Wednesday night in early March the restaurant was less than half full, mostly with people they knew by name. They seated themselves before the big cathedral window that overlooked the ocean, where, for about ten minutes, they had a spectacular view of purple-shadowed surf tumbling against the shore while the last of the daylight faded away. Now the only view they had was of the dancing flames from the central freestanding fireplace reflected in the dark window glass, and a corner of the bar that angled off in the room next door.

"Things are looking up," said Laura with a firm approving nod of her head. "Porpoise Watch is rented for the season, and we've got somebody coming tomorrow to look at Pelican Perch—another full-season rental—and here it is barely March. Another month like this and we might be able to make our quarterly tax payment."

Before the economic meltdown, Beachside Realty had owned and managed between twelve and fifteen ocean-front houses. Now they were down to the five, of which Porpoise Watch and Pelican Perch were the original two. Although Laura was only half-joking about the quarterly tax payment, there had been times when the office expenses and both their salaries depended entirely upon the rental income from those houses. It was always a relief to have them occupied.

Still, Carol said glumly, "Another month like this and we might have to start selling T-shirts to make the mortgage payments."

Laura lifted an eyebrow playfully, twirling a pineapple spear in her drink. "Well, if it's only T-shirts…"

At Carol's lack of response, she shrugged and said, "Come on, kid, so you lost a couple of sales. It's not like you can't make them up before summer ends. Beach real estate is on the upswing, don't you listen to the news? Why are you so down on yourself lately?"

"Low self-esteem."

"Oh, right, that's always been your biggest problem. That must be why you've been president of the board of realtors only three times in the past five years, not to mention the ranking member of the million-dollar club for two years running and, frankly, I don't think I'll go on. I'm starting to depress myself. How's the swordfish?"

Carol shrugged disinterestedly.

Laura looked at her sympathetically. "Do you know what you need? A vacation. I mean, business isn't going to pick up here for another month at least. You know what spring break is going to do to the traffic around here in another month, and with your back acting up again, why don't you just take off for a couple of weeks?" She speared another forkful of pasta.

"But that's the trouble with living in Paradise, isn't it?" replied Carol wryly. "There's no place to go on vacation." Then, with an obvious effort to hold up her end of the conversation, Carol said, "Why don't you have a date tonight, anyway? I thought you and that pony-tailed fellow were on your way to becoming an item."

"Winston?" She waved a dismissive hand in the air. "Too weird."

Weird, in reference to Laura's dates, was a relative term, but Carol chose not to point that out. "I thought he was nice."

"He played with dolls, for heaven's sake."

"He collected," Carol corrected, "priceless antique porcelains."

"Which I suppose means he was in touch with his feminine side."

"What it means is that he had a steady income, which is a vast improvement over most of your gentlemen friends."

Laura shrugged. "Maybe that was the problem. I like my men a little more dependent."

Carol rolled her eyes helplessly.

A male voice spoke behind them. "Evening, ladies. Buy a sailor a drink?"

Laura glanced around, pretended to spot someone up front, and beckoned. "Oh, bouncer."

Guy pulled up a chair between them and straddled it backward. "Mind if I join you?" He reached for a roll from the basket.

Laura returned, "If you don't mind picking up the check."

Carol was constantly surprised by the way the sound of his voice could still make her heartbeat speed— sometimes with anger, sometimes with agitation or surprise, but always with anticipation. It was an instinctive thing, like a blush, that she could neither control nor explain. There was chemistry between them still, she supposed, and always would be.

At forty-two, Guy was lean and lanky—too lean, occasionally, because he sometimes forgot to eat—with brown hair that was thinner than it had been when Carol had married him, and a long, thoughtful face that disguised an acerbic wit. From her father Kelly had gotten her dark hair and her impish sense of humor; from Carol she had gotten green eyes and a tendency to worry. Guy never worried. That was only one on a long, long list of reasons their marriage had not worked.

Carol said, "What do you want, Guy?"

"A double scotch and a rare rib eye will do me just fine. Or don't they serve anything but pasta here?"

Laura smiled sweetly. "No carnivores allowed."

Sometimes it still gave Carol a strange feeling to look up and see Guy. Right after he had moved out, Carol kept tripping over the empty place in her life where Guy had once been. But knowing that she could see him, accidentally or on purpose, any time of the day or night, was both reassuring and disconcerting. When he had moved to Tallahassee, and Kelly was gone, too, the emptiness had taken on a life of its own, threatening to consume everything in its path. A world without Guy seemed to be a world that was very wrong indeed, like a world without stars or in which tides flowed backward.

But that was a long time ago. Carol had changed, Guy had changed, life had changed. And even after a year, Carol wasn't quite sure how she felt about having him back in town.

Guy said, "So how about inviting me over for a soak in the hot tub?"

Laura lifted her wineglass in a small salute. "In your dreams."

"Don't flatter yourself. I was talking to your friend."

Carol mimicked Laura's sweet smile. "What she said."

"Hey, I used to own that hot tub."

"You also used to have hair," Laura returned tartly.

"I resent that. Besides, I still have hair ... more or less."

"Not for long, sweetheart."

Guy glanced at Carol. "You know she really adores me, don't you?"

It was then that Carol noticed that Guy had torn a roll into three pieces, littering the white tablecloth with crumbs, but he hadn't eaten a bite. This was so unlike Guy that Carol's stomach contracted once, sharply, with consternation and concern. And then Carol glanced sharply at Laura. Was it possible that Laura had called Guy, after all, and told him about the distressing phone call? The only time Guy ever fidgeted was when he didn't know what to say—which was virtually never. But if he were trying to find a way to reason with his near-hysterical ex-wife before she fell over the edge of a breakdown, that might well put him at a loss for words—however temporarily.

The waitress stopped by and Guy ordered his drink. Carol discreetly nudged a bread plate toward Guy and waited until the waitress was gone to ask coolly, "What's on your mind, Guy?"

"The national debt, Mideast tensions, the decline of family values ..."

Laura raised her eyebrow to an exaggerated height. "All that in that tiny space? I'm impressed."

Guy said, "One of these days you're going to go too far, Capstone."

"Excuse me." Carol raised her hand in a plea for peace. "Who divorced this man, anyway?"

Laura retorted, "It's beginning to look as though no one did."

Carol decided that if Laura had set this up, she was a better actress than Carol had ever guessed.

The waitress returned with Guy's drink and he dropped the mangled pieces of bread onto the bread plate Carol had provided, looking mildly surprised as he realized the damage he had done.

Carol said, trying to neutralize the conversation, "So, Guy. Now that you're managing editor, what are the chances of featuring Beachside Realty in the Focus on St. T. section of the paper this June?"

He seemed to relax a little. "No can do. No favoritism under my command."

"Oh yeah, right." Laura's voice was heavy with her familiar sarcasm. "Like that feature you did on Walt

Marshall's marina wasn't favoritism. Everybody knows he gives you your slip for free."

Guy grinned. "Yeah, but I was never married to him."

"There's been speculation about that, too."

Guy ignored her, sipping his scotch. He said, in the same mild, almost casual tone, "Speaking of the newspaper business, I know you two charming ladies have followed the ups and downs of my career with rapt interest—"

Laura made a muffled sound of derision.

"So in that context I wonder if the words 'Mary had a little lamb' might mean anything to either of you."

Laura put on a pensive face. "Aside from the obvious connection between your writing style and the intellectual challenges of a nursery rhyme..."

Carol looked at him curiously. "Why?"

Guy turned to her and for a moment she thought he was going to answer. Then he tossed back another swallow of scotch and replied, "No reason. Just trying to see if you were paying attention."

But now even Laura looked interested. "Is something going on?"

Guy hesitated. "Interest rates are rising. Three thousand college students are set to descend on the Gulf Coast next weekend. Arlene Campbell is having a hysterectomy."

Laura tilted her head toward Carol confidentially. "I can't imagine why you ever left him. He's better than a radio."

Carol said to Guy, "Sometimes Laura has difficulty expressing herself. I think what she wants to know— what we both want to know—is what you're doing here,

Guy. Did you just stop by to annoy Laura, or is there something in particular we can do for you?"

"Yes to both. I realized it had been far too long since I had annoyed Laura, and I thought since I was in the neighborhood, I could walk you home."

"I drove."

"All the more reason. A walk on the beach will do you good."

Laura said, "I'm not sure I see the logic in that." But her gaze was alert and interested as she watched Guy. Carol knew then she wasn't imagining it. Something was wrong.

She forced herself to take a final bite of the tasteless swordfish, crumpled her napkin beside her plate and said, "Let's go."

"I haven't finished my drink," he protested, but took a final swallow and reached for his wallet.

"Whatever happened to leaving with the girl that brought you?" Laura objected, but not very energetically. The curiosity in her eyes only fueled Carol's own.

Guy said, "I think that only applies to barn dances and weddings." He placed two bills on the table and touched Carol's elbow, absently and protectively, as she rose.

Laura said to Carol, "If you're not in by nine in the morning, I will be calling the police."

And Guy replied, "Be sure to get my description right."

They walked down the fog-shrouded boardwalk that crossed the dunes between the parking lot and the building, and Carol hugged her arms briefly against the cold and damp. The wind, blowing over the water at fifteen or twenty miles per hour, could turn a March evening on the Gulf into one in New England.

"You were kidding about that walk on the beach, weren't you?" Carol said.

Guy, in his shirtsleeves, pretended to ignore the cold. "You used to love to walk in the wind."

"This seems to be your night for things that used to be, Guy." They reached the end of the boardwalk and Carol turned toward her car.

Michael's was upscale enough to have a parking lot that was both paved and lighted, and she did not need an escort. St. T was not the kind of place where women worried about anything except breaking a heel when they walked alone across parking lots at night.

Nonetheless, Guy escorted Carol to her car. Carol kept glancing at him, growing more and more curious about what was on his mind, but he walked with his head down, hands in his pockets, and his face in shadows, and he gave no hint as to what he was thinking.

When they reached her car Carol turned to him. "Just tell me. Did Laura call you?"

His frown was puzzled and distracted. "Laura wouldn't call me a son of a bitch if it took more than a minute of her time. Why?"

Carol was growing exasperated. "Then I really don't understand what all this is about, Guy. You track me down while I'm having dinner, spend twenty minutes exchanging insults with Laura, and all this just to walk me to my car? Is there a point to this at all?"

"Actually, I wanted to talk to you." His voice sounded tense, though he tried to make his tone casual.

"I wouldn't have guessed." She shivered again.

Guy opened her car door. "I'll follow you home."

Carol searched his face, but she knew from long experience that whatever Guy had to say would be said when he was ready and not before. She shrugged and got into the car. "Don't expect coffee."

He stepped out of the way as she closed the car door, and stood watching as she backed out of the parking space. Only then did he go to his own car.

Chapter Five

G uy didn't like to admit it, but his ex-wife made him nervous. He told himself she had made him even more nervous when she was his wife, but that wasn't true. The rules of marriage were simple and easy to follow: faithfulness, patience, compromise. But there were no rules to divorce, or if there were, he had not yet discovered them. And he never knew how to act around Carol anymore.

He was already feeling foolish for making a big deal out of what was doubtless nothing more than a feeble practical joke. After the initial shock, he had been able to shrug it off in front of Ed, and even minimize the whole thing in his own mind, until he heard that voice again, *Do you know where your little girl is?* and he felt sick inside. Because anyone who could joke about a thing like that was twisted indeed, and he was running around loose and he knew where Carol lived.

He pulled his ten-year-old Honda onto the under-house parking pad beside Carol's SUV—all the real estate people were driving sports utility vehicles this year, he had noticed—just as she was getting out. She waited for him at the bottom of the stairs that led to the front door. The security lights were on a motion sensor and had been triggered by her arrival. Guy could clearly see the impatience and irritation on her face as she stood shivering behind the windbreak at the bottom of the stairs. Her shoulders were hunched, her skirt plastered to her slim legs by the wind; her curls, tugged and tossed by the weather, fluffed around her face like a kewpie doll's. She looked small and fragile and deceptively vulnerable. Guy was glad he hadn't ignored the threat, however absurd it might turn out to be.

He hurried to join her and they went quickly up the twenty-foot-tall staircase. There was no point in trying to talk in the wind. Carol unlocked the heavy glass door on the first deck, and they stepped inside.

Guy did not miss the house and hadn't even thought to ask for any part of it in the divorce. It had always been Carol's place: She had earned it, she had chosen it, she had decorated it. He had never been much more than a guest there, which was probably why he had spent so little time at home. It was only when he came here now, after all these years of being away, did he realize there was something he missed about it: the smell. It smelled like Carol—a combination of her delicate jasmine perfume, salty breezes, and warm things baking in the kitchen—and that smell, he supposed, would always mean home to him.

Carol, still shivering, hurried toward kitchen. "All right, so I lied. I'll make coffee. I'm freezing."

The house, when it was built in 1998, had won a number of architectural awards for its open floor plan and innovative features. The entry level was basically one grand room with a vaulted teak ceiling, cypress walls, and gleaming parquet floors. A bank of windows, all different sizes and shapes, faced the ocean, and two sets of glass doors opened onto a circular deck. A spiral wooden staircase was set on either side of the cathedral-like room, one leading to two medium-sized bedrooms and baths, and the other to the master bedroom tower with its glass-enclosed garden tub. An open gallery, which Carol had decorated with green plants, bookshelves, and cozy reading areas accented with Greek statuary, overlooked the main level, with sliding glass doors opening onto a second set of outside decks. Access to the widow's walk, with its hot tub and observation telescope, was via another staircase tower in the master suite.

Carol had decorated the master suite in sea blues and greens, and the lower level in the warm tones of the beach—driftwood gray and sea-oat beige and pale coral. The kitchen area, which flowed off the great room, was a pleasant surprise of yellows and whites, copper pots, and hanging greenery. The kitchen had been the only part of the house Guy had really liked when he lived there—with the possible exception of the rooftop hot tub. Everything else had always seemed too put together, too magazine-cover perfect. Carol, ever the salesperson, was far more concerned with presentation than with livability, and always had been.

Guy said, "I'm surprised you've held on to this place for so long."

Carol replied from the kitchen, "I guess I just don't have the energy for a move. Besides, it's not a good time to sell."

Guy had made the same observation more than once over the years, and her reply was always the same. It would never be a good time to sell as long as the memories lived here.

There was a freestanding fireplace in the center of the room and Guy automatically started toward it and the basket of split wood on the hearth. Then he stopped, feeling foolish. It wasn't his job to build fires any longer, and he wasn't sure Carol would appreciate the intimacy of the gesture. It occurred to him that he would have felt far more comfortable building a fire in a stranger's fireplace on the first date than he would performing the same service for this woman who had shared his bed for fifteen years, and the knowledge irritated him.

He stood for a moment uncertainly a few steps inside the room, defeated once again by the intricacies of the rules of divorce. Scowling, he went to the kitchen and pulled out a stool at the counter.

"I'm not staying for coffee," he said abruptly, straddling the stool. "I just wanted to talk to you about something and I didn't know if you'd want Laura to hear. Truth is, I didn't think it was any of her business."

Carol turned with the coffeepot in her hand, curiosity and alarm darkening her eyes. But she kept her expression neutral, even light, as she poured the water into the coffeemaker. "Let me guess. You're filing for bankruptcy? You've come down with a social disease? Although I can't figure out why either of those should affect me."

"This is pretty serious, Carol."

"I know." She wiped her hands on a towel, but did not turn to face him. "That's probably why I don't want to hear it."

Guy felt bad then. Carol had had enough trouble in her life—God knew, they both had—and he didn't like to think he could be the cause of more. Maybe he shouldn't say anything. He didn't want to worry her needlessly. But if he said nothing and later something happened to her...

She was a grown woman, damn it. She could worry or not worry for herself.

He said, "It's just this. Some nut called me this afternoon at the paper. He claimed to know me from some time in the past, and I got the impression he didn't much like what he knew. He mentioned you, made some reference to you living up here all by yourself. I just thought you ought to know."

Carol turned slowly, the dishtowel still in her hand, her eyes big. "What?"

"It's probably nothing. Like I said, he was some nut. He wouldn't even give me his name."

"What exactly," Carol demanded, quietly and distinctly, "did he say?"

Guy wished intensely that he had never come. But it was too late to do anything now except answer. "Something about how I was hard to track down, and how was my pretty little wife, and were you still living up there in that great big house by yourself—that's fairly close, I think. And when I asked who he was, he seemed insulted that I didn't remember, and then he started singing 'Mary had a little lamb.' Said it would refresh my memory. I don't mind telling you, it was creepy."

He looked at Carol. She was frowning, clearly no more enlightened about the identity of the caller than he had been. He wished he could stop there. He probably should have. But he couldn't.

"Then he said," Guy finished, "he said, 'Do you know where your daughter is?' And he kind of laughed, and hung up."

He watched the color drain out of Carol's face, leaving it pinched and dry and paper-white. She said hoarsely, "My God." and the way she said it, the way she looked when she said it, told Guy that she was scared—and by more than just his recounting of a bizarre phone call.

He said, "Carol?"

She turned her back to him, bracing her hands on the counter before her and stiffening her elbows as though only by supreme effort could she keep herself upright. Guy got to his feet, but at the scraping sound the stool made, she threw up a hand to stay him.

"Wait." Her voice sounded choked. "Wait, I have to think."

He came around the counter, his muscles tense. "Listen, I don't think you should give this thing more weight than it deserves. You know how it is in the news business, you make enemies, you get threats, but none of it ever amounts to much. The only reason I told you was because—"

Carol turned, her expression composed, but her eyes still dark with turmoil. "Last night," she said, "someone called—a girl. She was crying. She called me 'Mama', and she asked me to help her and—then we were cut off."

The words hit Guy like a blow to the stomach, because his first instinct was to believe—of course, he believed, just as Carol did—it was Kelly. But it was an instant, just long enough to leave him feeling hooked and sore, a sailfish crashing onto the deck, and then his reporter's rationality reasserted itself.

He said, "Son of a bitch."

Surprise looked out of place on Carol's face. Clearly this was not the reaction she had expected from him. "What?"

Guy paced back to the counter, absently rubbing the back of his neck as he tried to put order to his thoughts. "This is—damn it, this psychopath, whoever he is, obviously has some kind of plan. Why the hell he would want to torment you—"

Carol said, confusion still heavy in her voice, "It was a girl who called. I told you, she—"

Guy gave a sharp shake of his head, turning back to her. "No, it's a setup. The same guy has got to be responsible for both phone calls. For some reason he hates us enough to use the one thing against us we're most vulnerable about. Carol, don't you have any idea who it could be? Think!"

Carol stared at him as though he were a creature she was seeing for the first time and she could not imagine how he had suddenly materialized in her kitchen. She said nothing for the longest moment; she just stared at him while the coffeemaker hissed and gurgled and the room slowly filled with the aroma of Jamaican brew.

Then she said, clearly and coolly, "Isn't there any room in your scenario at all for the possibility—just the possibility—that it might have been Kelly? That it might have been your daughter who was calling for help and that the man who called you today might know why? That he might even be responsible for whatever trouble she's in?"

Guy drew in a breath and for a moment he had absolutely no idea of what to say. In that moment the doors of time had somehow opened and he had stepped over the threshold and two and a half years into the past; same kitchen, same pain and accusation in Carol's eyes, same helplessness churning in his stomach.

The only way he could react was with frustration. "For God's sake, Carol, you can't be serious! Kelly's been gone two and a half years without a word. Now, suddenly, for no reason at all, she picks up the phone in the middle of the night and calls home—"

"It wasn't for no reason!" she cried. "She was asking for help, she was in trouble—"

"And this phone call just happens to coincide with one I get from somebody singing nursery rhymes and making veiled threats against my family—"

"Are you listening to yourself?" Her voice was shrill. "Do you hear what you're saying? Of course, the two calls are connected, and of course, the man who called you knows where Kelly is or maybe he even has her, maybe he's holding her against her will—and that's why she called me! Damn you, Guy, I can't believe you're taking this so lightly! Why didn't you call the police?"

He stared at her incredulously, his head reeling. It was two and a half years ago. He had stepped back in time. And he was just as horrified, just as miserable and helpless and enraged as he had been then. God, how long could she keep doing this to him? How long was he going to keep letting her?

He spoke coolly and deliberately to mask his anger. "I am not responsible for this, Carol."

"Oh, no, of course not! You're not responsible for anything are you?"

They stood with stormy eyes and tight lips, and the wall of hurt and anger between them was so thick it practically colored the air. He thought, this isn't right. They both were grieving, they both were scared, and instead of turning to one another, they were turning on each other, just as they had always done. Suddenly he was very tired.

His tone was subdued as he said, "You're probably right. We should talk to the police—separately. I'll have

Sheriff Case call you tomorrow. Meanwhile ..." He turned for the door. "Just be careful, okay?"

She said, "You think she's dead, don't you?"

He felt the words like sharpened knives strike between his shoulder blades. He stiffened his muscles against the pain, but did not turn around. He said, "I've thought about it, yes. After all these years with no word ... life is rough for a kid on the streets and, yeah, I've thought about it."

"You bastard."

Guy drew in another sharp breath but stopped himself from answering. He left the house without another word.

Carol stood there in the kitchen after he was gone, flushed with emotion and cold with fear, hating herself for the way she had behaved and hating him because he hadn't been able to stop her ... or because he couldn't keep the hurt away or he didn't know how to comfort her or simply because she was scared and he was there.

"Damn," she muttered softly and pressed her fingers briefly against her eyes to stop the sudden sting of tears.

She squared her shoulders and took one cleansing breath, then turned to pour a cup of coffee. That was when she noticed the blink of the answering machine light from the desk across the room.

She had never been able to ignore that blinking light, not in the deepest depression or most urgent moment, and she certainly couldn't ignore it now. She crossed the room and pushed the button. The tape rewound, beeped, and began to play.

The husky, desperately familiar voice took her breath away.

"Mama? Mama, I was outside today and I could see you. I could see our house. It was still there, just like it's always been. You've got to come get me, Mama. I can't get out of here by myself. Why don't you come get me?"

Carol could hear her heart beat, the air rushing in and out of her lungs, the last sputtering drip of the coffeemaker, the distant thunder of wind and surf outside. What she could not hear was anything else on the message tape, even though the reel continued to spin and she could tell by the blinking light that another message was now playing. The only voice she could hear was that voice, the same voice, over and over again. Kelly's voice. And those words, *You've got to come get me, Mama... . Why don't you come get me?*

Carol ran to the door and flung it open. "Guy!" she cried into the wind. "Guy!"

Chapter Six

SPRING BREAK COMES TO ST. THERESA-BY-THE-SEA

St. Theresa-by-the-Sea was discovered by the Spanish in 1716, forgotten for another hundred fifty years, then rediscovered by railroad magnate Henry Morrison Flagler. It has since remained the private paradise of a select few who call this part of the world home. But St. T. is now in the process of being discovered all over again—this time by the thousands of college students destined to descend on St. T next week.

According to the St. Theresa County Chamber of Commerce, St. T. has been playing host to more and more of these sun-and-fun-seeking youngsters since the toll gate on the F. W. Jackson bridge was eliminated in 2009. Last year, an estimated eight hundred young people crowded the streets, shops, and restaurants of St. T. at the height of spring break.

The students are attracted by St. T.'s pristine beaches and casual lifestyle, as well as the abundance of beachfront homes available for rent at off season prices during the month of March.

Although some residents express concern about the traffic problems, property damage, and general disorder attributed to raucous spring breakers, few merchants have been heard to complain. Ed Williams of Earth Treasures Book and Gift Shop reported an increased profit of almost one hundred percent in March of last year as opposed to the previous month. Earth Treasures features inexpensive jewelry, crystals, and semiprecious stones which have special appeal to young adults. Pizza-to-Go and Beach Combers reported a similar surge in business during spring break, as did most of the fast food and casual dining establishments in the city.

Sheriff John Case estimates a possible three thousand students will visit St. T. this year during the middle two weeks of March. Although the vast majority of students will be day tourists ...

He had to stop then, and reread that last paragraph. A possible three thousand students. Three thousand. The streets would be crowded with lithe, tan bodies, the music of laughter, the flash of flirtatious smiles, the air redolent with the scent of sweat and coconut oil and sweet young sexuality ... three thousand. Three thousand baby dolls, his for the choosing. His for the taking, his for the cherishing. His for the keeping.

His breath was coming fast and he felt a fine film of perspiration begin to form on his upper lip. He closed his eyes, took a few deep, cleansing breaths, and found his center. It was important to stay centered. Balance was at the core of all things. Those without balance were doomed to failure, for nature itself abhorred inequity.

Balance. It was a concept worth meditating upon.

He was startled out of his reverie by a beeping sound coming from the vicinity of his briefcase. Startled, yes, but he refused to be annoyed. He opened the case and took out his cell phone, which was emitting a high-pitched rhythmic alarm warning of low batteries.

Now he was close to becoming annoyed. The battery charger was on the boat, which meant he would have to do without his phone all day and two or three hours tonight while it recharged. This was particularly irritating, since he had charged it fully only two days ago and the battery was supposed to last for over forty-eight hours of continuous use. He hadn't used it at all.

He liked his phone; he didn't need it, but he liked it. And he wasn't at all pleased at the thought that it might be defective.

And then he noticed something odd. The power switch was on, which was why the battery was low. He must have left it on the last time he had used it. But no. He had recharged it since then. He couldn't possibly have left the telephone on.

Which could only mean that someone else had.

Hesitantly, hardly daring to believe what must have happened, he pushed the redial button.

A connection was made, and an answering machine picked up. He listened to the message in its entirety, and disconnected.

Breathing slowly and deeply, he put the phone aside. He focused on the blue, blue water, sand and shore, clean salt breeze. This was unexpected. But sometimes the unexpected was good. It forced one to reexamine, regroup to meet the challenge and sometimes, to allow wonderful surprises into one's life.

He could deal with this. He certainly could. In a moment, he opened the phone again and made another call.

Sheriff John Case estimates a possible three thousand students will visit St. T. this year during the middle two weeks of March. Although the vast majority of students will be day tourists, the sheriff's department points out that, under present innkeeping laws, the possibility exists for a serious overcrowding of the county's overnight facilities. Municipal agencies, points out Case, are unprepared to deal with those kinds of numbers. "St. Theresa County welcomes all visitors," said Case, "as long as they abide by the law."

Sheriff John Case pushed the newspaper away with a barely suppressed sigh and reached for his coffee cup. It was his fifth cup of the morning, but the morning had already lasted six hours too long.

He had worked an accident until midnight—a gruesome thing, with two dead—and had returned to the office to find the report filed by the Dennisons waiting on his desk. It had been too late to interview them last night, but he hadn't slept too well, thinking about it. Then at four A.M., he had been called back to the office with the report of a missing resident from Shady Homes Retirement Center. A three-hour manhunt had yielded the ninety-two-year-old man, perfectly safe and extremely confused, trying to break into an empty trailer a mile and a half away.

Case wasn't able to get both Dennisons in until nine o'clock, and he didn't like the story they told. He didn't like it because it opened up too many doors, left too many possibilities, presented too little evidence of anything at all. And because all of the possibilities were bad.

"So," said Derrick Long, the investigator he had assigned to the case, "you want to assume the incidents are related—the phone call to Mr. Dennison from the male, and the one to Mrs. Dennison from a female she believes to be her daughter?"

"Until you get some evidence to prove otherwise," said Case, "that's exactly what we have to assume."

Long flipped back through his notes. Long had only been with the department for a year, and he was a meticulous, deadly serious young man—an attitude, Case suspected, that was born out of a determination to prove himself worthy of the title "investigator" with the St. Theresa County Sheriff's Department. He needn't have worried. John Case had found him to be not only competent, but one of the brightest men under his command—otherwise, he would never have assigned him the Dennison case.

"Not much to go on," Long admitted after a moment. "I'll have wiretaps put on both their phones and do some checking into Dennison's background—who he might have pissed off bad enough to play this kind of practical joke—but my guess is we're not going to find much. Most of the time these things just wear themselves out."

Case glanced absently at the newspaper again. Focusing for a moment or two on unrelated matters was a way of keeping his mind clear for the task at hand. It was a trick he had used for years.

He said, "What about the girl?"

"That is disturbing," said Long, glancing back at his notes. "If it is Kelly Dennison—and what I've heard so far gives me no reason to believe it is—then we could have a real mess on our hands."

Case seized on his first statement. "What you mean, you have no reason to believe it's her?"

Long shrugged. "You heard the tape. She doesn't give her name. The father didn't even pretend to recognize her voice, and I think the mother would have started to back down if we'd questioned her a little longer."

Case frowned. "You an only child, Long?"

The detective looked a little taken aback by the change of subject. "Well, no, as a matter of fact. Two brothers."

Case grunted. "Me, I'm an only child. And I'll tell you what. I never, for as long as she lived, God rest her soul, called up my mother and said, 'Mama, this is John.' Who the hell else was going to be calling her 'Mama,' huh? Kelly Dennison was an only child. She wouldn't have given her name to her own mother."

"But somebody trying to make Carol Dennison think it was her daughter might have," Long observed slowly.

Case shrugged. Possibilities. They could drive a person crazy.

Long hesitated. "I've looked at the old case file, when Kelly Dennison was first listed as a runaway."

"She wasn't the first," Case said, "and God knows not the last. You grow up in a place like St. T., your opportunities are limited, if you know what I mean. The boys can look forward to a lifetime standing knee deep in fish guts and the girls to having a baby every year and getting knocked around no more than twice a year if they're lucky. They live on an island, for God's sake, and all they can see is life passing them by everywhere they turn. They best we can hope for is that they stay 'til they finish high school, but that doesn't happen very often either."

"Kelly Dennison didn't really fit that profile," Long pointed out cautiously. "She lived on the beach. Her folks were rich. She had pretty good grades, would have gone to college. She had it made."

"Yeah, well it might have looked a little different from the point of view of a fourteen-year-old. Her parents had just gotten a divorce, her grades were dropping, her friends were dropping her...."

"Drugs?"

"Could be. It doesn't make a lot of difference, though. She was messed up. A good kid deep down, but she just let everything get the best of her. Maybe she thought she could run away from her problems, maybe she was just trying to get some attention. But she had enough money to get her just about as far as she wanted to go, and there's nobody harder to find than a kid who's made up her mind she's not going to be found. You know that yourself. Anyway, after her mama got that second letter from her, postmarked Tallahassee, saying she was off to California to become a movie star or some such, it seemed pretty cut and dried to us. Another one bites the dust."

"Yeah." Long was frowning thoughtfully. "Except this one has a change of heart two and a half years later and calls her mama for help."

"Maybe."

"Begs her to come get her, only forgets to tell her where to come."

"Looks that way."

"What are the chances it is Kelly Dennison calling her mother and she's in collusion with this other dude somehow—hitting her daddy up for ransom or something?"

Case shrugged. Possibilities.

"Because she's going to a certain amount of trouble for a plausible story here. She says she can see the house. That means she's somewhere on the island, but she can't get to her mama."

"Fishy," said Case. "That's how the whole thing smells. Real fishy."

Long nodded in agreement. "I sure would hate for the kid to be involved in this. Those poor folks have been through enough."

"I won't argue with you there."

"My gut tells me we've got a hoaxster and a paid accomplice. But I'll check out all the possibilities." Long hesitated, then said, "I noticed that when the girl first disappeared, you investigated it as a possible kidnapping."

"Not for long. Her mother was hysterical, and you can't take chances. We had to follow up on every possibility, and I tell you, there were a few rough days and nights there before we got that second note."

Long looked down at his notebook, although it was clear he wasn't reading anything, just buying time. When he looked up again, his expression was reluctant and unhappy. He said, "I also noticed, during the first part of the investigation, Guy Dennison was a suspect."

Case did not respond for a moment. He sipped his coffee, he glanced at the newspaper, and he thought, Three thousand students. Jesus, what a mess.

He pushed up from the desk and walked over to the window, coffee cup in hand. He spent a moment looking out, searching for some way to get a handhold on a day that had already begun to spiral out of control. Then he said, scowling, "Get to work, Deputy. If this is a hoax, you bring me the prankster's balls on a platter. If it's not. . . just get me some answers, and get them soon. This time next week all hell will be breaking loose on our little island and we're not going to have any time to waste looking for ghosts."

"St. Theresa County welcomes all visitors," said Case, "as long as they abide by the law."

Sheriff Case goes on to add that, while his department will be fully staffed during the two weeks of spring break, no extraordinary measures are planned to deal with the crowds.

He smiled as he read the article for the third time. First there had been anger, then there had been amazement, then there had been simple amusement. Because it was funny, how things had a way of working themselves out for those who were patient enough. For those who had a plan.

And he had one hell of a plan.

At the center of it all, as he had been for three solid years, was Guy Dennison.

Before Dennison, he had had a wife, a kid, a job, and a house. Now he had nothing.

The most important thing in his life—the only thing in his life—was to make sure Guy Dennison ended up the same way. And he knew just how to start.

He smiled again as he glanced at the headlines. SPRING BREAK COMES TO ST. T and the subhead OFFICIALS PREDICT RECORD CROWDS. Three thousand kids, and an undermanned, under-budgeted sheriff's department. The law officers in this county were going to have more than they could handle the next couple of weeks.

A lot more.

Chapter Seven

L aura had finished the lead article and was just starting on COCAINE HELD PRISONER IN THE COUNTY JAIL, when she heard Carol come in. She folded the paper and went quickly into the outer office.

"How'd it go?" she demanded anxiously.

Carol noticed the empty receptionist's desk with dismay. "God, Laura, I'd forgotten Tammy had that dentist's appointment this morning. I hope you didn't miss any appointments waiting for me."

Laura waved an impatient, dismissive hand. "Don't worry about it. What did the police say?"

Carol slipped off her linen blazer and hung it on the rack by the door. She was scheduled to show second-and-third-tier property today and she had dressed appropriately: designer jeans, sturdy walking shoes, white silk blouse with a lace ascot, and navy blazer. The one thing Laura had always envied about Carol was her effortless sense of style. The second thing, perhaps, was her ability to look charmingly feminine even in jeans and a blazer, even with windblown hair and puffy eyes. Laura could have put on the same outfit and looked perfectly ordinary. But then Laura wouldn't have thought about the lace ascot.

Grimacing, Carol replied, "Me? I got a pat on the hand and a 'there, there.' For my big strong ex-husband, however, they practically issued an all-points bulletin for anyone who knows the lyrics to 'Mary Had a Little Lamb.' "

Laura stared at her. "You've got to be kidding. Did you take the answering-machine recording?"

Carol poured a cup of coffee with only slightly unsteady hands. "God, I didn't sleep a wink last night, thinking, worrying. Yes, I took the answering machine, and no, they didn't take me seriously. That is—let me see if I can get this right—they think it's unlikely that it is Kelly's voice on the machine. If it is, however, it's out of their jurisdiction because she was never officially considered a victim of a crime. As far as they're concerned, the telephone calls are family business—like Thanksgiving greetings or Mother's Day cards."

"Wait a minute." Laura's voice was incredulous. "Do you mean to say they actually stood there and told you that the message on that machine wasn't important?"

Carol sighed tiredly, pushing a hand through her curls as she sipped her coffee. "Not exactly. What they said was that it was probably a hoax—part of some scheme somebody out there has to intimidate Guy."

Laura frowned a little. "I didn't entirely get that part when you were explaining it to me over the phone this morning. They think this person who called Guy yesterday with the Mary-Had-a-Little-Lamb line is involved with Kelly somehow?"

Carol leaned against the receptionist's desk, sipping her coffee. "No. They don't think Kelly—the real Kelly—is a part of this at all. They think somebody is trying to get to Guy through me, and he's responsible for both sets of calls."

Laura's frown deepened. "That doesn't make a lot of sense, does it?"

"It's supposed to make sense?"

"What did Guy say?"

Carol dropped her gaze to her coffee cup. It was impossible to read her expression, but Laura could guess her feelings. Carol's emotions were the same whenever she had an encounter with Guy: anger, confusion, impatience, betrayal, hope, anxiety, and suspicion. Laura wondered how anyone who stirred up such strong emotions could ever be considered an "ex" anything, but she never said so. There were some subjects into which it was better not to delve too deeply with Carol.

"Guy thinks Kelly is dead," Carol responded briefly, and with the tone of a woman who has met the unforgivable.

"But—when he heard the voice..." Laura felt faltering and unsure, afraid that whatever she said would be the wrong thing. Kelly had been the closest thing to a daughter she would ever have and losing her had torn apart Laura's world with as much force as it had either Carol's or Guy's. With Carol, Laura hoped desperately that Kelly was alive and well somewhere, living out the life she had chosen when she left home. But with Guy, she saw too much on the news, knew too much about what life was like on the streets to hold out much hope.

Carol said, "He says it's not her voice. As though he should know! He probably wouldn't have recognized her voice three years ago, much less now."

Laura said quietly, "That's not fair, Carol. You know Guy adored Kelly."

Carol hesitated, then released a short soft breath of frustration. "I know. It's just—damn it, I don't understand that man! He's so sure this is some kind of trick and it's all tied in to someone he's involved with in some way—and he's got the police believing it too! They're so busy inventing conspiracy theories and tracking down strangers that they can't see the simple truth. Is this a prime example of tangled male logic and twisted male ego or what?"

"I wish I had heard that message," Laura said.

"God, it would turn your blood cold. The way she said 'I got to go outside today' as though it's not something she can do every day. And she said…" Carol's hands gripped the coffee mug as her voice tightened with intensity and barely repressed excitement. "Laura, she said she could see my house! That means she's close. With a clue like that the police should be able to find her in a matter of hours, if they'd only look!"

"Well, not necessarily," Laura answered with a note of apology in her tone. "You can see your house from almost any place on the island, you know, and from some places across the bridge with a telescope."

Carol frowned thoughtfully. "Telescope. I hadn't thought of that. But still, it does mean she's close—whether she's on the island or across the bridge, at least she's not in California or New York, for heaven's sake. Why won't they look for her?"

"What I don't understand," Laura said, "is that if she's close enough to see your house, on the island or even over the bridge, why she doesn't just come home? Why call when she could walk to your door?"

The only possible answer to that was evident in the strained, tight lines of Carol's face, and it was horrible to see. Carol answered simply, "She said she can't."

"So what do you think happened?" insisted Laura. "I mean, why no contact for all these years and now, all of a sudden..."

She let the rest of the sentence trail off as Carol shook her head impatiently. "Who knows? It doesn't matter. She's been away, but she was on her way back and now she's in trouble. She sounds—" Carol swallowed, and Laura could tell the next words were hard for her. "She sounds strange, Laura. Something is really wrong. I've got to find her. She needs my help."

Laura hesitated. She still wasn't convinced it was Kelly who had made the phone calls, and she had no idea how this business with Guy's mysterious caller fit in. In the back of her mind remained the uncomfortable suspicion that it was all just a little bit too cryptic, too patly intriguing, to be genuine. And if even Guy didn't believe it.... Guy was Kelly's father. He was an investigative reporter. Surely he should know when he was being scammed, shouldn't he? And shouldn't Carol then take his—and the sheriff's—word for it?

The answer to that was simple and unqualified. Carol was a mother, and when it came to her child, she would rely on no one but herself. And Laura was Carol's best friend. She couldn't let her go through this alone.

She looked Carol in the eyes and she said, "What can I do to help?"

Carol smiled gratefully. "You've already done it. Just knowing that someone is on my side is more help than you can guess."

"I can do more than that," Laura said with sudden resolution. She went into Carol's office and returned in a moment with a framed, five-by-seven copy of the same photograph of Kelly that Carol kept beside her bed. "If she's in the county, someone has got to have seen her," she announced. "The one thing we know for sure is that she's got access to a phone, and where there are telephones, there are people. We'll have copies made of her picture and take them to every place of business on the island, and beyond if we have to. Someone has seen her," she finished with resolve. "All we have to do is find that person." Laura knew what an extreme possibility that was, and she suspected Carol did, too. But the hope she saw in her friend's eyes was worth any chance.

"She's close," Carol said, trying hard to keep the enthusiasm out of her voice. "She has to be, if she can see the house. Maybe—do you think one of the other realtors on the island could have rented her a place, or rented to someone she's staying with?"

"It's possible," agreed Laura, though they both knew it wasn't very likely. "We'll take her picture around to every office, and the hotels, too. At least we'll be doing something."

Carol looked hesitant, hope warring with the all too familiar defeat in her eyes. "It's an old photograph."

"I know. But teenage girls don't change that much between fourteen and sixteen. And a lot of people will remember Kelly when they see her picture."

Then Carol smiled. "I know this is really a long shot. And I can't tell you how much it means to me that you thought of it."

Laura felt a flush start at the base of her neck, and knowing she was blushing embarrassed her more. She said quickly, "Meantime, you won't believe who called for you this morning. Ken Carlton!"

Carol looked blank.

"You know, the architect?"

It took a moment, but Carol made the connection. One couldn't be seriously involved in real estate development in Florida without having at least heard of Carlton. He had become famous for his cluster community designs, which adapted themselves particularly well to the flat, featureless land of south Florida, and now was receiving acclaim for his spectacular waterfront innovations. Where Ken Carlton went, it was well known, money surely followed.

Carol was intrigued despite herself. "What did he want with me?"

Laura shrugged. "That's what I wanted to know, particularly when there was someone much more attractive, available and, er, open to suggestion if you know what I mean—right here in the office when he called, all of which I took care to point out, of course. But he insisted on you. Did you know he's not even married?"

"Always a plus," murmured Carol.

"Maybe. But if he turned me down, he's probably gay. On the other hand, he hasn't even seen me yet. Anyway, apparently he saw your name on the sign in front of Sea Dunes, and says he's interested in renting it for the season. Can you believe that? I mean, with his money, wouldn't you think he'd just whip out a checkbook and buy a house?"

"Well, I'll see what I can do about persuading him of the wisdom of that. What time is he coming by?"

"I told him eleven-thirty. That way, I thought if you hit it off, you'd be more or less obligated to have lunch."

"You're too kind."

"Oh, I'm not being generous," Laura assured her. "I expect you to invite me." She grinned and waved the photo at her. "Meantime, I'll drop these off at the one-hour photo place and get some copies. We'll divide them up and we should be able to hit ten or twelve places each before close of business today. Tammy should be in at eleven, so if Mr. Moneybags gets here early, go ahead and leave."

"Don't worry, I'll give him the full treatment. But before he gets here, I can start calling realtors and see if any of them have rented to a family with teenage children in the last week or two—or to a group of teenagers. Whatever we do, we'll have to do it fast because spring break starts next week and——"

"Three thousand students," Laura remembered from the article. Her face reflected her dismay. "More than half of them girls."

Carol nodded soberly. "After this weekend, it'll be like looking for a needle in a haystack."

Chapter Eight

Ken Carlton was a nice-looking man, younger than Carol had expected, with auburn hair and gray eyes, and a friendly, direct gaze. He drove a Maserati and wore a Cartier watch—exactly the kind of client Beachside Realty liked to cultivate. He explained that he was investigating a possible development project in the area and wanted a convenient temporary location from which to conduct business. The careful way in which he avoided giving details about the project suggested a deal of major significance, and at any other time Carol's curiosity would have been excited to a fever pitch. Today she was barely able to arouse courteous interest.

Repeatedly, she tried to get the phone calls out of her mind and concentrate on the work, which was always her salvation from dark tormenting thoughts. But she found herself merely going through the motions as she gave the routine island tour, went into her sales pitch, showed the property, and waited for a decision.

And when he spoke, she literally did not hear what he said; she merely stared back blankly.

"I said it's more than I expected," Ken Carlton repeated with a smile.

Carol snatched herself back with irritation and consternation from the dark corridor of her thoughts, putting on a pleasant face for her client. For a moment she couldn't be sure whether "more than I expected" referred to the price or the view, but the contented expression on his face as he looked out over the ocean suggested it was a good thing. Carol relaxed.

They were on the upper deck of the property listed in their brochure as "Sea Dunes"—a spacious Mediterranean three bedroom with an infinity pool and Italian marble in the foyer—and the view was, in fact, spectacular. The water was that clear sun-sparked blue peculiar to the Gulf of Mexico and the sky a shade lighter. The March wind had just the hint of a bite to it, but the sun was warm enough to burn unprotected skin. Laura was fond of saying that the St. T. weather was the best salesperson in the world, and a day like this proved it.

Carol smiled and turned to the rail, gesturing up the beach. "My house is that gray one with the turrets and the widow's walks. It's a great house, but I bought it for the view."

Ken Carlton returned her smile, tilting up his sunglasses as he moved his gaze from the beach to her face.

"I must be moving into a good neighborhood, then, if the realtor lives up the street," he said.

"Does that mean you'll take it?"

"I can't think of any reason not to. It looks like just what I had in mind. And since I'm going to have to be here for a while, it's bound to beat living on my boat—or in a tent on the beach. I've done so much of both these past few years I'm not sure I'll be able to adjust to having a real roof over my head again."

Carol responded lightly, "No camping on the beach. Also, no open fires or glass containers. This part of the beach," she went on when he chuckled, "is under private homeowner's association rules. And since every lot is a half-acre or more and only residents are allowed to use the beach, you'll find it's the quietest place on the island, even in summer. In the winter or spring, you practically have the place to yourself."

"How long have you lived here?"

"About fifteen years."

He raised an eyebrow in surprise and Carol laughed. "Some days it seems longer. We didn't even have cable TV out here for the first ten years, and they only put in the cell tower last year. If you can believe it, up until then we had to rely on the tower on the other side of the bridge, which means we didn't have cell service if there was so much as a heavy fog. We've been petitioning for a cell tower out here for almost five years, but the environmentalists held it up. I guess it finally got to the point that even tree huggers couldn't live without their cell phones."

"It can be a mixed blessing," said Ken with a shrug. "The places in the world where you can get away from modern technology are growing few and farther between every day."

"That's certainly true. Will you be commuting to Tallahassee much this summer, Mr. Carlton?" She had done enough quick research to determine that his office address was in the state capitol.

"I certainly hope not. I try to stay out of the city as much as possible."

They stood in companionable silence for a time, enjoying the sun. Carol watched as a small blue-and-green lizard made its way with quick darting motions up the rail between them, then said, "We'll circle around by the river on our way to the office. There are some beautiful properties there, if you prefer a marsh view."

He turned his attention for a moment toward the antics of the little lizard, which had reached the top of the rail and was now poised, head cocked intelligently, as it surveyed its surroundings. Carlton smiled and leaned on the rail again, looking at the ocean. "How many lots are still available in this section? Maybe we could take a look at a few of them after I get settled."

That was generally the kind of question Carol held her breath waiting for. An award-winning architect—one who had already admitted he was here to pursue development possibilities—building his dream home on one of Beachside Realty's prime oceanfront lots could bring a dozen times the price of the lot in new business and free publicity. Not to mention the fact that, if she played her cards right, Carlton might be easily persuaded to trust exclusive listing rights on his development project to Beachside, or even consider going into partnership with them on other major development plans. The possibilities were dizzying, and Carol had made her reputation and her success by assessing and exploiting just such opportunities.

But when Ken Carlton spoke, Carol didn't hear him. Her attention was on the beach, where a young girl with long dark hair tied back in a pony-tail jogged by in a pink sweatsuit. For a moment Carol's breath caught and she thought … incredibly, she thought…

But then the girl glanced in their direction, and there was no resemblance at all. Her face was too narrow, her eyes almond shaped, her skin dark; she was obviously of Asian descent. When Carol looked more closely, she realized the girl was shorter and plumper than Kelly and she wondered why she had ever thought there was a similarity.

Of course, as Laura had pointed out only this morning, it had been two and a half years. Carol had no idea what her daughter looked like now. If Kelly was still alive....

"Carol? Is that a problem?"

Belatedly, Carol registered his question and turned back to him with a smooth smile to hide her confusion. "Not at all. I was just trying to decide which lots you might like best. We have about a dozen beachfront listings now, but you might also want to look at some of the second-tier lots. They're bigger and even more private, and run about half the price of beachfront. Best of all, because of the building restrictions, you would always have an ocean view, even on second tier. Of course the second-tier lots are so lush with natural vegetation that they're practically pre-landscaped for you. That can be a real advantage with the price of landscaping these days, and you know how hard it is to get anything to grow at the beach."

He made a thoughtful sound of agreement. "I guess there are strict building restrictions about tearing up the vegetation."

"Some of the strictest in the state. We're on such a shallow little island here that the ecosystem is very fragile. Interestingly enough, the very sternness of the restrictions attract some of the most creative architects in the country. They like the challenge, I guess."

He grinned at her. "You're quite a salesperson, aren't you?"

Carol replied modestly, "It's what I do."

He said, "I might like to take a look at what some of those other architects are doing. Of course," he added apologetically, "I've already taken up a lot of your time and I don't want to inconvenience you."

"I've got all the time in the world," Carol assured him. "Especially since you're taking this house, because I won't have to show it again. And if you decide to pick up a couple of lots on the side, too, all the better."

He chuckled, once again favoring her with a smile that crinkled his eyes at the edges of his sunglasses. "I might just do that. I always liked this area."

"It's a great place to build a part-time home," Carol agreed, "or even raise a family."

"You must work for the chamber of commerce in your spare time."

She laughed. "Sometimes I think they should give me a cut."

"Do you have children, Carol?"

The question caught her off guard and something must have been reflected on her face because he explained, "You mentioned something about raising a family here. I thought you might have children of your own."

"Oh," she said, without expression. "One daughter. She—um, she doesn't live with me."

It was always uncomfortable, that moment of explanation, and Carol avoided it whenever she could. Carlton quickly sensed the shields she put up, and did not pursue the subject. In a moment he said, "Well, then. How soon can I move in?"

Carol relaxed. "As soon as you sign the rental contract. The house is ready for occupancy now."

"It will take me a couple of days to get things together. Is the weekend okay?"

"Of course. We'll prorate the rent from the day you move in."

"Great." He glanced at his watch. "We could get the paperwork taken care of now and if you're free, I'd like to take you to lunch."

"I was about to suggest the same thing—only the other way around. Taking clients to lunch is what I do, after all."

"We'll argue about the check later. And I'll still want to look at some lots when I get settled, so don't sell all the best ones before next week."

She said, "No promises. These are prime lots and they go fast."

"Shall we go then?" He touched her shoulder lightly.

"Sure," Carol said, and returned his smile. The day, she told herself, was definitely off to a good start.

But that did not help her get the memory of the voice of the girl on the telephone out of her mind.

Chapter Nine

The girl in the tower had lived a long, long time; longer than any of the others, longer than she deserved to live, longer, she sometimes thought, than she had ever wanted to. She had no way to measure the passage of days, or perhaps it was months or even years, so she could not say how long long was. Forever, or yesterday. It was all the same to her.

She was confused a great deal of the time, and she had forgotten a lot. She remembered almost nothing of the early days, and now she realized—in a dim uncertain way that she did not entirely trust—that the confusion and the lethargy were due to the drugs he gave her. That he still gave her drugs was almost certain, hidden in her food or in the bottled water that always tasted strange, but somehow they didn't affect her the way they used to. She could think more clearly now. And she was remembering.

She thought it all began when he brought her to this place. She wasn't even sure where this place was, but she knew she remembered it, or remembered things about it. She didn't like remembering. Most of the time it was a painful thing. It made her cry out inside for the things she remembered. It made her desperate and helpless; it made it hard sometimes to pretend. And pretending was how she survived.

At first she had screamed in the dark, alone and terrified in the small closed space. She had screamed and screamed until she became aware there was no one to hear her except the wind and the sea, and she had screamed still. She screamed giant silent puffs of air until finally she screamed the last of her spirit away and all that was left of her was a husky breath of air, like the remnants of her ruined voice. Sometimes, after that, she used to hear the others scream, in voices that never left her dreams, but she was never tempted to join them. No one had screamed here in a long time.

She thought about killing him. She dreamed of it sometimes and she awoke from those dreams feeling peaceful and quiet, believing for those first few moments of wakefulness that she had really done it, that it was over and she was free. She knew just how she would do it, too. With something sharp. She would hurt him like he had hurt the others. She would see the look of terror in his eyes just as she had seen the terror in other eyes, and then she would kill him. In her dreams she always killed him more than once, killed him even after he was dead because dying just once did not seem like enough.

She knew she would never do it, though. She knew she wouldn't because she had had chances—a paring knife left carelessly in an apple, a heavy tool put down within easy reach, a line cutter or fillet knife merely waiting to be tucked into the folds of her skirt when she went on deck—but she had never taken them. She would never kill him, any more than she would ever try to get away. And the worst part was that he knew it.

But things were changing now. She was stronger. Things made sense to her more often now; horrible, terrifying sense. But it was like cloud patterns: If you looked at them long enough, pictures began to form, and it was better to see dragons than to see nothing at all.

Possibilities began to form when she discovered the telephone. It was a tiny thing, barely bigger than a credit card, and he carried it in his briefcase. When it rang, he unfolded it and spoke into it. It was amazing. He made calls from it. He spoke to people outside this place on it. For the first time she began to believe—really believe— that there were people outside this place, a world that existed apart from the one he ruled, and slowly, in bits and pieces, memories of that world began to come back to her.

It took many tries before she figured out how to work the phone. She kept pushing buttons, the same seven digits over and over again, and nothing happened, not even a dial tone. Finally she noticed the "power" button. When she pushed it, she got a dial tone, but still she couldn't make the call go through, and she was frustrated to tears. Before that day, it had never occurred to her that she could pick up a telephone and someone would come to help. Before that day it hadn't been possible, and how could she imagine what wasn't possible? Perhaps, early on, she had fantasized about freedom, about home, about escape, but those days were so very long ago, the possibility so dim and remote, that she could barely remember wanting it. Now, all of a sudden, the possibility of freedom was in her hands—she understood its potential, and she wanted it with such a blind obsessive intensity that she could barely breathe.

She did not figure out how to put a call through that first time.

How many days passed between his visits she had no way of telling, but on his third visit after she had discovered the telephone he brought lumber and tools and worked outside. But he left his briefcase in the boat. Two visits after that, he left the briefcase in the building with her. When she was alone, it took her a long time to work up the courage to open it, to take out the telephone. She hid it until he was asleep.

That time she noticed the "Send" button. And when the call went through, when the voice answered, it was as though something broke inside her and all kinds of memories came flooding through: memories too fast and full and furious to even be captured or understood, as though a door had opened on a galaxy faraway where another girl lived another life at twice the speed of light. And then she couldn't do anything but cry. Then, just when she thought she could remember what to say, could make the words that she needed come out of her mouth, he made a sound as though waking. She panicked, and she turned the phone off and put it away, but he hadn't been waking up after all.

She sank to the floor, hugging her knees and shaking hard, and she didn't think she would ever be brave enough to use the phone again.

What was strange, though, was that after that first time, after hearing that voice once, a lot of things began to become clear to her. She felt smarter. She even, in some ways, felt stronger. Sometimes she even started to make plans, but it was hard to hold on to more than one thought at a time, and when he was with her, all her thoughts went away and the world became small again.

Then she went outside again. She saw the house and she held on to that picture and it gave her the courage to take the telephone again, and push the buttons. And this time she knew what she wanted to say.

But ever since then she had been afraid, terribly afraid. She was afraid the machine that had recorded her voice would be used against her somehow, that he would find out, that she would be punished. Then she was afraid that no one would ever hear her plea, that the machine had swallowed it up, that no one cared and she had gone through all of this, taken such terrible chances for nothing. It was hard to think when she was afraid, impossible to remember. And the thing she was most afraid of was that she had forgotten something—something very important.

She didn't feel strong anymore. She didn't feel smart.

It was when she felt small and confused and helpless like this that she missed Tanya the most. Tanya was never afraid. She always knew what to do. She had taken care of them all. But Tanya was faraway now, her voice very small in the dark, and she could not help.

But there was the telephone. And he never bothered to hide his briefcase from her. That fact, in some strange inexplicable way, made her unafraid of him.

When she heard him coming, black despair did not fill her chest the way it usually did. Now she thought of the telephone, and her heart speeded, and it was easy to pretend.

When he saw her, he would smile. "Hello, precious. Would you like to play a game?"

She would smile back. "Yes. I'd like that."

And then he would kneel down and open his arms to her, and he would leave his briefcase on the floor.

He would leave his briefcase on the floor.

Chapter Ten

G uy, along with everyone in the office who could come up with an excuse to stop by, watched as Deputy Long attached the trace-and-record device to his telephone. It was hardly state-of-the-art equipment—big and bulky and conspicuous as hell—but Guy was mildly impressed that St. Theresa County possessed any kind of surveillance equipment at all.

"So what you do when a call comes in," Long was explaining, "and you think it's him, you just press this button here. That turns the recorder on, just like an answering machine, forwards the call to the police station, and starts a trace on the line. Of course, with the St. Theresa telephone system it's going to take awhile to trace a call, particularly if it's coming from outside this exchange, so you need to try to keep him on as long as you can."

Guy said, "How long?"

"About three to five minutes."

Long looked apologetic when he said it, and Guy nodded. Three minutes was a long time when you were trying to make conversation with a crazy person.

"I work outside my office a lot," Guy reminded him. "What happens if he calls and I'm not here?"

"Your secretary should put him on hold, come in here and turn on the equipment. Then tell him she's looking for you. The trick is to keep him on hold as long as possible. I'll talk to her about it and show her how to use the equipment. What about your home phone?"

Guy reached into his pocket and pulled out the cellular. "This is it."

"Well, we can't put a tap on a cell phone," Long said. "And unless he forgot to block his caller i.d..." He finished with a small shrug. "Our best bet is to hope he calls the office again."

Guy said, "What about my wife?"

Long noted the slip. "Ex-wife, you mean."

Guy said impatiently, "I've only got one, and believe me that's enough misery for any man. I don't need to add to it by having her hurt by some nut who's out to get me. So is she in danger or what?"

"There's really no evidence that either one of you is in danger," responded Long. "As I told you before, most telephone threats are just that—threats."

Guy said, "Then why are you tapping our phones and investigating this like a crime?"

Long began to pack up the metal case in which he had transported the equipment and tools. He said, "When your daughter first ran away, your wife had you investigated as a suspect in a kidnapping."

Guy frowned sharply. "What the hell has that got to do with anything?"

Long's tone was casual. "You just seem awfully worried about a woman who almost tagged you with a criminal record."

Again Guy's tone was impatient, but his expression was alert and cautious. "I was the noncustodial parent. Carol thought I was hiding Kelly from her and she was hysterical. It didn't amount to anything."

"No hard feelings, huh?"

Guy said, "I think I could probably help you out a lot more if I had even the smallest idea of what you were getting at."

Long answered in an easy, almost convincing way, "I'm just trying to get a feel for the case, and the people involved. So there's never been a doubt in your mind that your daughter left home of her own free will?"

If there was a hesitation on Guy's part, it was barely noticeable. "No."

"And you haven't heard from her at all in the almost three years?"

"No."

"Why do you think the man on the phone would bring up your daughter at all? How many people knew about the situation with her?"

Guy shook his head impatiently as he began to understand the line of questioning. "It was in the paper for God's sake. We thought she'd been kidnapped or had an accident. Carol started a poster campaign. Everybody knew. As for why he'd bring her up..." Guy shrugged. "For the same reason he brought up Carol. To make me nervous."

"So you don't think your daughter could be involved in this in any way?"

Guy looked at the deputy for a thoughtful moment before answering. "These are the same questions you asked me yesterday, Deputy. Why is this starting to sound like an interrogation?"

Long answered, "I understand this is a tight-knit community, and you and your ex-wife have been a part of it for a long time. But I've only been here a year, and the only way I know to find out anything is to ask questions. I'm sorry if those questions make you uncomfortable."

Guy started to form an irritated protest, but then he caught the watchfulness in the officer's mild, steady gaze. He fought with a wry grin, and for the most part, lost. "You're good," he admitted. "Where're you from?"

"St. Petersburg, most recently."

"Thought you'd opt for the peace and quiet of the Forgotten Coast, huh?"

"Something like that."

Guy abandoned his interviewer's tone. He said, quietly, "When you lose a child—particularly when you don't know what you've lost her to, whether she's dead or alive—it's hard to think about, much less talk about. Carol and I can't even talk about it without..." He ended the sentence with a frustrated breath. "Look, I can't answer your question. It didn't sound like Kelly's voice on the tape, but maybe I didn't want it to sound like her. Carol's so sure it is, maybe you should listen to her. She never did think I was much of a father."

"Was it a bitter divorce?"

"Is there any other kind?" Then Guy frowned, annoyed with his own plunge into irrelevancy, and said, "The only thing I know is that whoever is behind this knows how to push my buttons. I can take care of myself, but he brought my family into it. I'm not going to have other people put in danger because of me."

Long nodded. "Like I said, I don't think anyone is in danger yet, and most likely nothing will come of this.

But it's best to be on the safe side. Have you thought any more about the 'Mary Had a Little Lamb' connection?"

"I haven't thought of much else." Guy walked with him toward the door. "I figured it might have something to do with a story I've covered, but I've been in this business a long time. I can't remember every single story."

"That's funny," said Long.

"What?"

"It's a nursery rhyme, something most folks would associate with their kids. But you think it's related to work." He opened the door and paused, looking at Guy. "You really don't want to believe your daughter is involved, do you?"

Guy had no answer to that. Long put on his hat, nodded to Guy, and left.

Chapter Eleven

By the time Carol got home that evening, her back was hurting so badly she could barely climb the stairs. After leaving Carlton in Laura's hands after lunch, she had spent the next three hours pushing through brambles and picking sand spurs out of her clothes, showing property to two rather unpromising prospective buyers. Midafternoon she had rushed home to meet Deputy Long, who wanted to install a tap on her phone and show her how to work it. His attitude, as it had been before, was condescending, and he left her with the distinct impression that, if her ex-husband had not been a reporter whose favor he wished to curry, he would have considered the wiretaps an unnecessary extravagance. He left her feeling furious, patronized, and uncertain. To offset her own sense of growing impotence, she spent the remainder of the day combing the island, leaving photographs of Kelly with realtors, shopkeepers and transient vendors who had already begun to set up booths on the streets. Between herself and Laura, they had covered all but the west side of Main

Street and, of course, the seasonal lessors who hadn't opened their stores yet.

Every single query had been met with a blank look, and Carol had never felt more foolish, more tired and defeated, in her life. Maybe Guy was right, maybe the police were right. She was wasting her time. After all, if anything could be helped by circulating a few photographs, wouldn't the sheriff's department have done it already? Wouldn't the previous fliers have brought Kelly home?

Carol turned on the light and stepped out of her shoes, wincing a little as she shifted her weight from her right foot to her left and a spasm of pain grabbed at her waist. Even after all this time she couldn't get used to coming in to an empty house, especially at night. The bank of windows was like the eyes of a monstrous giant, giving back her own reflection in prismed fractions and distorted pieces. The sterile silence was unwelcoming, and seemed to overwhelm even the background sigh and splash of the surf. When Guy and Kelly lived here, there was never a silent moment; it used to drive her crazy, the noise they made.

She moved forward to draw the blinds over the beachside windows, and stopped, her heart leaping absurdly to her throat when the phone rang. Her eyes went quickly to the instrument and the ugly police machinery attached to it and for a moment she was gripped by a paralysis of indecision, of anticipation, dread, hope, and reluctance. Her phone rang all the time, eighty percent of her business was initiated through the telephone and there was no reason to believe that this call would be different from any other. That just because the police had installed a tracing device only hours ago, she might have a chance to use it with the first call—

there was no reason to believe, none at all, that it might be Kelly.

Energy galvanized her limbs in a rush and she went quickly to the desk that held the telephone attached to the machine. Her finger was poised over the activation button as she picked up the receiver on the third ring and said breathlessly, "Hello?"

From the beach below he watched, his shoulders hunched against the wind inside his nylon jacket, resentment rising inside him like bile with each passing moment. It never failed to irritate him, walking down the beach and looking at the big gaudy houses that rambled over the dunes, each one of them representing an investment of a million dollars or more. Who the hell made that kind of money? Who the hell deserved that kind of luck? And the worst of it was, for most of those rich assholes the million-dollar piece of real estate was just a part-time residence, a weekend retreat, something they barely thought about until it came time to pay the taxes. Hell, most of them didn't even bother paying taxes.

Sometimes he'd walk for hours up and down the beach, looking at the big houses and wondering about the people who were in them, trying to figure out why they deserved everything and he ended up with nothing. Sometimes he'd walk right up the boardwalk and try the doors and windows, and sometimes—he himself was amazed at how often—a door was left unlocked or a window open and he'd just walk right in and make himself at home. Marble foyers, Jacuzzi tubs, expensive scotch, he was no stranger to any of it. He had to be careful though, and he couldn't enjoy his forays into the upper crust as much as he might have liked because the last thing he needed was to be hassled by the cops for small shit when he was working on something big.

He walked mostly at night, when lighted windows turned those expensive beachfront homes into fishbowls and their aristocratic occupants went about their business completely oblivious to any other life form, supremely confident that their money could protect them from anything. He liked to stand on the beach and watch them, taking a kind of scornful satisfaction in nothing more than the fact that they didn't know he was watching. He always ended up here, in front of the gray castle. He would have done so even if he hadn't known who lived there. Because it was bad enough to have to deal with the rich arrogant assholes who had more than they knew what to do with, but when the bitches started taking over ... well, that was when something had to be done.

This one, he knew, would have to be taught a lesson.

He watched her come in, turn on the lights, and stand illuminated in front of the bank of multishaped windows that faced the beach. He watched her kick off her shoes and run her fingers through her hair. He watched the way her shirt tightened over her breasts when she lifted her arm and that made him smile. He watched the way she moved in those tight jeans, slim hips, small waist, tapered legs. Showing off. It was almost as though she knew he was there watching, wanted him to see, and the thought both irritated and excited him. When she moved toward the window, for a moment, he was convinced that she could see him, and then she stopped, and turned away.

He realized a moment later that it was the telephone that had distracted her. She went to answer it, and he smiled, his mind made up.

He waited until she had finished her telephone conversation and started up the stairs. He knew if he stayed where he was and waited long enough, he could watch her undress in front of the second-floor window, but he had more interesting plans.

Tonight's the night, baby, he thought. *Payback time.* He moved, boldly and silently, toward the steps that led to her private boardwalk from the beach.

The call was from a customer who was driving down from Atlanta over the weekend to look at property. Carol hung up the phone feeling disappointed and impatient. It wasn't outrageous of her to expect Kelly to call tonight—after all, she had called two days in a row—but she couldn't keep jumping every time the phone rang. She had to remain calm and clear-headed so that when Kelly did call again, she would know what to listen for, how to keep her talking long enough for the trace to work, or at least how to get Kelly to tell her where she was before she hung up.

Before leaving the house that morning, Carol had activated Call Forwarding to send all her calls to her cell. She wanted to take no chance on missing Kelly's call, even though she might not always be able to activate the police's tracing device. She debated for a moment now whether to stay downstairs so that she would be close to the machine, but her back was killing her and the important thing was not tracing or recording the call, but talking to Kelly. She took the cordless phone with her as she went upstairs to change into her swimsuit, and from there to the rooftop hot tub.

A widow's walk enclosed the deck, and a glass windbreak surrounded the hot tub on three sides, protecting it from the harsh sea winds, which were strong year-round, and in the winter and spring far too cold for comfort. Carol hugged her terry robe close around her until she reached the protection of the windbreak, then placed the phone on the bench next to the tub and tossed her robe beside it. Wincing a little at the twinge in her back as she bent over, she folded back the cover on the tub and stepped gratefully into the warm, bubbling water.

The wind was loud, occasionally rattling the three-sided-glass partition or funneling around it to create a low-pitched roar, which effectively screened out even the sound of the whirlpool motor and the surge of the surf. Carol glanced at the telephone once again, making sure it was close enough for her to hear if it should ring. Then she sank back into the water, positioning a jet against the small of her back, and relaxed.

The stars were brilliant, as they can only be in an absolutely black sky viewed miles from the nearest light source. Guy used to say that being up here was like being in a space capsule with the earth and all its troubles light-years away. For a moment that was how Carol allowed herself to feel—insulated by water and sound, isolated by height, protected by the sky and the sea from all that troubled her. But it was only for a moment.

The first indication she had of anything unusual was a sound too vague to be identifiable, and so muffled by the wind that she couldn't be sure she had heard anything at all. A slamming door? Something bumping against the side of the house? She listened for a moment and was just about to decide she had imagined it when she felt a definite, distinct vibration. For a moment she couldn't move.

The house was tall, supported at the base by twenty-foot-high pillars that were designed to give and sway with structural stress. In the very highest winds or most severe storms, one could actually feel the sway of the house, much like a boat at sea. Most of the time, however, the house was as solid as Gibraltar—with one notable exception. Even the lightest footfall on the spiral staircase in the master bedroom tower would cause the entire tower to pick up the percussive vibration, a sensation which was particularly noticeable on the rooftop deck. The tower was vibrating now, in rhythm with forceful and determined footsteps.

Someone was in the house. And he was coming toward her fast.

Carol snapped her head around toward the door that opened onto the roof. It was the only exit and an intruder was on the staircase. There was no lock, no way to keep him on his side of the door. Her eyes moved quickly toward the telephone, and she was levering herself out of the water, turning toward it, as the door swung open.

The square of light from the door widened and Carol's heart slammed against her ribs. Her foot slipped on the step as she tried to scramble over the side of the tub and she banged her knee hard. A shooting pain went through her back and she cried out. She pushed herself up again and was on the ledge, propelling herself toward the bench and the telephone, when his shadow, long and grotesque and horribly exaggerated by the glare of light from the open tower door, fell over her.

Shattered

Chapter Twelve

Carol had one brief flash of stark terror that came with the realization of how vulnerable she was, alone and almost naked on a rooftop four stories above the ground, isolated by distance and wind from anyone who might hear her cries for help. Even if she could get to the telephone, it would be too late. Still, she tried to run, her heart closing up in her throat, but her wet feet slipped on the plank floor and she plunged forward. Then he was upon her, his hand hard on her shoulder, jerking her upright.

Carol whirled and struck out hard with her fist just as he exclaimed, "Jesus Christ, Carol, what's the matter with you?"

Her blow landed in the center of his chest and she drew back for another, but he stepped back and her fist just grazed his shoulder. "Damn it, Guy, are you crazy? You scared me half to death!"

"Serves you right," he responded, scowling. "I've been shouting for you for five minutes. Why didn't you answer? You could have been unconscious in the bathtub or held hostage at gunpoint as far as I knew."

"Oh, for God's sake! I can't believe you'd just walk in without knocking! You know I hate it when you do that." Her heart was still racing and her face was hot; she felt foolish and mortified and awkward, standing there in her wet swimsuit with water dripping on the floor and her skin prickling with cold. She pushed past him to get her robe.

"That's what keys are for." He dangled his set in front of her face. "And I did knock, for your information." And then he must have noticed the stiffness in her movements because his tone changed as he inquired, "Is your back bothering you again?"

Carol pushed a damp hand through her hair, tying the sash of her robe. "What do you want, Guy?"

He hesitated, in that way he had when what he was about to say was not exactly the truth. "I just wanted to see if the police got the equipment installed on your phone."

"You could have called to ask me that." She walked toward the open door. To her surprise, he did not follow her.

"Yeah, I guess I could have. I guess I was feeling a little edgy, wanted to see for myself."

"Well, the answer is yes. Is that all?" She had reached the door and she looked back impatiently, but he was half-turned from her now, gazing down at the beach.

"No," he said.

She went into the house and down the spiral staircase.

She changed into a soft warm-up suit and half expected Guy to be waiting for her in the master suite when she came out of the bathroom. He was not, and she retraced her steps to the roof.

At first she didn't see him. She moved to make sure the cover had been replaced on the hot tub and that the controls had been reset, and when she turned, Guy was sitting on the bench, his head tilted back toward the starry sky.

"Remember that contest we had to see who could name the constellations?"

After a moment, Carol answered with only a slight stiffness in her voice, "You drove all the way to Tallahassee to get a book on astronomy."

"Kelly was one tough kid. She hated it when she thought you were letting her win at anything."

Carol almost smiled. "Well, you gave her a run for her money that summer. I wasn't even in the game."

"I was going to surprise her by naming a star after her on her next birthday. But by that time, there was so much going on, and she seemed to have lost interest in the stars."

Carol knew exactly what had been going on. Kelly's parents were getting a divorce, her world was shattered, and she wasn't interested in much of anything.

She came and sat beside Guy on the bench. "Kids of that age outgrow things pretty quickly."

Guy said softly, "She was the best thing you and I ever did."

Carol felt her throat tighten. "Yes," she agreed. "But not the only good thing."

He was silent for a moment. Then, "What happened to the telescope?"

"The wind knocked it over a couple of years ago. I never got around to putting it back up."

"You should have called me."

"It's probably broken."

Again silence fell. The wind rattled the glass partition and hissed around the corners; the stars hung brilliant and profuse overhead, as though suspended in a net. They were alone at the top of the world and Carol discovered, in the silence and darkness, that she didn't mind.

Then Guy said, "I wanted to explain about the other night. What I said. No, how I acted." He didn't turn his head to look at her, but spoke straight ahead toward the sea. It was easier that way for both of them. "When you told me about the phone call, I know I cut you off at the knees. But if you think it was because I didn't think it was Kelly—that I didn't consider the possibility it could be Kelly—you're wrong. I did. Just like you, it was the only thing I could think.

"But after all this time, I've kind of gotten into the habit, a bad habit, of closing that door hard and fast before it ever completely opens. And yeah, I guess it's easier for me to think she's dead than to believe she's out there somewhere and I can't reach her."

Carol knew how hard that must have been for him to say. She said, "I know you tried, Guy. I don't think I ever thanked you for that."

When Kelly had first disappeared, Guy had called in every favor, used every contact, brought to bear the investigative resources of every news agency and law enforcement office with which he had ever worked, but to no avail. He had had his street contacts in Tallahassee reporting to him on an almost hourly basis for the first two weeks; undercover cops who owed him favors put out the word over their own networks with the drug and countercultures of the city. The bus stations were watched, airline manifests called up, police, hospital, and maritime records all over the state were opened to him.

But Carol, intent and absorbed with her own desperation, had been unable to understand just how much he was doing until it was all over, and he was gone. They hadn't been able to speak to one another back then without fury or accusations; instead of the tragedy bringing them together it had only pushed them further apart.

That was why Carol had been so disappointed in the way their last encounter had turned out. She had hoped they might be able to deal with one another more maturely by now. And perhaps tonight was a start.

Guy said, "You didn't have to thank me. She's my daughter, too."

Carol said nothing.

In a moment he added, "I said some pretty harsh things to you back then."

"Nothing I hadn't already said to myself."

Now he looked at her, his face merely a sketch in the darkness, but his voice was firm. "It wasn't your fault, Carol. Not the divorce, not Kelly. I know I waited too long to say it, but that was because it took me this long to get over feeling it was all my fault. Hell, maybe I'm still not over it. But I want you to know ... I've been hearing that message from your answering machine over and over in my head, and I don't think you're crazy for believing it's Kelly."

Carol tried to see what was in his eyes, but it was dark, and she was out of practice. She said, "Thank you," and meant it.

He reached into his pocket and brought out a photograph. Carol did not have to see it to know it was one of the prints of Kelly she and Laura had circulated that afternoon.

"Do you think it will help?" he asked. There was nothing judgmental in his voice.

Carol drew in her breath for a quick reply, but changed it to a slow and simple shake of her head. "No," she said softly. And she leaned her head back, fixing her gaze on the stars. "It's too little and too late. It wasn't even my idea, it was Laura's. All day long I've been asking myself why we didn't do more when she first disappeared, why we didn't blanket the state—the country—with fliers and pictures, and I didn't much like the answer I got."

"You were following the advice of the police."

"Yes." It was little above a whisper. "I did what they told me because there was always a part of me that thought they might be right, that Kelly was just an ordinary runaway and that we couldn't find her because she didn't want to be found ... and that made me angry. All the time I was screaming at the police for being incompetent, demanding that they make more of an effort to find her, all that time there was this part of me that was just so mad at her I was almost hoping we didn't find her. Mad and hurt and scared and ashamed of myself because I wasn't sure. In the end, I wasn't as sure as I pretended that Kelly wasn't just hiding out from us. That she hated me that much."

Silence passed, not comfortable, but not painful either. Guy said, "We both made some mistakes." Then he looked at her again. "Let's not let the past affect our judgment now, okay?"

After a moment, Carol nodded.

Guy stood up. "Come down and lock the door after me. And keep it locked from now on, day and night."

Carol shivered in a gust of wind as they left the shelter of the partition. "Come on, Guy, you know if somebody wanted to get in, a lock wouldn't keep him out. This house was built for an island with a higher incidence of hurricanes than crime. What do you want me to do, get metal shutters and doors?"

Guy frowned. "I just want you to be careful."

At the top of the stairs he paused, his expression altering slightly. His eyes were troubled but quietly confident as he said, "Kelly wouldn't have written that second note. She never would have said she was going to Hollywood."

"She wanted to be a musician, not a movie star," Carol agreed softly.

Guy looked away. "I never told you—but I flew to Los Angeles, right after that second note. I don't know what I was thinking. That she'd be hanging out in the airport or bus station, that I'd be walking down the street and see her ... it was crazy. What I saw was so many girls, dozens of them, hundreds of them, runaways living on the street. I flew back that same day. Like I say, it was crazy."

Their eyes met in a moment that was as close to understanding as they had reached in three years, perhaps more. Then, together, they went down the stairs.

He was angry. He hated the anger for the ugly, consuming thing it was, for the energy it wasted and the time it took. There had been a time when the anger had power over him, when he let it control his actions and therefore his life. In anger, he had broken, crushed, destroyed ... and lost. That was in the time before he had come to understand that anger was his enemy.

Now when he felt the familiar stirring of rage, the bite of frustration and the heat of blood lust, he knew what to do. He knew how to put that power to work for him. Anger, given its head, was waste. Anger properly channeled could result in enlightenment.

Enlightenment came tonight when he realized his anger was, in fact, foolish. He felt angry because he felt betrayed, but betrayal was impossible. The girl was incapable of it. She had followed her instincts, that was all, and she couldn't be blamed for that. It wasn't as though she had plotted to anger him, given measured and considered thought as to how best to betray him. Such complex reasoning was completely beyond her, and to attribute blame to her was to also give credit.

That was, of course, unthinkable.

She had acted from curiosity and impulse, and those were not malicious characteristics. In fact, when he thought about it, he realized it was not her actions he objected to so much as the fact that she had acted independently of him, without his permission or knowledge. That was not acceptable behavior, and for it she would have to be corrected.

That was when he began to appreciate the advantages of letting his anger work for him. Because when he thought about it, he began to see opportunities here, the ladder of learning unfolding, a chance to shape and mold his precious pet into an even more perfect specimen. In the end, he was almost grateful for her transgression. It couldn't have come at a more opportune time.

She had been alone too long, that was all. It was time he brought her a companion. And with that companion would come a built-in object lesson.

It felt good to be on the prowl again.

Chapter Thirteen

Mickie Anderson had been wasted for the past three days. The first two nights she had spent on the beach; the third one she spent with a guy she didn't know in a Panama City motel room with six other kids. It didn't matter. She wasn't going home again anyway. She was twenty years old and she didn't have to account to anyone for what she did.

She was flunking out of the University of Virginia, and her parents had made it clear she would either make it in college or she'd have to come home and get a job. Well, screw them. She could make it on her own. She didn't need their house and she didn't need their bullshit.

She'd planned spring break in Panama City for weeks, long before she knew that even perfect scores on her midterms—fat chance—wouldn't bring her average up enough to keep her off scholastic probation. She'd seen no reason to change her plans after her folks had given her their ultimatum, and she and a bunch of kids had taken turns driving down, making it in just over twelve hours. Since then, it had been one long party, a few good drugs, a lot of cheap booze, and a hell of a good time.

Today she'd hooked up with two of the kids she'd driven down with and they had picked up some Penn State hotshots who decided it might be cool to cruise on out of the city in search of bigger beaches. One of the Penn State guys, Donny, was kind of cute and had an eye for her, and Mickie sat on his lap on the drive to St. Theresa-by-the-Sea, where somebody had heard there was some action.

The beaches were bigger and not nearly as crowded as the ones they'd left, and Mickie was anxious for Donny to see her in her bikini, but he went off in search of beer with two of the other guys and left her behind. The girls wanted to cruise the beach anyway, but Mickie was mad. She blew them off and decided to try her luck on the streets.

She was feeling pretty good about herself—though still mad at Donny—when she stopped for a butterscotch-almond cone next door to a funky shop with Indian dream catchers, turquoise beads, and jeweled incense burners displayed in the window. With her frayed denim shorts slung low on her hips, and her shirt stuffed into her backpack purse to display her colorful bikini top, she got quite a few whistles, a lot of "whoa, Baby's" and more than enough stupid grins. One bicycler pretended to run into a telephone pole while twisting his head to watch her, which made her laugh. A carful of guys cruised the curb for half a block, hanging out of the windows and calling to her. She was ready for a break.

Mickie was a good-looking girl and she knew it. She had long dark hair that she wore in a braid for the beach, perfect skin, great legs and cute, C-cup breasts that looked good in skinny tank tops and skinnier bikinis. She tanned honey-gold, and except for a slight ruddiness on one shoulder that would even out with one more day on the beach, that tan was now at its peak. She turned heads, and she liked it. She knew she could walk into any bar on the strip and have a waitress job today, so what did she have to worry about? Her folks thought they were so smart. Hell, she might even try hooking if worse came to worse—or maybe if it didn't. There was good money on the street, and she knew that for a fact.

Licking her cone, looking for a place to be out of the sun, she went into the shop with the Indian junk in the window. It smelled like sandalwood and hashish, and a tuneless, rambling melody was being played from a stringed instrument on a CD somewhere. A man with a dark tan and gray hair pulled back into a braid that was almost as long as Mickie's looked up from behind the counter when she came in, smiled at her, and said, "How're you doin'?"

Mickie smiled back. He was kind of a cool-looking dude, his face younger than the gray hair would indicate, and he didn't give her any hassle about the cone. She appreciated that.

She wandered around the shop for a while, looking at quartz crystal pendants on leather thongs, beaded earrings, books with titles like *Heal Yourself with Magic* and Mother *Earth's Guide to Inner Peace*, and checked out some CDs from the tower. There were three or four kids in there with her and a man in a baseball cap and shorts. Nice buns on that one, though he was a little older than she generally liked.

One girl bought two fat violet candles, and a boy, who was loud and so stoned he had trouble counting out two tens, bought a leather bracelet studded with turquoise. Mickie was trying on silver rings shaped like dragons, dolphins, cats, and snakes, and she sensed the guy in the shorts watching her from across the aisle.

Probably thinks I'm going to cop one, she thought sourly, and returned a ring.

But to her surprise, he smiled at her and said in a friendly, easy tone, "It looked good on you. You should buy it."

Warm for my form, thought Mickie, relaxing. She knew the signs, and if she played it right, she was likely to get more than a cheap silver ring out of this one.

"No dough," she said, smiling, then giving him the full view of her tongue as she swept it across the ice cream cone.

"Shame." The guy smiled back and came over to her. "It's no fun to go on vacation and run out of money."

The guy wasn't even being subtle about it. This was going to be easy. "Bet that never happens to you," she said, running her tongue around the ice cream again.

He chuckled. "Not often."

She looked him over flirtatiously, lips pursed for a moment around the melting tip of the cone. He was your better-than-average-looking old dude, that was for sure. She wouldn't be embarrassed to be seen cruising in his Corvette.

"Cool necklace," she commented, noticing the pendant on the leather thong he wore around his neck. Definitely not your average old dude.

Obligingly, he slipped it over his head to show it to her. Mickie took it, frowning a little as she examined the pendant. It was unusual, all right. It was a figurine of a woman in a long waistless dress with her hands tied behind her back and her eyes blindfolded. Mickie was a little creeped out, and glanced up at him warily. "So what are you, into S&M or something?"

But he just smiled. "You don't recognize it? It's from the Tarot. It represents a young woman on the brink of discovery, yet held back by forces beyond her control. Paralyzed, you might say, by indecision, fear, uncertainty, what have you. Ready to go out and make her mark in the world—but not quite able to."

"Cool," Mickie said and looked at the pendant again. That was interesting. When she looked at it like that, it wasn't creepy at all. It was—well, it was a lot like her.

"The pendant is actually a charm—or so people say. It's supposed to be particularly effective for young women in times of crisis. Brings them good luck."

"No kidding?" She looked down at the necklace again. "Well, I guess I could use some of that."

"Try it on," he suggested.

Mickie pretended reluctance. "I don't know," she said. But the pendant was heavy, probably real silver, one of those collector's items. No one she knew had ever had anything like it.

"Go on," he insisted, and she slipped it over her head, making sure the figurine rested in the shallow between her breasts, where he could enjoy it.

"Does this mean we're going steady?" she asked playfully, and he laughed.

She wandered off down the aisle, licking the cone, making sure he'd follow. "So anyway, what makes you think I'm on vacation?"

He gestured toward the crowded streets, the busy little shop. "Isn't everyone?"

"What about you?"

"Nah. I'm on business."

She looked him up and down, taking care to pay special attention to his legs, which weren't half bad at that. "Oh, yeah? Funny way to dress for business."

"I'm in a funny business."

"What's that?"

"I'm a director. You know, commercials and stuff."

"Is that right?" Skepticism and disinterest mingled in her voice and she thought, *Sure you are, dude. Sure you are.*

He said, "As a matter of fact, I'm going to be shooting here for the next couple of days. You want to be in it? I need all the pretty girls I can get."

"Yeah, I just bet you do."

"It's nothing much, won't make you famous or anything. Just a promo for the chamber of commerce. But I could pay you, say, fifty bucks for a half hour's work?"

If he had said he was filming a Coke commercial or a rock video, Mickie wouldn't have bought it for a minute. But the chamber of commerce … it sounded just hokey enough to be on the level. And fifty bucks was fifty bucks.

She said, "No shit?"

And he responded solemnly, "No shit."

She giggled, then turned a provocative shoulder to him and strolled a few more steps down the aisle. "So, like, what would I have to do?"

"Play volleyball on the beach. You can even wear what you've got on."

"I'm no good at volleyball. I hate getting all sweaty."

He laughed. "You don't really play. You just pretend. And don't worry about getting sweaty, that's what we have makeup people for."

"Could I bring my friends? I'm here with friends."

A momentary annoyance seemed to cross his face, but it was quickly gone again. "Sorry," he said smoothly. "Closed set."

Mickie shrugged disinterestedly and turned back to her cone.

He said in a moment, "Truth is—I wasn't going to mention this—but if you weren't on vacation, and if you were in the market for something a little more permanent, I'm looking for a production assistant, and I thought maybe we could talk about it after I finish shooting this afternoon. I start filming in Daytona next week though, so whoever I got would have to be able to travel on pretty short notice."

Daytona. Production assistant. She was interested, oh, yes, she was, but it wouldn't do to let him know that.

She said casually, "So what kind of money are we talking about there?"

"Five hundred a week plus expenses."

She stared at him, big eyed. Whatever hope she had of nonchalance was abandoned. "Whoa. Making commercials must pay some okay bucks."

He grinned. "That's why they call it 'commercial.' Anyway, you might mention it to your friends. I'll interview anyone who's interested."

Mickie made sure that was one thing she would not do. The less competition the better.

She said, "Why can't we talk about it now?"

He glanced at his watch. It was gold, and looked to be the real thing. "Sorry, I have to go set up for the shoot. But if you're interested, I'll be at the pier—you know the one by the public parking lot—at four. I'm picking up a few other kids there and driving them to the site. I'll have you back by six."

She thought it over. "Maybe I'll see you there."

He smiled. "I hope so." He turned toward the door.

"Hey, wait." She reached to slip the necklace over her head. "Don't you want this back?"

He smiled. "Keep it," he said, "for good luck. And maybe it will remind you to think about that job."

"Hey, thanks." She grinned as he turned toward the door. "And I will—think about it, I mean."

He waved at her. "You know where to find me."

She finished off the cone, browsed a little more, and went back out on the street, feeling pretty damn good about life in general. Then she saw Donny across the street, and she thought maybe that good luck charm was starting to work already. She waved at him, and he waved back enthusiastically. She dodged traffic to get to him, then jumped in his arms and clamped her legs around his waist. He laughed and whirled her around and for the next hour or so she forgot all about commercials and trips to Daytona and the man in the Indian shop.

But he did not forget about her.

Chapter Fourteen

BRIDGE CONSTRUCTION CAUSES TRAFFIC DELAYS
TEEN RESCUED FROM NEAR DROWNING
TWELVE ARRESTED FOR ORDINANCE VIOLATIONS
BICYCLIST INJURED IN COLLISION

Guy manipulated the various headlines on his computer, trying to decide on a lead story, but only half his attention was on his work. The weekend had come and gone, and the machine attached to his telephone had not been activated once, nor had Carol's. He was beginning to feel foolish, more than a little impatient, and perhaps worst of all, to wonder about the soundness of his judgment.

They said survivors of tragedy—be it violent crime, war, even an airplane crash—were never afterward to achieve the same level of security they had known before the event. It was as though, once that barrier of "it can't happen to me" was removed, they almost began to expect the worst, to take it as their due. He and Carol had survived a tragedy. Would he have been so quick to assume the call was more than an idle prank if he hadn't stepped over that line of "it can't happen to me" once before, and seen what was on the other side?

"Shall we do a layout meeting today or do you just want to sit and brood?"

Guy glanced up to see Ed Jenkins leaning against the frame of his open door. He frowned a little. "Yeah, I'm on my way."

"So what's your lead?"

"They're paving the parking lot at the Piggly Wiggly."

Jenkins lifted an eyebrow. "I'll stop the presses."

"Well, it's a lot more relevant to our readers than what we've been running all weekend. Personally, I want to know when the last three lanes of the parking lot are going to be closed so I can schedule my beer runs accordingly. Can you believe we live in a place where the feature story is accompanied by pictures of some teenage girl pushing her boobs into the camera for three days in a row?"

"I don't know about you, but that's why I live here. I'd take a guess that's why the photographer lives here, too."

"Let's run the bridge construction story. If we do one more spring break headline, I'm going to quit."

"Now that'd be a shame." He waited as Guy lined up the stories and locked them in. Then he said, in a tone that was carefully casual, "So how's Carol holding up?"

"Great, just great. You ought to have us over to dinner some time."

Jenkins nodded toward the machine attached to his telephone. "Look, nobody likes to ask but——"

"Yeah, I know." Guy released a breath that was both frustrated and apologetic. "It's the waiting that's making me crazy. I'm starting to think the whole thing doesn't amount to anything."

"That'd be good, right?"

"Right." But Guy was frowning. "Wrong. Hell, I don't know." He picked up his notebook and left the desk. "I just don't like unanswered questions, you know? I've got too many of them floating around in my head as it is."

Ed nodded sympathetically, and turned away from the door just as Rachel was coming through it. She was carrying a colorful arrangement of pink and blue flowers.

Guy feigned delight, though not very well. "For me? Sweetie, I didn't know you cared."

"I care all right," Rachel retorted, and set the arrangement on his desk. "I care a lot about knowing who your new sweetheart is, and why she doesn't know any better than to make sure the florist doesn't send baby shower flowers to a gentleman. Or is there something you'd like to tell us?"

"Just what I need at eight o'clock on a Monday morning, a secretary with a sense of humor." He took the card off its forked holder and read it. Ed came back into the office and waited, a half-curious, half-amused smile on his lips.

The card read: *Just didn't want you to think you were forgotten.* There was no signature.

He handed the card to Ed, and told Rachel in a carefully calm tone, "Why don't you give the florist a call and see who paid for these?"

"On it." She left the office with a purposeful stride.

Ed handed the card back to Guy with a puzzled expression, but Guy didn't take it. He had just noticed the small stuffed lamb nestled at the base of the blossoms.

Guy picked up the toy and turned it over in his hand. He could feel the blood drain out of his face as he looked at it. "Oh, shit," he said. His voice sounded weak and he felt sick inside.

He looked up at Ed slowly. "Jesus Christ, I know who it is," he said. "I know who the son of a bitch is."

Chapter Fifteen

S he heard him arrive, but a long time passed before he came to her. Enough time so that anticipation turned to dread and dread turned to resignation and resignation turned to simple waiting. She could hear things from the dark place where she was: his muffled voice, the occasional thump. She didn't know what the sounds meant. Long ago she had learned it was best not to listen.

She heard the scrape of the key in the lock and he swung open the plank door. She lifted an arm to shield her eyes from the dim glow of the camping lantern he carried. He always held it high so that it shown in her eyes, hurting her, blinding her.

He said pleasantly, "Hello, lovely."

She answered, because she knew what would happen if she didn't, "Hello."

He smiled. Sometimes his smiles were cold, but this one was filled with genuine pleasure. And that pleasure terrified her.

"I brought you a present," he said. But he stood blocking the door with the lantern held up so that she could see nothing but his face, his smile.

"Well, not a present, really," he corrected himself. "An object lesson, really. But it's for your own good. Because you've been very naughty, haven't you, darling?"

She shook her head slowly, pressing back against the wall. "No," she whispered, eyes wide and fixed on him. "No, I haven't done anything, I haven't."

He smiled. "Oh, yes, you have. And you want to know something, little darling? I've thought about it a great deal and I've decided this is exactly why I love you so. Because you're always doing and saying the unpredictable. Because you're never boring. You're a challenge, love, and that's why I've kept you so long. Even though you make me very, very angry sometimes."

With no warning, he grabbed the leather thong around her neck and jerked her out of the enclosure into the open room. Now his face was dark and tight; she read him well and let herself grow limp, offering no resistance. He jerked her upright and gave her a shake, startling a cry of pain from her.

"You took my telephone without permission, didn't you? You called that nice Mrs. Dennison, bothering her in the middle of the night, upsetting her so, getting her hopes up about her poor lost Kelly. That was a bad thing to do, wasn't it?" His fist tightened on the thong, cutting off her breath, and he shook her again. "Wasn't it?"

"Yes!" she gasped. "It was bad!"

He twisted his fist another turn, and two. The leather dug into her neck, spots of light danced before her eyes. "Do you know why it was bad?" he demanded.

She nodded wordlessly, eyes blurred with pain.

"Tell me!"

"Because," she managed, gasping, "because—Kelly is dead!"

He released her so abruptly that she stumbled. Bright throbs of red-hot pain from newly awakened nerve endings burst through her neck and throat. Her lungs felt as though they would explode.

But that wasn't the worst. The worst was that when he released her, when he stepped away, and she saw what he had brought.

The girl was naked, blindfolded, and lashed with her hands tied behind her back to an upright post in the center of the room. One cheek was purple and swollen and her lip was split. She was drunk or drugged or simply unconscious. Her head lolled sideways on her shoulder.

He said, smiling, "She looks a little like you. Don't you think?"

"No," she whispered. "No, please..."

He hooked his fingers over the leather-thong necklace he made her wear and jerked it over her head. She lost several strands of hair to the effort, but hardly felt the sting. She watched in horror as he went to the naked girl and dropped the necklace over her head.

"Stupid bitch," he commented carelessly. "She lost the one I gave her." Then, smiling, "Don't worry. I'll get you another."

Then he took out the knife.

An involuntary moan was wrenched from her and she sank to her knees. She drew up her arms to cover her head, and the sounds she made were low and animal-like, helpless and terrified. "No. No, please don't make me watch, don't make me please..."

But he made her watch. He made her listen to the screams. And afterward he didn't lock her up. He left her in the big room with the telephone in plain view and waited to see if she would touch it.

She never did.

Chapter Sixteen

L iving on the Gulf Coast, one got used to expecting every day to be perfect. It was always refreshing for full-time residents to discover Mother Nature still had a few tricks up her sleeve, and that some of them were reserved for St. Theresa-by-the-Sea ... yes, even during spring break.

The day was gray and misty, cold enough for a fleece running suit, and so fogged in that not even an outline of the lighthouse was visible from the beach. Carol had manned the office over the weekend, putting up with endless phone and walk-in inquires from groups of students looking for houses to rent, and she was entitled to Monday and Tuesday off. Generally, she would have simply taken a few hours off in the mornings to run errands, but under the circumstances, she had decided to take the entire Monday off. She hadn't decided about Tuesday yet.

She pulled the hood of her jacket over her head and walked down to the end of the boardwalk, frowning a little as she noticed that hers were not the only footprints that had disturbed the damp, filmy coating of sand over the boards. She hadn't been down to the beach in almost a week, which meant that sometime—probably over the weekend—someone had come up onto her private walk and had gone at least halfway to her door. Perhaps he had stood there, looking into her windows or, perhaps, in a drunken confusion, had stumbled all the way to her garage before he realized he had the wrong house.

That was far, far too close for comfort.

Carol tried not to make too much of it. Homeowners with beachfront boardwalks were constantly fending off tourists who mistook the PRIVATE RESIDENCE sign for a shortcut to the parking lot, even in this protected community. And with all the kids who had crowded the beaches that weekend, she was lucky she hadn't been disturbed by more than a few footprints. Still, it made her uneasy in a way it wouldn't have if Guy hadn't started making such a production over security.

Neither one of them had received any more phone calls. For Guy's part, that was good news. To Carol, it meant only heartbreak, anxiety, and sleeplessness.

She went down the steps and onto the soft sand. Her back had been helped by all the time she had spent sitting in her contour chair at the office that weekend, but she still wasn't strong enough to resume her morning run. Instead, she started down the beach at a moderate walking pace, seeking out the firm sand, stretching her legs. There were a few vague shapes far down the beach—intrepid spring breakers determined to get to the beach even if it was raining—but for all intents and purposes she was alone.

Or so she thought.

The sound of the surf was muffled by the fog, so that the thud of running footsteps, as they approached her from behind, were perfectly audible. Glancing over her shoulder, Carol had a glimpse of a tall man in a gray hooded sweatshirt and running shorts, his face lost in the mist and the folds of his hood. She stepped aside to let him past. He veered in her direction. Carol kept walking, faster now, moving into softer sand so that he could pass on the water side. He didn't.

Her stride was slowed by the heavy sand and she could hear his heavy breathing now. Her fists tightened at her sides and she thought, *Damn you, Guy. Damn you for making me afraid.*

She stopped and whirled around, her fists clenched and her heart pounding. He stopped, and pushed back his hood.

"Hi," he said, smiling.

It was a moment before Carol could speak. "Mr. Carlton," she said. "I mean—Ken." She hoped he mistook her quickness of breath for the aftereffects of exertion. She felt like a fool, particularly since it took her so long to remember—"That's right, you're a full-time resident now."

She had given him his key personally on Saturday, but the office had been so busy they had not had a chance to talk. She gestured around rather aimlessly. "So, how do you like it so far?"

He laughed. "The weather could use some improvement. Other than that, it's perfect."

Now Carol laughed. "Obviously, you haven't been to town since you got here."

"Do you mean the traffic problem?"

"I'd say having to park across the bridge to get to the post office constitutes a problem, yes."

He grinned. "I live in Tallahassee, I'm used to it." He gestured back toward her house. "That's yours, right?"

"That's right."

"I thought I recognized it the first time I passed."

Carol said cautiously, "The first time?" Had it been his footprints she had seen on the boardwalk? And if so, why hadn't he simply come up and rung the bell?

He nodded. "I've been running for an hour. It's an Adam Jackson design, isn't it?"

"Yes, it is," Carol said, pleased and flattered as always when someone recognized her house.

"I think I might have seen it in Architectural Digest some years back."

"It's been featured a couple of times." They started walking up the beach, and Carol said, "Don't let me interrupt your run."

He shook his head. "No, I'm cooling down."

Carol found she was glad for the company, and was surprised at how much safer she felt in the company of a man, even on the beach—her own beach. She hated the fact that some unknown monster somewhere out there had that much power over her, robbing her of her security before she even knew it was gone.

They talked for a few minutes about her house, about architecture, about design in general, and she enjoyed it. It was good to think about something besides her troubles for a while, and Ken was an interesting and articulate companion.

He said, "So how far is it to the end of the beach?"

"To the Cut, you mean? Too far for me to walk. Maybe five miles."

He considered that. "I guess I could walk down there okay. But I don't know how I'd get back."

Carol laughed. "That's what a lot of people forget when they start out for that great camera shot of the lighthouse."

"Too bad it's so foggy though. I'd like to drive down there. Good fishing?"

"My husband—ex-husband"—she hated it when she did that—"says it's the best. He used to fish right off the sea break. Marlin, grouper, sea bass—and an awful lot of sharks." She wrinkled her nose. "I guess 'good fishing' is in the eye of the beholder."

He chuckled. "Maybe I'll pass on the fishing. So listen, how soon do you think we could get together for a property tour?"

Carol didn't even hesitate. In matters of business, instinct took over. "How about today? The weather's too lousy to do much of anything else."

"Sounds good. Maybe if the weather clears, we can see some of it by boat."

"Nothing much to see except deserted islands," she pointed out, "but I'm game."

"Great. I'll just go change."

She glanced at her watch. "Is an hour okay? I'll pick you up at your place."

He grinned. "That's right, you know where I live. See you in an hour then."

They parted with a wave, and Carol hurried back to her house.

The blinking light on the answering machine was still, and Carol was glad she was getting out of the house. She didn't know how much more of the waiting she could take.

Still, she didn't leave without transferring her calls to her cell.

Chapter Seventeen

Deputy Derrick Long knew that the Dennisons— particularly Carol Dennison— thought his interest in their case was purely perfunctory. They couldn't have been more wrong.

Since Friday afternoon he had patrolled the beachside streets of St. T. thirty-seven times. He had arrested twelve drunks—three of whom had thrown up in the back of his patrol car— four kids for lewd and lascivious behavior, six for possession of less than an ounce of a controlled substance, and two because he was just plain out of patience and they made him mad. He had issued forty-three traffic citations and sixty-two warnings. And he had accomplished all of that while spending what felt like half of his life caught in a slow-moving melange of honking horns, rebel yells, and scantily clad teenage girls hanging out of sun roofs. When the call from Guy Dennison was relayed to him, he had to restrain himself from falling to his knees and thanking God for deliverance.

"Richard Wakefield Saddler," Long reported to the sheriff late that afternoon. It had taken disappointingly little time to run down the details. "A construction worker from Fiddler's Cove, divorced, one son. He worked a circuit that took him just about all over the Panhandle—Tallahassee, Appalach, Panama City, Port St. Joe, the islands. And just about everywhere he went, there was one sad young lady left behind. In 1993, Guy Dennison was working as a crime reporter for that TV station in Tallahassee, and he latched on to the story about this thirteen-year-old girl that was assaulted in her house while her parents were out. He did the report from her room, where the attack supposedly took place. I haven't seen the tape yet, but apparently it was some powerful stuff. There was a collection of stuffed animals on a shelf over the bed, and at the end of the report, he took down a toy lamb and held it up to the camera, you know like reporters do when they want to tug at old ladies' heart strings, and he said something about lost innocence. I don't have a quote and he couldn't remember. Anyway, the girl's name was Mary Lynn White."

"Mary had a little lamb," Sheriff Case said softly. "This is one sick bastard."

Long nodded. "Well, that report and the ones that followed ignited a real firestorm of public outrage, and eventually Saddler was tracked down and charged with that assault and linked to eight others around the Panhandle. I should mention, by the way, that little Mary was no lamb, if you know what I mean, but she was just thirteen years old and she claimed he raped her. Anyway, the prosecutor got over-zealous, tried to charge him with nine counts of rape and child molestation. The jury would only convict on one. He got out on early release last month, address 1482 Cherrybrook Drive, Gainesville. I called the sheriff's department over there and asked them to check it out for me. Turns out there's nothing at 1482 Cherrybrook but a car wash. Saddler's parole officer was real sad to hear that."

"Son of a bitch," said Case.

"Right."

Case was silent for a long time. His face, profiled in the harsh light of the window that overlooked the parking lot, looked drawn and rough-shaven; they had all worked double shifts since Friday.

Finally he said, "There's a lot of things about this I don't like, Deputy."

"Yes, sir."

The sheriff looked at him. "We've got a child molester and a rapist running around our town during spring break. That's the number one thing I don't like."

"I'm having mug shots faxed over. That should be some help tracking him down. And we don't really know that he's in town. The florist said that the order was charged to a credit card, but my guess is it's going to turn up stolen."

Case heard him out patiently. "Two and a half years ago," he said, "Guy Dennison's daughter takes off to see a concert in Tallahassee, and never comes back. Now we've got this convicted child molester calling up Dennison and asking him if he knows where his daughter is. That's the second thing I don't like. And I don't like it a lot."

This time when the sheriff looked up, there was a kind of dread resignation in his eyes. Long knew what he was going to ask before he said it.

"I don't suppose we know where Saddler was the summer Dennison's daughter took off, do we?"

Long swallowed, then nodded. "He was in Tallahassee." That was the first thing he'd checked.

Sheriff Case said nothing for a moment. "That," he said at last," is the third thing I don't like." Then, "Get to work on tracking down that credit card. Start spreading those mug shots around when they come in. As of now, you're on this one full-time."

Long's shoulders straightened smartly. "Yes, sir." He turned for the door, then hesitated. "Should I tell Dennison what we've found?"

After a moment Case sighed. "No," he said, "I will."

Chapter Eighteen

They had taken refuge in the Tahoe from a brief cold downpour when Carol's car phone rang. Afterward, she would think a lot about the fate that was at work then. She and Ken had spent the morning walking deep beachfront lots, lunched at Michael's, and in the afternoon, wandered far and deep into the interior of the island, mostly on foot. She hadn't thought about the car phone once, nor had she remembered to remove it from the console and slip it into her pocket when they left the Tahoe.

So as they hurried inside the SUV, laughing in the silly way people do when they unexpectedly become drenched, trying to wipe the water from their eyes and squeeze it from their hair, the squeal of the phone was an alien, intrusive sound. Carol had barely closed the driver's side door and was fumbling in her purse for the car keys so that she could start up the heater, and she answered the phone in an absent impatient tone that was due mostly to the fact that she was trying to keep her teeth from chattering.

"Carol Dennison," she said and made an apologetic gesture to Ken, who grinned good-naturedly and slicked his hair back with both hands, looking like an old-time mobster.

The silence on the other end of the line hissed. Carol found the key and started to put it in the ignition.

"You're—Kelly's mother, right?"

Carol froze in place. The voice. The voice...

"Yes," she said, or thought she said, or perhaps merely whispered on the last of the choked-back breath that glided past her lips. "Yes."

"Listen, you've got to help her. She wants to come home, but she can't get out of here. He watches her all the time. She can't even call you anymore. She thought you'd be here by now. Why didn't you come?"

No, it wasn't the same voice. This woman sounded older, stronger, more in control. The accent was different, the words more clipped. It wasn't Kelly. But it was someone who knew her.

Carol's hand tightened on the phone. Her chest ached with breathlessness. "Who is this?" she demanded hoarsely. " Who are you?"

She was aware, very dimly, of Ken's growing still in the passenger seat, of his look of concern and interest. Mostly she was aware of the silence on the other end, and how long it seemed to drag on, although in truth it probably lasted no more than a couple of seconds.

The voice returned, a little impatiently, "My name is Tanya. I'm trying to help you and I don't have much time—"

"Who? Who are you?"

"Tanya. Tanya Little. I told you that. The important thing—"

"You know where my daughter is? You know Kelly?"

"Of course, I know! I'm here with her, didn't I just tell you that? Look, I can't talk long. The last time he caught her on the phone he did something..." A catch in her voice. "He hurt her real bad."

"Who?" The word was screaming in her head, everything was screaming in her head, but when she spoke it out loud, it was little more than a strained croak. "Who hurt her?"

There was a sharp breath and Carol thought the woman wouldn't answer, that she was going to lose her, but then she answered simply, in a flat, tight tone, "Him. He did."

Carol gripped the phone, focusing her strength. The windows had fogged with her breath and little rivulets of rain occasionally crawled snakelike down the outer glass. She could hear the thud of drops on the roof and the thud of her heart in her ears.

She said, "Where are you? I'll come right now. Just tell me where Kelly is."

Silence. Rain pelted. The seat leather rustled as Ken leaned closer, propping his arm along the back of the seat. Carol barely noticed him.

"Tell me," Carol said intensely. "Don't hang up, don't stop talking to me. Just tell me." Her voice was rising, desperation sharpened it to a near scream. "Tell me where my daughter is!"

The voice grew smaller, more uncertain. She answered, "I can't."

"No, don't! Don't hang up, please—"

But she was gone.

Ken said, "Carol? What's wrong? Is there something I can do?"

Carol sat there, clutching the telephone to her chest, her breathing quick and light. A dozen things went through her head. She should have been home. She was supposed to have been home. If she had been home and the call had come there, she could have activated the machine and traced the call and they would know where Kelly was now. Or maybe not. Maybe this woman had nothing to do with Kelly at all. Maybe it was some kind of sick joke after all. Maybe ...

She said, "I, uh..." Briefly she pressed two fingers to one temple, trying to clear her head, trying to think. "I have to call the police. No. I have to go home. I..." She looked at Ken in helpless apology. "Something has happened. I'm sorry."

She was shivering now, the cold seeping into her bones. Ken took the telephone from her stiff fingers. His concern was genuine, but his quiet control was reassuring. "Do you want me to drive you somewhere? Has someone been hurt?"

Carol took a breath. "My, um, daughter. She's been missing now for almost three years. Recently I started getting phone calls and—the police are investigating." She thought that made sense. Maybe it made sense. "That call..." Still shivering and trying not to show it, she nodded stiffly toward the telephone he was replacing in the console. "This woman—she said she knew where Kelly was. That some man wouldn't let her go. That he..." Now her voice caught on a ragged sound that felt like a sob but wasn't, not entirely. "That he hurt her."

Ken's shock was almost palpable and it filled the car. She realized too late what her story must sound like to a stranger, one who had no responsibility for her troubles nor obligation to listen to them, and she tried to be sorry, but couldn't. She was too shattered and hurting and confused inside.

"My God." Ken's voice sounded as stunned as his face, a bit pale in the interior dimness of the car, looked. In a moment, he seemed to recover himself, though, and his hand covered hers in a warm firm squeeze. "I'm sorry," he said.

Carol swallowed hard, dimly surprised by how good it felt to say the words to someone, to tell the story and not be met with suspicion or disbelief. She drew another long slow breath and Ken, with a gentle squeeze, released her hand.

"It may turn out to be nothing," she said. "But I should report it to the police. I'd better go home."

Ken glanced toward a clearing spot in the steamy side window. "The rain has almost stopped," he said. "But you'd better let me drive, anyway. You still look a little shaky."

Carol knew she should argue, but she didn't have the strength. She smiled gratefully and turned over the keys to him as they got out of the car to change places.

Chapter Nineteen

He was over being angry, and he was smart enough to realize that sometimes things worked out for the best. He had been halfway up the boardwalk and she was up on the roof in her swimsuit—not a bad-looking woman for her age, not bad at all—and he knew what he would have done if he'd gotten in the house. Guy Dennison's wife? Oh, yes. He wouldn't have been able to resist. It was inevitable. Almost predestined.

But then a car had pulled into the garage and its headlights had almost pinned him. He had swung over the boardwalk and onto the soft sand below and watched, cursing, as Guy Dennison himself got out of the car and walked boldly into the house.

It had taken him a long time to talk himself into walking away from that one.

But things had a way of working out. He wasn't ready to confront Dennison, not yet. He wanted him to suffer first, to worry, dread, and anticipate. He wanted him to feel safe and then realize he wasn't. He wanted him to fear waking up in the morning and going to bed at night. He wanted him to lose everything, piece by piece. Then he wanted to destroy him.

It was only fair.

The most vulnerable point of entry on a beach house was its windows. Destroying the view with bars was of course out of the question, and most of the time people didn't even bother to lock the windows, even in winter—perhaps especially in winter when the days were often warm enough to open the windows to the sea breeze. On a rainy gray day like this, no one was on the beach, and he walked casually and unobserved up the boardwalk and across the lower deck to a set of sliding windows. He popped the screen, slid the window open, and swung himself inside all in less than five seconds.

There was no alarm system. It was amazing, how few people bothered with them on the beach.

He knew she didn't keep regular work hours; that was part of the excitement. If she came in while he was there ... well, that would be just fine. But if she didn't, that would be fine, too. All he wanted to do was leave her a little present.

He took a casual look around the main floor, taking his time as he examined her possessions. Then he started up the stairs.

John Case called Guy at four-thirty. Guy wasn't surprised at anything he had to say, but it still gave him a sick, tight feeling in the pit of his stomach. The worst part was when Case told him Saddler had been in Tallahassee when Kelly disappeared. It was like a shot of ice water through his veins and he thought, *No, not possible. It couldn't be...*

But it was possible. Both Guy and the sheriff who had called the case closed two and a half years ago knew just how possible it was.

When he hung up, he sat at his desk a long time, hands flat on the surface, eyes fixed on the telephone. He didn't want to call Carol. How could he tell her this?

How could he not?

Tammy answered the phone. "Beachside Realty."

"This is Guy Dennison. Is Carol in?"

"Oh, hi, Guy. No, she had the office over the weekend. I think she was planning to spend the day at home. Do you want me to check with Laura?"

"No," he said. Laura was the last thing he needed. "I'll try her cell. If she checks in, have her call me."

"Will do."

Guy dialed her at home, his throat growing dry as he waited for it to ring. *I screwed up, babe,* he thought. *I screwed up bad, and now there's a convicted rapist and child molester out there with your name on his mind ... and Kelly's.* Kelly. Even her name sent a twisting tightness through his chest that made it hard to breathe.

Carol sounded strange when she answered, her voice hoarse and a little fuzzy, as though he had awakened her from a nap.

He tried to keep the strain out of his own voice. "Hey, sweetie. Are you going to be there for a while?"

"No, Guy, I'm not—"

"It's important." He gave up trying to sound casual. "I need to talk to you about something and I can't do it over the phone."

"Guy, something has happened."

Now he recognized the roughness in her voice as a high level of stress. His attention quickened, the alarm tightened a notch. "What? Are you okay?"

A hesitation, then, "Yes. I just—all right, come on over. I guess I need to talk to you, too."

"I'm on my way."

Chapter Twenty

K en pulled into the circular drive before his house as she hung up the phone. "Are you sure you'll be okay to drive home? I don't mind."

Carol tried to smile. "Don't be silly. It's only a mile. I'm just—well, I'm sorry you got caught in this. I'm usually much more professional."

He put the car in park, but left the engine running. "I know that," he assured her. "And listen, I know it's none of my business, but if there's anything at all I can do to make this easier for you, please let me know."

Carol thought he meant it. "Thank you," she said. "That's kind."

He sat there for another moment, smiling at her gently, until she felt compelled to say, "And we are going to finish that real estate tour, okay?"

"You bet. Maybe next time we can do it by boat. I brought my Donzi down Sunday. Hope the weather clears so I can try it out."

She said, "These little squalls never last long. The sun will be out again tomorrow."

He smiled. "A good thing to remember."

That made her smile, too. "Right. And it's always darkest just before dawn."

"Right."

The moment was becoming warm, almost comfortable. She glanced away. "I should go. Someone's meeting me at the house."

He nodded. "I heard. I wish you'd let me drive you to the police station."

"It's the county sheriff who has jurisdiction out here, and his office is on the other side of the river. I'll call as soon as I get home and make them come to me."

He opened his door. "Drive carefully then. And you know if you need anything, you can call. I'm here for the duration."

Carol slid across the seat as he got out and took her place behind the wheel. "Thank you," she said. "You've been great."

He rested an elbow on the open car door and looked down at her. "That's what neighbors are for," he told her.

He closed the door and watched her drive away.

Carol's car was not in the garage when Guy pulled up, and he tried not to let that alarm him. She had told him to meet her here; she was probably just running late. Nonetheless, she had said something had happened, and from the sound of her voice it had been serious. He had no compunction about going up the stairs and using his key when he found the door locked.

The first thing he noticed, when he let himself in, was the rush of cool damp air from an open window. That struck him as odd, because it wasn't the kind of day anyone would normally leave a window open. Then he noticed the screen was off, too. Then he was definitely alarmed.

He called out her name, but didn't wait for a reply. A quick glance around told him she wasn't downstairs, and he rushed up the tower staircase.

He emerged into the master suite and knew immediately something was wrong, even before his senses pinpointed what it was. First of all, the room reeked of perfume. It was Carol's jasmine scent, but it smelled as though she had broken an entire bottle and let it soak into the carpet. Directly across from him was the bank of windows that opened onto the upper deck, and the light that filtered through them was weak and gray. Centered on the adjacent wall was the white marble fireplace and directly opposite it was the king-size bed he and Carol had once shared. And that was where something was wrong.

At first he thought Carol had merely been uncharacteristically sloppy. In all the years he had known her, she had never left a towel unfolded or a garment out of its drawer; she always kept her house in "ready-to-show" condition. It was completely unlike her to leave her lingerie scattered on the bed. Then Guy realized the lingerie wasn't scattered, but arranged in a distinctly obscene pattern atop the aqua bed cover. A pink silk underwire bra and matching french-cut bikini panties were placed to resemble the figure of a woman on the bed; a pair of shimmering black stockings and lace garters were placed to resemble legs with one ankle crossed over the other in a blatantly seductive posture.

Repulsed and puzzled, Guy took a step toward the bed, then he heard something behind him. He had time to make a half turn and to fling up his arm in an instinctive protective gesture before the red-black pain exploded behind his eyes and he felt himself falling. He crashed against the bureau and heard glass breaking, saw a blur pushing past him. He struggled to hold on to consciousness, but lost in the battle in a wave of nausea and defeat.

The last thing he thought was, *Carol, don't come home now, Carol, run* ...

Chapter Twenty-one

Blood on the carpet. Blood in spatters on the stairs where he had fallen trying to get down, smeared on the hand rail where he had caught himself. Blood, it seemed, was everywhere. When Carol closed her eyes, she saw a whirling vortex of it and it was all she could do not to press her hands against her eyes and scream until it went away.

Because what she saw when she opened her eyes was no better.

"Damn it, he was here," Guy was muttering to the paramedic who was trying to bandage his head. "I could have had him. I can't believe I was that close and let him get away."

The sound of his voice brought the harsh sting of tears to Carol's eyes, filling her with terror and gratitude and irrational fury. She had to look away from him, blinking hard and breathing slowly, to keep from bursting into sobs.

The house was engulfed in chaos. Police photographers going up and down the stairs, the EMTs with all their equipment cluttering up the room, blood on the carpet, radios crackling, everyone talking at once. Carol was afraid if she even blinked, she would become so disoriented she would lose her balance and be forever sucked into this nightmare that had temporarily invaded her peaceful life.

She had seen the obscenity on the bed. The memory would bring a chill to her spine and bile to her throat for a long time to come. But no more than would the sight of Guy, with blood matting his hair and soaking into the collar of his shirt, lying crumpled on the floor.

Sheriff Case said, "Tell me again exactly what you saw, Mrs. Dennison."

Carol's fingers dug so tightly into her crossed arms that she could feel the bruises, but that was the only way she could bring the shivering under control. Her shirt and hair were still damp from rain, and even though the window had been closed, the room was cold. It was a deeper cold that chilled her, though, and it came from inside.

She said harshly, "I'd rather talk about what a maniac like that is doing running around loose, Sheriff. You said he just got out of prison? Why the hell isn't he still in prison?"

Guy made an involuntary sound of pain as the paramedic applied a strip of adhesive tape to the gash behind his ear, and Carol's attention immediately shot to him. Her fingers tightened on her arms.

Sheriff Case said, "We don't really know that the man we're talking about is the one who broke in here, so it might be better if we don't jump to conclusions just yet. Could you start at the beginning, please?"

Carol tightened her lips, and made herself look away from Guy. The paramedics had made him remove his shirt and from where she stood, she could see the long, welting red-purple bruise on his arm and shoulder, where he had deflected the full force of the fireplace poker as it came down on his head. If he had not, the blow would have crushed the base of his skull. Carol could not think about that without fighting back a new wave of nausea and shivers.

She said, in a carefully controlled, low and steady voice, "I got Guy's call on my cell phone, telling me he was on his way over and he needed to talk to me. When I got here, his car was in the garage and the door was unlocked. I assumed he had gone in."

The sheriff said, "And this didn't bother you."

"I was annoyed at him, I told you that. I had just recently asked him not to come in without an invitation."

"So something happened recently to make you say that? You had a fight?"

Carol could feel her color rising. "No, of course not! It's just—I've always asked him not to do that—"

"And he continued to ignore you?"

"For God's sake, John, leave her alone," Guy said shortly, with an edge to his voice that wasn't entirely pain-induced. "She didn't have anything to do with this, I told you that."

The paramedics began to pack up their equipment. "We'll need to take you in for x-rays, Mr. Dennison," the senior officer said. "We can bring up the gurney if you don't feel up to walking to the ambulance."

"No," Guy said. "Forget it." The stubbornness in his tone was unmistakable. "I'm not going anywhere." He reached for his bloodstained shirt.

Carol said in alarm, "Guy, please—"

And the paramedic added soberly. "A head injury is nothing to mess around with, sir. I'm afraid I have to insist."

Guy said impatiently, "And I'm afraid I—" But a sharp intake of breath cut off his words as he pulled on his shirt over his injured arm, and Carol took an involuntary step toward him.

"Don't be an idiot, Guy, go with them." She knelt beside him and eased the shirt over his shoulder. "I'll be right behind you."

And Case added, "We've got all we need from you, Guy. Go on."

Guy glared at him. "Not until you stop wasting time trying to intimidate Carol and put some effort into investigating this case. I told you, I saw him."

"But not well enough to identify him."

"Well enough to know it was him. Jesus, common sense should tell you that. Carol at her maddest couldn't have done this to my arm, I don't care how hard she swung that poker. And I've seen her plenty mad, let me tell you."

That drew a rueful smile from Case. "I'll tell you the truth, I'm inclined to agree with you. But..." And he fixed a meaningful look on Carol. "It's important to remember there are no clear answers here. If you could just go on with what happened after you came inside."

Carol looked anxiously at Guy, then got to her feet again. She repeated, brusquely and matter-of-factly—or at least as matter-of-factly as she was able—"I saw the window was open and it was cold. I closed it."

"When you went to the window, did you see anything? Think hard."

This time Carol hesitated, trying to replay the moment in her head. The shock of entering her bedroom, of seeing what she had seen on the bed and of finding Guy, had all but erased the previous moments from her head.

"It had been raining off and on all day. It was still misty, and visibility wasn't very good. There may have been someone running on the beach, far down. I didn't really pay any attention."

She knew the intruder had made his escape beachside. There were footprints on the deck, and on the beach at the end of the boardwalk, which were fresh enough to have been made after the rain.

She went on, "I called out Guy's name and when he didn't answer, I went upstairs. I thought he might be on the deck or the roof. When I went into the bedroom I saw—" Here she had to swallow. The thought of filthy hands going through her underthings, selecting, arranging, forming an imaginary woman on her bed— she made herself go on. "I saw the clothes on the bed, and I knew someone had been there. I was scared. When I moved toward the bed, I saw the poker on the floor, and the blood."

"But you didn't pick it up."

She shook her head. "I might have, but then I saw Guy. I—at first I thought he was... But then I saw he was semiconscious. He kept muttering something about the man who was getting away. I called the paramedics, then you. Can we go now?"

Guy said, waving away the offer of assistance from the paramedic as he got to his feet, "What about the phone call Carol got? Do you think it could have been made from here?"

"It was a woman's voice, I told you that. It couldn't have been the same person who attacked you." Carol couldn't help noticing how pale Guy was growing, and that he leaned heavily against the wall for support. She knew any offer of help would only make him more stubborn about going to the hospital, though, so she bit her tongue.

Case said, "And it wasn't the same person who called before?"

"No. I don't think so." At this point she wasn't sure of anything.

"She gave a name, damn it," Guy said with a display of energy that seemed to come close to depleting his reserves. He frowned as though trying to remember. "It was—you wrote it down. Why don't you check it out?"

Case glanced at him sympathetically. "We will. And we'll also check out the possibility that the call was made from here. I know you're upset, but we have done this kind of thing before. Some people might even say we're specialists in this business."

Deputy Long came down the stairs with the fireplace poker carefully wrapped in an oversized evidence bag. He believed in doing things right, it was plain to see. He said, "I think we've got everything here, Sheriff. We'll need a set of elimination prints from both victims, of course, and anyone else who might have handled objects in the bedroom, particularly the poker."

Case nodded. "Guy, get yourself over to the hospital and get checked out. If I need anything else, I'll be in touch."

"Don't worry," Guy said. His voice was starting to sound tired. "I'll make sure you do."

The paramedic took Guy's arm in a firm grip and this time he didn't object. Carol hurried to get her purse and opened the door for them.

Sheriff Case said, "Mrs. Dennison."

She looked back.

"I'll be sending a team over to dust for prints, and the place might be kind of a mess tonight. You might want to think about staying somewhere else overnight, just for your own comfort."

She knew, from the look on his face, that what he meant to say was, "for your own safety". She started to like him a little better, not because he was concerned about her, but because he didn't say so in front of Guy.

She said, "Yes. I think I will."

She saw Guy and the paramedics safely out the door, then hurried behind them. She knew it would be a long time before she would be comfortable staying alone in that house again.

Chapter Twenty-two

But he's going to be okay?" Laura insisted worriedly as she brought a tray of coffee and sandwiches into the living room, where Carol sat huddled by the fire.

She nodded. "They always keep head injuries overnight for observation. It's routine. They think he has a mild concussion, nothing's broken. God, Laura, I'll have to borrow a nightgown. I couldn't even go back there to pack." She couldn't entirely suppress a shudder. "I'm not sure I'll ever be able to wear anything in my closet again anyway. Not knowing what he touched or ... rubbed over himself."

Laura sank swiftly to the hassock at Carol's feet and placed a hand over hers. "Don't do that," she commanded firmly. "I know you can't just put it out of your mind, but there's no need to make it easy for that sleaze to drive you crazy, either. Besides,"—she tried to coax a smile— "I don't think your homeowner's insurance will cover replacing your wardrobe under these circumstances."

Carol tried to smile. "You're probably right."

Laura gave Carol's hand a final reassuring squeeze and got up.

Her house was located on the marsh side of town; she claimed she didn't mind the occasional cottonmouth in her windowbox or alligator in the fishpond in exchange for the spectacular morning and evening views. The house itself was a cozy traditional design of stone and columns, with wraparound porches and dormer windows. Her second husband, a contractor, had built it as a wedding present, and Laura had shamelessly brought husband number three to live there for the six months it took her to discover his problem with alcohol and other women. Sometimes it brought a wry smile to Carol's face when she thought of the symbols they each had retained of marriages long failed, times from which they both should have moved on. But she wasn't smiling tonight.

Carol pulled the wooly afghan a little tighter about her shoulders, frowning into the flames. "I should have stayed at the hospital," she said worriedly. "I shouldn't have left him."

"There was nothing you could do."

"I know, but it just seems—wrong, somehow, to leave him. He wouldn't be hurt if it wasn't for me."

Laura fixed her attention on the coffee she was pouring. "And you wouldn't be in danger if it wasn't for him."

Carol rubbed a hand across her forehead. "I guess."

Laura brought two cups of coffee over to the fire and handed one to Carol before she resumed her seat on the hassock near Carol's feet. "What did the police say about the woman who called you?"

Carol shook her head, staring thoughtfully into the coffee mug. Its heat was welcome, but her throat was still so dry she didn't think she could swallow anything, not even coffee.

"They couldn't figure out how it was related to the intruder," she said. "Neither can I." She shrugged clumsily. "Of course, the police never tell you what they're thinking. So I guess the answer is, "who knows?"

Laura said, "Maybe they're not related."

Carol tried to follow her, but she could barely make her thoughts focus on one sentence at a time. She kept thinking about Guy, and the black and swelling imprint the poker had left on his arm. The way he'd put on his tough-guy act at the hospital, joking with the nurses and chatting with the other patients in the emergency room. He had done it so she wouldn't worry. He shouldn't have wasted his strength. Carol would never stop worrying, not now.

She made herself look at Laura, her expression helpless and apologetic. "I'm afraid I don't..."

Laura gave a brief dismissive shake of her head, although it was clear her impatience was not directed at Carol. "It's just that—men. They always have to have everything all tied up in a neat little package. Sometimes I think it's because their brains can't handle more than one concept at a time. The man that broke in today— why does he have to be this same ex-con who's been threatening Guy? And why does he have to be behind the phone calls you've been getting? I mean, there are hundreds of college kids swarming over this island and yours isn't the first empty beach house that's been broken into this week. As for the lingerie—well, just because you're a burglar doesn't mean you can't be a pervert."

Carol lifted the coffee cup to her face and inhaled the steam, but couldn't bring herself to drink. "I don't think I like your theory."

"It's no more cockeyed than anything Guy or the police have come up with. They don't have a single piece of evidence to link all three of these things together."

"I know." Carol raised her eyes from the cup to look at Laura, her expression bleak. "But if you're right, then I've got three people out there to worry about—four, if you count the woman who called me this afternoon—and that's at least three more than I can deal with."

Laura nodded glumly. "God, honey," she said, "what did you ever do to deserve this?"

Carol managed a dry grimace. "When I find out, I'll let you know, because I'm going to make sure I never do it again." And then she groaned. "Damn, the police are going to want to interview Ken Carlton. I hate to involve a client in something like this. But he was with me when the call came in."

"I don't suppose he made an offer on one of our beachfront lots before you distracted him, did he?"

Carol accepted her friend's attempt to cheer her up. "No. But he looked kind of interested in those three adjoining lots on Deer Trail. Then it started raining and..." She trailed off. Laura knew the rest of the story.

They sat in silence for a while, listening to the crackle of the fire and the rush of wind and rain against the windows. The clouds of the afternoon had gathered force for one last angry burst, and from the sound of it, a genuine coastal storm was on the way.

Carol realized she missed the sound of the surf. She wanted her house back, and she was angry, briefly and fiercely, at the intruder who had taken it from her—and who had taken, more importantly, the innocence of security she had always felt within its walls.

Then Laura said, "Whatever happened to you two anyway?"

Carol was confused. "Me and Ken Carlton?"

"You and the only man you've ever loved, fool," Laura said with a mixture of indulgence and exasperation that made Carol smile.

"We broke up," she said.

Laura looked at her steadily. "No, you didn't."

Carol closed her eyes for a moment. When she spoke, her voice was low and strained. "God, I don't know. We always had more passion than sense. We were so different, we knew exactly how to get on each other's nerves, and after all those years it just got so hard, you know? Hard to keep fighting, hard to keep explaining, hard to keep overlooking things and forgiving things." Her lips tightened with a brief sharp shake of her head, and her voice grew abruptly thick as she said, "Stupid things, all of them, the kinds of things every marriage goes through and none of them were worth losing our daughter over."

It took a moment to collect herself and she didn't look at Laura. She tasted her coffee and finished in a calmer, more tired voice, "I don't know what happened. I never knew what happened. We just—let it get away from us, somehow, the anger and the stress and the stupidity. But the thing is—the really strange thing is—if it hadn't been for Kelly, and what happened, I don't think it would have been permanent. I think we would have gotten back together." She shrugged and almost managed a wry smile. "Another thing we let get away from us."

Rain slammed against the windows and sputtered down the chimney. Carol shivered. Laura put a comforting hand on Carol's knee, then sat back.

In a moment Laura said, "This woman, girl, whoever she was—she gave you her name?"

Carol nodded. "The police didn't seem nearly as impressed by that as you might think."

"Well, maybe not, but it seems to me it's a place to start."

Carol frowned again into her coffee cup. Small flames, reflected from the fireplace, danced within its black depths like eyes glittering in the jungle. She said, "I don't know, Laura. When I first got the call, when I listened to her, I was convinced she was just who she said she was and that she did know something about Kelly. But now … I mean, this man was a child molester, a rapist. He was…" She had to catch her breath and then swallow hard, because she had not even had the courage to say the words to herself until now. "He was in Tallahassee when Kelly disappeared and it's possible he—knew her and now he wants to get back at Guy for putting him in prison and it's all just so crazy. I mean, the things this girl said—that Kelly couldn't get away, like she was being held prisoner, that she knew where Kelly was but she couldn't tell me any more than Kelly—the first caller—could. It's crazy. The kinds of things you would say if you wanted to torment someone. And the voice … the more I think about it, the more I think it might have been the same one—kind of hoarse and husky like." She looked at Laura and drew a breath. "It might have been a man, disguising his voice."

Laura nodded, understanding. "Maybe you're right. Maybe this has been just one long sick joke designed to torment you and Guy, and now they've got the fingerprints of the man who's behind it. He'll be back in jail in no time."

Carol dropped her eyes. "Maybe." And it was awful. Because she wanted to believe it, and she didn't. She wanted it to be that simple ... and she couldn't bear it if it were.

"On the one hand," Carol said quietly, needing to voice her thoughts out loud. "Kelly never called me at all. She walked away all those years ago and never looked back, or—or she's dead. On the other hand"—and she had to draw another long and calming breath— "she's being held prisoner somewhere—and not just her, but this Tanya girl, God, maybe even more than that ... all this time, kidnapped, locked up, tortured by some maniac, and all within viewing distance of my house."

She looked at her friend, her eyes haunted and torn. "Pick one," she said simply.

Laura reached up and closed her fingers over Carol's hand, but she did not reply. There was nothing to say.

They both knew that.

Chapter Twenty-three

For two weeks every March and September, Chip Sanders and his wife rented a beach cottage on the channel end of St. T. He spent his days fishing while Margaret read on the beach, and at the end of the day, they met for a good dinner at Bay Breezes. Sometimes they went the entire day without hearing another human voice. In the real world Chip was a fifty-eight-year-old building contractor, and Margaret was a telephone operator. Those weeks at St. T. were the most peaceful of their lives.

Chip walked down early the morning after the rain, carrying his fishing tackle, a yellow bait bucket, and a cooler filled with ice for his catch. The beach was deserted in that cool purplish dawn, the shoreline slightly rearranged from the pounding it had taken during the night, and the surf dark and noisy. The fish would be jumping today.

He wore a pair of bright red hip waders and a straw hat. By the time Margaret came down with his lunch, the sun would be hot and he would have been standing thigh-high in the surf for four or five hours, if he was lucky.

When they weren't biting, he fished from the sand. But if anything was swimming out there at all, the only way to go for it was to get right out there with them.

In March, whiting and flounder were beginning their spawning behavior, redfish were abundant, and so were speckled trout. And he could always look forward to the thrill—sometimes once or twice a week—of hooking a baby shark, particularly after a good storm like they had had last night.

Chip set up his camp chair and cooler on the sand far enough away from the tide line so that he wouldn't have to worry about moving it when the tide came in—which he had been known to forget to do on more than one occasion—and started to bait his hook. He scanned the surf, speculating on what might be biting, and decided to start out with the shrimp he had bought fresh from the bait shop last night.

Then something in the surf caught his eyes and he swore. A dolphin. He hated it when they fed this close to shore. They were always breaking his lines, not to mention driving the fish away. On the other hand, dolphins only went where the fish were, which could mean good news.

But it wasn't a dolphin. Chip's eyes narrowed and he took a couple of steps forward, searching the tide. He saw it again, and his throat went dry. Slowly, still not quite believing what he saw, he put his fishing pole down and moved closer to the surf.

There was no mistaking it this time. Long dark hair swirling around like seaweed, a white hand flip-flopping back and forth with the surge and crash of the tide. Chip took a few purely instinctive running steps into the surf, then stopped.

He shouted, "Hey!" for no reason at all. He looked frantically over his shoulder, calling again, "Hey!" But the beach was deserted, and Margaret, still asleep in their cottage across the dunes, was too far away to hear.

Lacking no other options, Chip splashed forward grimly to retrieve what the sea offered up.

Chapter Twenty-four

Derrick Long was thirty-two-years old, married, no children. Patsy, his wife of nine years, had M.S., dormant now and perhaps for years to come, but never far from their minds, never out of their lives.

Maybe because of Patsy's illness, maybe because of Patsy herself, every day was precious to him. He was grateful when he woke up beside her. He was grateful when he sat down across the table from her. He was grateful when he walked into a room and she was there and it didn't matter what he had been through during the day, it was all worth it because she was there. He would have felt like a sentimental idiot saying these things, of course. And perhaps the best thing about Patsy was that he didn't have to.

She was a nurse at Mid County Hospital, a job she loved even though Derrick worried it was too stressful for her. Still, with their combined incomes, they could barely afford the split-level house on three acres off County Line Road. Patsy wanted to live in the country, which was one of the reasons that when the job with the St. Theresa County Sheriff's Department opened up, he had jumped at it. He had never regretted the decision.

A lot of officers made it a policy never to discuss their cases with their family. Derrick made it a policy always to discuss his cases with Patsy. She had been so proud of him when he made investigator; he knew he wouldn't have made it without her. Sometimes he called her Mrs. Colombo and she laughed, but there was more truth to that than she knew. Things didn't really make sense to Derrick until he talked them over with Patsy.

But they had been discussing the Dennison case for days now, and it still didn't make much sense.

"I told you," said Patsy, thoughtfully munching on a piece of toast, "that it wasn't the husband trying to get back at the wife. Not after all these years."

Derrick shrugged uncomfortably. "That was never a serious theory."

Patsy was working three to eleven this week, so she had been in the emergency room when Guy Dennison was brought in. She now felt she had a special involvement in the case, which was evident as she informed Derrick a trifle smugly, "And there's no way that tiny Mrs. Dennison did that kind of damage to her husband with a fireplace poker—not even if he was sound asleep at the time and she had been working out for six months."

He gave her a dry look. "You're pushing it, baby."

"Well, at least now you have a real criminal to track down—and a pretty good idea of who he is."

Derrick nodded. "That was always the thing that bothered me," he admitted, glancing at the clock on the wall over her head before he refilled his coffee cup. "That was the thing that never made sense. Why would the Dennison girl call now, after all these years, with those crazy messages? She was doing just fine living on the streets, but almost three years later, she comes home and gets into so much trouble she has to call her mother for help. But she can't tell her mother where she is or what kind of trouble she's in or how anybody can help her. Well, I mean, nothing about the whole thing made sense, but it's a relief to know we don't have a lost girl out there to track down."

Patsy lifted her coffee cup to her lips with both hands, fingers delicately curved around the mug, "You don't?"

Derrick frowned a little. That was one of the things he still hadn't quite worked out. "Well, no. I mean obviously it had to be Saddler, disguising his voice somehow or using an accomplice to make the calls. He just got out of prison, that's when this whole thing started. He blamed Dennison for his arrest. He's probably been brooding on it all these years, planning how he was going to get his revenge."

Patsy said, "And one way to get that revenge couldn't be to seduce Dennison's daughter? To drag her into his scheme for revenge?"

Derrick's frown deepened. "Do you mean Kelly Dennison herself might be his accomplice?"

"Why not?"

"Kind of a coincidence, don't you think?"

"It's only a coincidence until you find out the real explanation."

"Did somebody say that?"

She smiled. "Me." Then, "Anyway, what about that other girl—that Tanya whoever? Why would he make up another name—one that means nothing to the

Dennisons? Wouldn't he just stick with Kelly if he wanted to scare them?"

"So you're saying there really are two girls out there for us to worry about?"

She shook her head. "Not necessarily. One is all you need."

'Tanya Little," Derrick said thoughtfully. "Saddler's accomplice. But why would she give her real name?"

"Well, she wouldn't," Patsy pointed out equitably, "if she were Saddler's accomplice—or at least his willing accomplice."

"You're not being very helpful."

"Sure, I am. Now you have two leads on Saddler—Tanya Little and Kelly Dennison. Find either one of them and you'll have Saddler."

"Maybe." His tone was doubtful. "Seems to me it would be easier to just find Saddler in the first place." And he grinned, getting up to clear the table. "Of course, I'm just an amateur."

"But gifted," she allowed generously, then her expression sobered. "I don't know, honey. There's an awful lot about this case that still doesn't add up. I just can't help but wonder if you're not giving Saddler too much credit. Are you sure it was him who was in Carol Dennison's house yesterday?"

"We'll know as soon as the report on the fingerprints come back from the lab—which should be first thing this morning." The phone rang just as he passed it, and he scooped it up. "Maybe that's the office now. I told them to call as soon as the report came in."

It was the office, but not with the fingerprint report. Two minutes later, Derrick Long was out the door and on his way to what he knew already was going to be a very bad day.

Chapter Twenty-five

By the time the day nurse came on duty, Guy had showered, shaved—albeit a little shakily—and dressed in the wrinkled, bloodstained clothes he'd found stashed in a plastic bag in his closet. Carol had said something about bringing a change of clothes by for him that morning when she came to take him home, but he couldn't wait. He spent a few minutes arguing absently with the nurse who had some fixation about patients being dismissed by their doctors before they went home and Walt was waiting for him when he went outside.

"Man, you gotta start hanging out at better bars," was all the big man said as Guy got into the Jeep.

"Yeah, tell me about it." Guy gingerly touched the bandage on the back of his head. It still throbbed dully, but if he remembered not to make any sudden movements, the pain was manageable.

Walt pulled out onto the highway and the light traffic that constituted rush hour in St. Theresa County, chomping down on a tattered cigar. Walt Marshall had long hair, a bushy beard, and weighed three hundred pounds on a light day. He favored Jimmy Buffett T-shirts that were always too tight on him, and was rarely seen without the cigar, which Guy had never known him to light. He was arguably the wealthiest full-time resident of St. Theresa County, but most nights ate dinner from a TV tray in front of a fuzzy-pictured, nineteen-inch television set. That was why Guy liked him. Except for the part about being wealthy, they had a lot in common.

Walt said, "A sheriff's deputy was by last week with mug shots of some dude they said was gunning for you. Guess he found you, huh?"

"More like I found him."

"Good going, Slick."

"He got away."

"Yeah, I heard about your troubles last night on the police scanner. I was going to send you flowers."

"Thanks for not."

"Shaping up to be one of them weeks," Walt went on, chewing the cigar. "Moon's in Scorpio."

Guy leaned his head back gingerly and closed his eyes. "Oh, yeah?"

"Damn straight. Had a floater wash up before sunrise this morning."

Guy opened his eyes. "What?"

"Some kid, probably drunk, swum out too far. Girl, I think. Fisherman found her near the channel cut, what was left of her anyway."

"Jesus." Guy stared at him. Everything inside him went cold. A girl, dead. He would never hear those words, never in all his life, without thinking first of his daughter. "Who was it? One of ours?" By "ours" he meant a local, and he knew how self-serving it sounded the moment the word was out. But he was, first and foremost, a reporter.

"Don't know. That was when you called, and I had to leave."

Guy said, "Listen, Walt, forget the marina. Take me straight to the office."

But one of Walt's eccentricities was his peculiar notion of propriety. He refused to take Guy to the office looking, in his words, "like a bad highway wreck," and he insisted on waiting while Guy changed clothes and then driving him to Carol's house to pick up his car.

Guy was glad to see Carol wasn't home; she had said she was spending the night with Laura. He scrawled a note—"Sweetie—I'm okay, call me at work. G." and pinned it between the storm door and the frame to protect it from the wind. In the end, it was nine o'clock before he got to the office.

"I've heard of devotion to duty," said Rachel when he came in, "but this is ridiculous. You look like death warmed over. Aren't you supposed to be in the hospital or something?"

"My, how news does travel." Everyone was staring at him and Guy was embarrassed. He beckoned Rachel to follow him into his office.

"Maybe that's why they call us a newspaper?" she said, coming inside and closing the door. Concern was on her face, and Guy was touched—and even more embarrassed. "Are you okay?" she asked.

"A little headache, that's all. Listen, I need a favor. Tanya Little—that name sounds familiar to me. Get somebody to look it up, will you? Lindy, if she's free."

Rachel had her notebook out. "Local?"

"I don't know. I doubt it. Seems like—oh, I don't know." He pinched the bridge of his nose between his fingers, trying to concentrate. "Three or four years ago."

"Got it," Rachel said briskly. "Anything else?"

"Yeah. Get Deputy Long on the phone and if my"—— he stopped himself before saying "wife"—— "Carol calls, transfer her to my cell phone. I'm going to be out of the office most of the morning."

Rachel closed the notebook, a stubborn look on her face. "We have reporters——" began a familiar argument.

"And I'll call one if I need one. Now try the sheriff's office, will you? If Long's not there, try to find out where he is."

Ed Jenkins came in the door just as Rachel was leaving. They shared a look——hers fraught with meaning, his bland. Ed said, "How're you feeling?"

"Like shit."

"Better than you look."

"Thanks."

"Carol okay?"

"Yeah. She stayed over with Laura."

"Any word on the perp, as we say in the biz?"

"They're waiting for a fingerprint match, but if you took a wild guess, you wouldn't be wrong."

Ed's face was grim. "So I figured. Listen, it's your call. The radio station has news about the break-in, but all they know is that you, and I quote, surprised a burglar in your ex-wife's home. They've been calling, but we haven't told them anything. If you want to keep it quiet, it never happened. You want headlines, you got them."

Guy thought only a moment. "Quiet, for now," he said. Then he added, "Thanks, Ed."

"You bet. Now go home."

Guy said, "What's the word on that kid who washed up on the beach?"

"I've got someone covering it."

"Yeah. Me."

"I don't think so." Ed looked uncomfortable. "They, uh—well not much is coming in yet but apparently the body's in pretty bad shape. Sharks and, well, you know."

"Come on, I'm not in that bad a shape. I can hold my cookies if that's what you're worried about." But in truth he wasn't as anxious to get on the story as he once had been.

"Maybe, but that's not it." Ed looked increasingly reluctant. "I just don't think you need this right now, okay?"

"Need what?"

Ed released a tense breath. "Look," he said. "The kid—she was about Kelly's age. And they think she was murdered."

Chapter Twenty-six

For Sheriff John Case, it was every spring break nightmare come true. News vans from as far away as Mexico Beach and Tallahassee were parked outside his office. A convicted rapist and child molester was on the loose, a young student was dead, his waiting room was brimming over with reporters and microphones and there on the front row, looking gray and grim and as alert as ever, was the man who was at the center of it all, Guy Dennison. And Sheriff John Case, dry-mouthed and sweating like a pig, had to stand up before them all and say, "We are withholding the name of the victim pending notification of next of kin. Though we won't have any details until we receive the autopsy report, we can tell you that the victim was a female, eighteen years old, and a student from the University of Virginia. It does appear at this time that she has been dead for at least twelve hours. She had, uh, been sexually assaulted before death."

Someone called out. "Are you calling this an ordinary drowning, Sheriff?"

A trickle of sweat rolled down the back of his neck. He did not lift his hand to wipe it. "No," he said, "we're not."

A babble of voices then. What, where, when, who...

Sheriff Case said loudly, "We are interviewing friends of the victim and others connected with this case. I have no other information for you at this time."

He went quickly through the crowd and into his office, shutting the door firmly behind him. He thought, *I reckon I could have handled that better. About a million times better.*

The door opened on a cacophony of murmurs and clatters and he looked up sharply. Guy Dennison came in and closed the door. Case scowled.

"I thought we were rid of you for at least a week."

"Nice attitude toward a crime victim. No wonder those vultures out there are after your blood."

Sheriff Case noted Guy's pallor, the set of his jaw, the flat dark color of his eyes, and he correctly attributed all to symptoms of something more than the aftermath of injury. Guy Dennison had the look of a man forcing himself to walk through hell for the simple reason that no one else was willing to do it, and Case was instantly sympathetic. This story had to be Dennison's worst nightmare; the one reason he had left big-city reporting for the small-time news of St. T. Yet even here it followed him: the assault and murder of a teenage girl who could have been his daughter, and no one could cover the story as well as the man who had lived through it already.

Case gestured him to be seated. "The girl's name was Mickie Anderson, from Wilmington, West Virginia. Her folks are on their way, but I'd rather not have them trampled by reporters until we get a chance to talk to them."

Guy nodded, making note of the name and knowing without being told to keep it to himself. The paper would release a special edition at four-thirty. That was all the lead time he got.

Case went on wearily, "One of her girlfriends reported her missing night before last. They had driven up for the day from Panama City. Apparently she was bragging all day about some guy she'd met who was going to make her a star or some shit."

Something tickled in the back of Guy's mind, but he couldn't quite catch it.

The sheriff went on tiredly, "Then she had a fight with her boyfriend and as far as I can tell, she went off to meet this guy and that was the last anyone saw of her. When she wasn't at the meeting place when they all got ready to go home this kid had the sense—God only knows how—to call our office. We didn't think much of it, just jotted down her name and school and where the caller could be reached. Like this was the only kid that didn't show up to catch her ride home? But anyway, we got a positive i.d. a few minutes ago. Mickie Anderson, eighteen years old."

The last words were uttered heavily, with an effort. His gaze was fixed on his desk blotter, where there was nothing to hold his attention but his own thoughts. He added quietly, "Do you know how long it's been since I had to deal with anything like this? Hell, that's why I live here."

Guy said carefully, "We have drowning and boat accidents every year."

Case looked up at him sharply. "This was no fucking boat accident. That kid was murdered. She was tied up, raped, tortured, then strangled to death. Her nipples had been sliced off. Finger tips. There were cuts all over her body. Of course, the fish..." He had to stop and clear his throat. "Well, it was hard to tell a lot by looking at her. We're bringing in a state forensic pathologist for more grisly details, but that's enough to make sure I don't sleep at night for a while. We've got a convicted rapist walking around loose looking for trouble and we've got a dead teenager who was tortured and raped before somebody tossed her in the water. And we've got a definite match between Saddler's on-file prints and the ones on the poker that brained you last night. What we don't have is Saddler."

Guy said softly, "Shit."

"You're telling me."

The two men looked at each other silently for a time. Then Case said, "There is another possibility. Seems like this Mickie was a real wild card. Picked up this guy in Panama City, rode down here with him, ended up balling him on the beach, having a big fight, stalking off. That was the last anybody saw of her. Long brought him in with the girlfriend to identify the body. He's questioning him now."

The tone of his voice suggested he did not anticipate helpful results.

Guy said tersely, "A man like Saddler can't hide out forever. The county's not that damn big."

Case returned, "You want my goddamn job? You're welcome to it." Then, rubbing his forehead, he added, "We're getting help from the state police. Something's got to break soon."

Guy said, " 'Spring Break Turns Tragic.' We'll play down the rape angle until you have more details." He hesitated. "What was she wearing when she was found?"

Case consulted a file on his desk. "She was reported missing wearing denim shorts and a red bandanna top. She was found nude."

Guy looked somber. "That makes it a little harder to gloss over sexual assault."

"Right." He was silent for a moment. "How's your head?"

"It's been better." Guy stood to go. "I'm going to try to talk to the kids who made the i.d." He hesitated. "How bad was the body?"

"The face wasn't so bad. The legs and torso were pretty chewed up. The witnesses aren't in great shape. I told Long to keep them away from reporters until they calm down."

"Good call," Guy said absently, starting for the door.

"Guy, listen." Case looked and sounded old for the first time since Guy had known him. "We're doing the best we can but—better keep an eye on Carol until we get this creep behind bars, okay? And watch your own ass, too."

Guy's phone rang as he was leaving the office. He answered it absently.

"You stubborn, selfish son of a bitch," Carol said. "I always did say it would take more than a big stick to knock some sense into you and now I see I was right. I thought you were going to wait for me to take you home."

Guy walked a few steps down the corridor for privacy. "Thanks for caring, sweetheart."

"The police left the house a mess," she said tensely. "No one will tell me anything. It looks like they emptied an ashcan all over the bedroom and they took—they took my lingerie. Did you tell them they could do that?

Who's going to clean this place up? Why won't anybody tell me anything?"

Guy said, "Carol, I don't want you staying there alone."

"I live here, damn it! This is where I live!" He heard her sharp intake of breath. "I called a locksmith. He's replacing the locks today and putting security bolts on the windows. And I'm calling Elsie to give the place a good cleaning, top to bottom, so I hope the police are finished with their investigation. You might tell your good friend John Case I appreciate all his help if you see him."

Guy smiled a little. That sounded more like Carol. In control, on top of the situation, blindly—sometimes stupidly—sweeping away obstacles. He said, "Do I get a key?"

"What?"

"To the new locks. I should have a key."

"You're the main reason I'm having the locks replaced," she retorted. "I should have done it years ago."

Guy's smile faded and he lowered his voice a little as he said, "Listen, Carol, in all the excitement last night—I didn't get a chance to tell you how sorry I am."

Her silence was startled. "Sorry for what?"

"This." With his head ducked over the telephone he made a short and helpless gesture with his wrist that included the corridor, the jail, the world at large, just as though she could see him. "Everything. The trouble. You're in the middle of it because of me and I'm sorry."

The silence went on a beat or two. Her voice sounded thick and a little watery when she answered, "Only you would apologize for being knocked unconscious by a criminal who's looting my house. Get some backbone, will you?"

He heard her sniff, or thought he did, and he wished she could see the reassuring smile that came automatically to his lips. If he had been with her, he would have squeezed her hand, or touched her hair, or pulled her head onto his shoulder. They had been married too long not to want to comfort each other in times of pain—even when they themselves were the cause of that pain.

She said, in a little stronger tone, "And go home and go to bed like you were told to do. I don't want to have to worry about you collapsing with an aneurysm or hematoma on top of everything else."

A surprised laugh escaped him. "Where did you get ideas like that?"

"From the literature they gave me in the emergency room last night," she returned sharply. "Go home, Guy. And don't try telling me you are at home, because Rachel already told me you're covering a story. Believe me, it's not that important."

Obviously, she hadn't turned on the radio that morning. Guy decided she had enough on her mind without the news of the murdered teenager—and Saddler's involvement, too.

Guy said, "You're probably right. But I figured if I didn't show up for work today, the paper would be reporting me dead by this afternoon."

"Idiot," she said, but indulgently.

Guy thought, I love you, Carol. I really do. But it was not a new realization, and certainly did not require verbalization. He had had the same thought twice a week, twice a month, sometimes twice a day, almost from the moment he'd met her. He supposed he always would.

He said, "Listen, honey..." He was about to do something stupid and embarrassing, like asking her to lunch or admonishing her, once again, to be careful. But he was saved from himself by the passage of a deputy, who opened a door a few feet down the hall and gave Guy an intriguing glimpse of the two people inside. He finished, "I've got to go. Let me call you this afternoon, okay?"

Her voice had an edge. "Don't put yourself out."

The deputy came back out of the room, and Guy saw that one of the occupants was definitely Deputy Long. The other was a young, blond man who seemed very upset. Guy disconnected almost absently and moved down the hall.

Chapter Twenty-seven

C arol replaced the receiver with a vengeance when she found herself listening to a dead line. "Damn him," she muttered, and then was embarrassed to look up and see Laura leaning against the doorframe.

"Come on, honey, you knew he was a snake when you picked him up."

That had never failed to make Carol smile. After Laura's first divorce, Carol had tried to cheer her up with the story of the woman who had found a snake frozen by the roadside. She had taken it home, warmed it by the fire, fed it, and nursed it back to health, then had been shocked and outraged when the reptile rewarded her with a poisonous bite. The moral of the story, whether having to do with the stupidity of women's nurturing instincts or the treachery of snakes of the male persuasion—or perhaps neither—was by that time lost at the bottom of a pina colada haze which dissolved into meaningless and uncontrollable giggles with the punch line, "You knew I was a snake when you picked me up." Since then the epithet, used back and forth as an admonition or an indictment or a mere statement of fact regarding men in general, had been an inside joke. But today Carol couldn't even manage a smile.

"I guess I did," she said with a sigh. "I just didn't expect to be reminded of it quite so often."

"You know what they say: We can't help who we fall in love with."

Carol looked at her friend questioningly, but Laura's expression was bland. "No. I didn't know they said that."

"I assume he's okay, and has no news on the apprehension of the suspect?"

"You assume correctly."

"Then I guess it's back to business. Ken Carlton called. He's at home."

Carol groaned. "Did he sound mad?"

"He sounded gorgeous."

"He's a client, Laura."

Laura lifted an eyebrow. "Why, my goodness. So he is." Then she said, "You want some advice? Push redial on that phone and ask your husband out to dinner. Let me take care of Carlton. You take care of what's important."

Carol looked at the telephone, her expression wan. "I guess I never have been very good at that, have I?"

"No," Laura said frankly, "you haven't." Then her expression softened. "I'm out of the office for a couple of hours. I've got to do an inspection on a couple of rentals and I thought I'd stop by the shops we missed the other day with Kelly's photo." She hesitated. "If it's all right, that is. I mean, if you think we should still…"

She trailed off, hesitance and question in her eyes and Carol smiled. "Did I ever tell you you're the best friend I've ever had?"

Laura shrugged lightly. "I thought it was assumed. Hold down the fort." At the door, she turned back. "On the subject of best friends, you know *mi casa es su casa* for as long as you need it, right?"

"I know. But I don't need it. I'm not going to let a cowardly pervert drive me out of my *casa* thank you very much. At least not yet."

Laura said in an exaggerated accent that resembled nothing familiar to Carol, "You've got spunk, kid. No wonder he's crazy about you."

"Who's crazy about me?"

But Laura just winked at her, and left.

When she was gone, Carol spent several long moments staring at her phone. But when she picked up the receiver, she did not push redial. Instead she scrolled down her contacts until she came to the number for Sea Dunes, and she dialed Ken Carlton's number.

When Guy opened the door, the kid was saying in an anguished voice, "I don't know what you want from me! I barely knew the girl!"

And Deputy Long replied smoothly, "Do you make it a habit to have sex on the beach with girls you barely know? Not very smart, you know, especially these days."

"Who told you that? We weren't having sex! It was broad damn daylight for God's sake!"

Then the kid noticed Guy and looked at him with a mixture of wretchedness and hope in his eyes. Long frowned at him.

Guy said, "Sorry, Deputy. They told me you were in here."

The boy said, "Are you a lawyer? Because he told me I didn't need a lawyer. But I don't see how they can keep me here—"

Long said patiently, "I told you Donny, we just want to ask you a few questions." To Guy he said, "If you'd just wait outside, Mr. Dennison..."

Guy told Donny, "No, I'm not a lawyer, but if you want one here while you talk to the deputy, I'll be glad to call somebody for you." He offered his hand. "My name is Guy Dennison. I'm with the local paper."

The kid looked confused. He wiped his palms on the hem of his shorts before accepting Guy's handshake. Long looked furious.

"I'm Donny, uh, Don Bradshaw," the boy said. "And like I was trying to explain I just met this girl Monday on the way down here. We had a few laughs, so what's the big deal? I mean she was a cute chick but really messed up in the head, you know what I mean? Hanging all over me one minute and biting my head off the next. And then all that crap about being in a commercial, about some famous director having the hots for her. You want to know who did her, you find him, that's what I say."

It clicked again, in the back of Guy's mind. Director. Movies. *I'm going to Hollywood.*

"Anyway, I've told everybody this, I've told them a dozen times. It's not that I didn't like her, but she was freaky, man. And when she got mad and walked off down the beach, I said to myself good riddance. Hell, I figured she had a way back, wouldn't you figure that? What was I, her keeper? I barely knew her!"

Guy said, "Have you called your folks, Donny?"

He caught a leather thong that he wore round his neck and started twisting it nervously. "Man, they're gonna kill me. Do I have to call them, man? Am I in some kind of trouble?"

Guy said, "I guess you'd have to ask the deputy here."

"Now that would be a nice change." Long's tone was mild but his jaw was tight. He glared at Guy.

Donny twisted the thong another turn. A red mark appeared near his collarbone but he didn't seem to notice. He said anxiously, "I just want to go home. Jesus, all I wanted was to come down here and hang out, have a little fun. If I got a lawyer, would it be one of those you have to pay? Couldn't you call somebody who takes, what do you call it, free cases? Because if my parents find out—"

Guy said, "Do you want a lawyer, Donny?"

Donny released his death grip on the leather necklace. He looked scared and defeated. "Yeah. I think I do."

Long bit back a curse and thrust his hands deep into his pockets, walking away. He said tightly, "Could I talk to you in the hall, Mr. Dennison?"

But Guy's attention was caught by the pendant that was suspended from the end of the leather thong around Donny's neck. He had seen it before, or something very much like it, but his head ached too fiercely for him to be certain where or when or if it even mattered. He said, "That's an unusual necklace. Where'd you get it?"

Donny looked down at the necklace as though he had never seen it before. Then his face cleared with memory and relief and he said, "She gave it to me. Doesn't that prove it? She wasn't mad at me, she liked me! She gave me this, didn't she?" He held up the little figurine pendant like a trophy.

Long closed his hand over Guy's arm authoritatively. Guy went with him to the door where Long said in a low angry tone, "Are you aware that you just blew my interrogation? What the hell's the matter with you?"

"The kid wants a lawyer," Guy said tiredly. His head really hurt. "He's got a right."

"And once he requests a lawyer, my interrogation is over until he gets one. But you knew that, didn't you?"

"That kid didn't murder the girl, you know that as well as I do," Guy said. "Let him go home."

"I don't have much choice now, do I?"

Long turned back to the boy and said abruptly, "Deputy Renkin will drive you and your friend back to your hotel when you're ready. Go out front and ask for her. But you remember what I said about you both being material witnesses in this case. You call this office before you leave Florida."

The boy, whose hurry to get out of the room was pathetic, now stopped with a look of panic on his face. "Man, I can't stay here forever! I mean, my ride's leaving at the end of the week and what am I supposed to do for money? This sucks, man!"

Long said unsympathetically, "I guess you'd better call your parents then, huh?"

Donny gave the deputy one last angry, despairing look, and then moved quickly past him into the hall. Guy followed.

"Hey, Dennison, I need to talk to you!" Long called after him.

Guy ignored him.

Guy caught up with Donny as he rounded the corner. There were still more reporters than officers crowding the room, but they were too busy speculating with one another to notice the boy.

"That's Deputy Renkin over there," Guy said, pointing to a female deputy who was talking with a weeping young girl. He assumed the girl was the friend of the deceased and he knew he should interview her, but he wasn't sure he had the energy.

Donny shot him a grateful look. "Thanks, man. I mean, for getting me out of there, too."

Guy shrugged. The motion sent a piercing pain through the back of his head. He said, "That necklace— when did she give it to you?"

He hesitated. "Well, that afternoon. Monday afternoon. She went shopping or something and when we hooked up again, she put it around my neck. Later she said something about some admirer, or some shit, giving it to her." He looked embarrassed. "I remember thinking at the time that she probably copped it, but what did I care? Anyway..." Suddenly he slipped the thong over his head and thrust the necklace to Guy. "I don't want it. It creeps me out. Maybe, I don't know, maybe you could give it to her folks or something."

Guy took the necklace. "Sure."

"Thanks, man. You're an okay dude."

That almost made Guy smile. "So I've been told."

When he was gone, Guy looked down at the odd little pendant in his hand, turning it over, testing its weight, trying to remember what was so familiar about it. But the only thing that occurred to him was what a convenient weapon that sturdy leather thong would make for strangulation. And he hoped he had not just made a mistake.

Chapter Twenty-eight

Ken Carlton said he had just been calling to check on her, which Carol found rather sweet and a little embarrassing. The police had indeed talked to him last night, for which Carol apologized profusely. Ken brushed it aside.

"We're neighbors," he reminded her. "Anything I can do to help." Then, "Listen, I know you've got a lot on your mind right now, but I've been thinking about your sales pitch—about St.T. being the resort of the future and the perfect showplace for an innovative architect."

"I'm glad to see you were paying attention."

"Oh, I was. The trouble is, you weren't selling the right thing."

"Oh?"

He chuckled. "All right, I confess. I've been taking advantage of your good nature when, as you've probably guessed, I'm far too tied up with this development deal to have any time left over for private investment."

Figures, Carol thought dryly.

"But maybe it won't be a complete loss. I'll have to talk to the other partners, of course, but right now I'm inclined to offer you the exclusive listing on all our properties, and we expect to get underway within the year."

Carol's heart skipped a beat. Jesus, she thought. A Ken Carlton exclusive listing. She felt like a child on Christmas morning, full of awe and disbelief, and wondering far back in a corner of her mind what she had done to deserve this. Exclusive. Jesus.

With all the self-discipline she possessed, she managed to keep her voice casual yet businesslike. "Where, exactly, is the development going to be?"

"Little Horse Island," he responded promptly. "I couldn't tell you before because we hadn't closed on the property and you know how quickly a great deal can go sour once word gets out."

"My goodness," murmured Carol, stunned. Her heart was still racing. In the midst of all this horror, was it possible something this incredible could actually happen to her? And because she was all too familiar with the eccentricities of life's dark humor, the answer had to be yes. It was possible.

"I didn't even know it was for sale," she added when she recovered her voice. "I don't think any of the realtors around here did. What a coup."

"We bought it directly from the state of Florida. It pays to have partners in high places. At any rate, that's what I'm doing here this summer, and I can tell you that I'm very excited about what we're going to be doing over there. I'd like to take you over and show you the plans."

"Well, of course. Let me just find a time…"

"Couldn't you get away this afternoon?"

Damn, she thought. And again, *Damn*. Of all days for her to be alone in the office. But she really had no choice.

"I'm really sorry, but my partner is out of the office and I don't know when she'll be back. I don't like to leave the office without an agent if I can help it." She added hopefully, frantically flipping through her book, "How about Thursday?"

It was an instinctive technique—never appear too anxious—and she used it automatically. Only after the words were out did she stop to wonder whether, for a Ken Carlton listing, a little anxiety might not have been appropriate.

He hesitated a moment, as though checking his calendar ... or wondering why she was not displaying more enthusiasm for the opportunity he had just offered her. "Eleven o'clock?"

"I'll meet you at the marina," she said quickly.

"See you then."

Carol hung up the phone with a long suppressed sigh of relief, and she thought, Wait until Laura hears this. It would almost, if not quite, make up for all she had put her friend through the past couple of weeks.

Almost.

Guy studied the photograph on his desk then withdrew the necklace from his pocket. The snapshot was too small to see the details of the necklace Kelly was wearing, but he remembered it clearly now. The figurine of a bound and blindfolded girl. He had questioned Kelly when she first acquired it, which was less than a week, maybe only a few days, before she disappeared. He hadn't liked the symbolism, or the vaguely S&M nature of the pendant, and he'd been afraid Kelly was hanging out with the wrong kind of crowd. When he tried to discuss it with Carol, though, she'd gotten defensive and taken his concern as a threat to her parenting skills, accusing him of paying more attention to Kelly's needs now that they were divorced than he ever had when they were married. And the significance of the necklace, if ever there had been any at all, was lost beneath the fight that followed. Now, all these years later, a young girl gives her boyfriend a necklace just like it right before she's murdered.

Guy hated coincidence.

Probably there were hundreds of little figurines like this, thousands. Probably it had some kind of special significance in the teen world, probably it was as popular today as ankhs and peace symbols had been in his time. Just because he didn't know about a trend didn't mean it didn't exist.

The Anderson girl's parents had released a photograph of their daughter—a graduation picture— smiling, happy, healthy, which the paper would run alongside the story of her murder tonight. She didn't really look like Kelly, Guy kept telling himself. Except for the long dark hair and the honey-colored skin and the dark lashes and the slim lithe figure and maybe a little in the smile. He had sent the photograph over to composing without looking at it more than once, perhaps twice.

He turned the little figurine over in his hand, frowning. He wondered what it meant, if anything, and why any young woman would be attracted to it. And why two young women, almost three years apart, had worn it and met with misfortune.

Coincidence. It was making his head throb with a blinding blue pain.

He looked up at a tap on his office door. Rachel came in with a file in her hand. "These were just faxed in for you. It's the information on that Little girl you wanted."

Guy moved too fast to grab the file and the pain was explosive. He determinedly ignored it. "Rachel, you're a genius. May the sun shine on you forever."

"Yeah, that's why they pay me the big bucks. Is that it for the day? Are you going home now?"

Guy waved her away absently. "Soon as I read this."

He opened the file. The top fax was a copy of a newspaper article from the Panama City Herald, and Guy saw immediately why the name had sounded familiar to him. He hadn't covered the story, but he had followed it, just as everyone in the news business had. LOCAL GIRL FOUND DEAD was the headline.

The mutilated body of a girl found in a cypress swamp Friday has been identified as eighteen-year-old Tanya Little, who has been missing from her Panama City home since last September. The girl had been dead less than a week, according to police.

The medical examiner reports that the girl had been sexually assaulted before her death by strangulation.

Guy stared at the words without reading them for several long moments. Then he drew in a breath and closed his eyes. "Shit," he whispered.

It was a long time before he could finish reading.

Chapter Twenty-nine

Guy smiled in the dark as he watched her come down the pier toward him. He shouldn't have smiled. She had no business running around after dark with all that was going on, and the marina was neither well lit nor well patrolled. Yet he wasn't surprised, and he wasn't angry. Carol had always done exactly as she pleased, and she could take care of herself as well as anybody he knew.

The night was mild and he was sitting on a lawn chair on the deck of his boat, trying to put things together in his head. The effort was made somewhat more difficult by the cooler of beer he had brought up with him, but his headache had in fact eased. It was quiet tonight; the sea lapped gently and the breeze was light and no one else was around. A yacht was docked at the other end of the pier, but the only sign of its presence was the occasional whiff of something tantalizing and expensive being prepared for dinner. Otherwise, he was alone.

Carol came aboard with only a slight assist of the guide rope for balance. She was carrying something in one hand.

"Chinese takeout, I hope," he said.

"Chicken soup. Don't worry, I didn't make it. Your friend Sal from the Seafood Shack sent it." She set the container on top of the beer cooler.

"He couldn't have sent fried clams?"

"I'll be sure to give him your complaints. How're you feeling?"

He tilted the beer bottle toward her. "Better."

"You're probably not supposed to drink that in your condition."

"Probably not," he agreed, and drank.

She pulled a waterproof cushion from one of the storage bins and sat down on the deck at his feet. She was wearing loose-fitting jeans and a long-sleeved knit cotton shirt with tiny buttons down the front, and she looked about twenty years old. She drew up her knees and encircled them with her arms. "It's nice out here tonight."

"Yeah. It will be for another couple of months, then the tourists start coming in and it's party central."

They were quiet for a while, enjoying the night. Then Carol said, with very little change in tone, "That girl they found this morning—they think Saddler's involved, don't they?"

He glanced at her as he brought the bottle to his mouth. "What makes you say that?"

"Your article in the paper."

"I didn't mention anything about—"

"I've been reading between the lines for over twenty years, Guy. I've always learned more from what you don't say than from what you do."

There was something oddly comforting in that. He said, "They don't have any evidence. Naturally, Case is worried. The girl was sexually assaulted and a known rapist is on the loose." He felt her tense, but her voice remained even. "So it was definitely him in the house yesterday."

"One good thing about convicted felons: Their fingerprints are on file. And his matched the ones on the poker to a tee."

"Careless of him."

"Keeping his identity a secret was never a priority with him," Guy reminded her.

"Too bad he doesn't feel the same way about where he's located."

Guy dropped a hand to her neck, giving it a light reassuring caress. The muscles there were like cable wire. "He's on his way back to prison as we speak, sweetie. It's just a matter of time. And if they can link him to the Anderson girl's murder, it'll be a long time before he sees daylight again."

Carol said, "She looked like Kelly a little, didn't she?"

Guy said, "No." He finished off the beer and put the bottle aside.

Carol didn't comment.

After a moment, he reached into his pocket and drew out the thong pendant. "Have you ever seen this before?"

She took it from him and held it up to the faint yellow light that was coming from the cabin before she said, "It's Kelly's." She turned a look on him that was half accusing, half afraid. "Guy, where—"

"It's not Kelly's," he told her. "The Anderson girl— apparently it belonged to her. She gave it to a boy just before she was killed."

Carol's eyes were big and worried, as though she dreaded to voice what she feared. The good thing about being married once was that she didn't have to.

She said, "That man she was last seen with, the one who said he was a director ... was anyone able to give a description?"

Guy shook his head. "We don't know that she was actually with him at all. She just told her friends about him. The sheriff asked me to put that in the story in case someone did see her with a man."

"No chance it was a real director?"

"No one has applied to film here since last September. But it would make a good line to lure young girls."

Carol swallowed hard. "He was going to take her to Hollywood, make her a star..." Her voice was barely above a whisper.

Guy couldn't reply.

Carol turned the pendant over in her hand. "I hated this thing," she said slowly. "When I think back on these days right before she disappeared, I always remember this, and it seems like a symbol of everything that went wrong. She wore it just to defy me, because she knew it annoyed me. I remember we argued about it, you and I." She returned the necklace to him. "The reason we argued about it was because I didn't want to admit to you how little control I had over Kelly."

"I always thought it was because you resented my interference."

"No. What I resented was your being right. You were right a lot more than you knew, Guy."

"I think I always suspected that."

"God, we made some awful mistakes, didn't we? And I blamed you for most of them."

"Just like I blamed you."

"Do you ever wonder, sometimes, how we got so far off the track?"

"Every waking moment of every day of my life."

"Any answers?"

"Do you want a list?" He began ticking off his fingers. "You were always shutting me out...."

She looked up at him. "I never meant to. I always thought you were pushing me away."

"Of course, I was. I thought it was self- defense."

"You made your life seem so much more important than mine, as though reporting the news were morally superior to selling real estate."

"And you never lost an opportunity to point out I would never make a fraction as much money as you did."

"As though you cared. You were so damn stubborn and independent—"

"Like you weren't?"

She looked up at him, her smile sad and gentle and filtered by starlight. "I really miss you sometimes."

"Yeah." His voice sounded a little husky when he said that, and he let the silence fall. The night was filled with the sound of water slapping the side of the boat, wind sighing far away. Sometimes in quiet such as this, he remembered how her heartbeat sounded against his ear. He almost told her that.

She said, "Did you ever notice how our lives have always been a study in extremes? Extreme poverty, extreme comfort, extreme happiness, extreme discontent..."

"Extreme longing," he said, "for something neither one of us seemed to be able to give the other."

She said softly, "I feel like I'm walking on the dark side of the moon right now, Guy. And it's scary."

He let his hand rested atop her head, stroking her hair. "You're not walking alone, babe."

She reached up and caught his fingers, turning her cheek into his hand. "I wish," she said after a moment, "I could reach back in time and make everything different."

"Me, too."

But after a time she released his fingers and turned away. He knew the real topic could not be avoided any longer.

"The Littles still live in Panama City," he said. "They agreed to see me tomorrow."

"Did you ask them about... ?"

"I didn't want to say too much over the phone. It was hard enough to get them to agree to see me."

Carol nodded. "I don't think it will help. I mean, I don't think it will make any more sense or seem any more real ... or be any easier to understand. What time?"

"He works until four."

"Pick me up at three."

He hesitated only a moment. "Sure."

They sat together, and listened to the sound of the waves, and after a time she rested her head on his knee. But they didn't talk much after that.

Chapter Thirty

The Littles lived in a Spanish-style house with a bougainvillea arbor providing shade over half the screened courtyard and a pool, tiled in deep Mediterranean blue, filling the other half. The double doors were paneled with stained glass, and the woman who opened them was slender and neatly groomed, but she looked fifteen years older than Carol had imagined her to be.

She dismissed their introductions and Carol's proffered hand with a nervous gesture, running her fingers through her short, tailored gray hair. "I'm Sandra Little," she said a little distractedly. "Come in, I suppose. Although I don't know what help we can be to you. My husband just got in. He's having a drink in the family room. It's just this way."

Her sentences were clipped and her voice thin, as though great reserves of energy were required for her to speak. As they followed her across the cool, Mexican-tiled foyer to the great room, Carol's eyes met Guy's and their thoughts were the same: How would they feel if two strangers invaded their life asking painful questions about their lost daughter?

The foyer gave way to a cathedral-ceilinged room with plush carpet and lemon silk- upholstered furniture. A set of glass doors looked out onto the pool courtyard, and the man who stood in front of them held a highball glass more than half filled with what might have been scotch, straight.

He turned when his wife said, "Henry, this is—" And then she faltered, turning to them with a faintly puzzled look, as though surprised by the fact that she could have forgotten their names so quickly.

"Guy Dennison, Mr. Little," Guy said, stepping forward and offering his hand. "This is my wife, Carol."

Carol did not correct him about their marital status.

After a moment, in which he seemed to assess both Carol and Guy, the man accepted Guy's handshake. "Henry Little."

Carol said, "Mr. Little, Mrs. Little..." She looked at the woman sympathetically. "I know this is difficult. It's not easy for us, either, to intrude on your grief like this. Please accept my sympathy on the loss of your daughter."

The wife averted her face, and it was a moment before Henry Little said quietly, "Life goes on. It doesn't feel like living sometimes, but ... life does go on." Then, with an abrupt change of tone, he gestured with his glass and said, "Can I offer you a drink?"

Guy said, "No, thank you. This isn't really a social occasion and we won't stay long."

Little nodded curtly. "After I talked to you yesterday, I started thinking this was a mistake. There's nothing we can do to help you and talking about it is only going to cause us both to relive things we're trying to put behind us."

"You never put it behind you," said his wife, softly and unexpectedly. "Never."

Then she turned to them and gestured to the yellow silk sofa. "Will you sit down?"

"Thank you." Carol sat at the end of the sofa next to a marble-topped table that held several photographs. They were all of the same girl. She glanced at the wife for permission, then picked up one of the framed photographs. "Is this Tanya?"

"Yes. It was taken—right before she disappeared."

Carol showed the photograph to Guy. A pretty smile, shoulder-length dark hair. Green eyes. Carol felt her chest constrict, and she saw Guy's jaw tighten with a reflection of her emotion. Carol whispered, "I am so sorry." Her hand was a little unsteady as she replaced the photograph.

Mrs. Little sank down onto a hassock opposite them and said anxiously, "You said—someone has been calling you, using our daughter's name ... that's obscene! Why would anyone do that? Why can't they just let her rest in peace?"

"We were hoping you could help us understand that," said Carol. "Our daughter—has been missing for over two years. A couple of weeks ago, I started getting calls from her, or someone who said she was her, crying and asking for help. Then the calls stopped and someone who gave her name as Tanya Little called and said she and Kelly were being held together against their will and that Kelly couldn't call me anymore. That was the day before yesterday. Then, of course, we found out that Tanya Little was ... had been..."

When she faltered, Henry Little supplied harshly, "Killed, Mrs. Dennison. That's what she was. Murdered.

Whoever called you was obviously aware of that fact and was playing some kind of twisted joke."

Guy said quietly, "We think there's a possibility it may be the same person who's responsible for your daughter's death. He was never apprehended, is that right?"

Henry Little said, "She had been gone so long, and she wasn't killed at the scene ... there was just no evidence. The case is still open."

Sandra Little's lips tightened. "We haven't given up hope. Someday that monster will be brought to justice. If you think you can help in any way..."

Carol said to the other woman, "Is there any chance at all that Kelly could have known Tanya?"

Sandra Little frowned, obviously not following her train of thinking. "You live in St. Theresa-by- the-Sea, is that right? I thought it was odd when Henry told me. You see, Tanya was working there that summer before she disappeared. But that was three years ago, and she was eighteen. I think it unlikely that she could have known your daughter."

"Where?" Guy said. "Where did she work?"

"A little shop on the strip. Blue Dolphin, it was called."

Guy glanced at Carol inquiringly and she shook her head, indicating she didn't recognize the name either.

Carol tried a different approach. "You said your daughter had been gone so long ... I don't understand. Where did she go?"

Mrs. Little dropped her gaze. "We don't know. She left a note one day, said she was leaving home. She was eighteen, we couldn't do much to stop her ... and to tell the truth, she was a rather difficult child and we thought—"

"I thought," interrupted Henry Little harshly. "I thought a taste of the real world would do her good."

The silence that fell was sharp with the guilt with which he had lived since that day—just as Carol and Guy had lived with their own guilt from the moment of Kelly's disappearance.

In a moment Sandra Little picked up the story. "After she left, we figured she was moving in with friends there, or someone she had met at work, but it turned out she quit her job the day before she left home. A week or so later, we got a letter from her, postmarked Tallahassee, saying she was on her way to Hollywood to become an actress. It was crazy." Her voice rose in indignation. "The last thing Tanya would do would be to go to Hollywood. She didn't even watch movies!"

Carol felt a chill go down her spine, and it was momentarily hard to breathe. Guy's hand covered hers on the sofa. It was the only spot of living warmth in a very, very cold world.

With his other hand, Guy reached into his pocket and pulled out the thong necklace. His voice sounded odd when he spoke. "Mrs. Little," he said, holding it out to her, "have you ever seen this before?"

She caught her breath sharply, and Carol could see the color drain from her face as she reached for the necklace. "My God," she whispered, "it's Tanya's!" She snatched the necklace from Guy's fingers and clutched it to her chest, her eyes big and dark and wild with pain and accusation. "Where did you get this?" she cried. "Where did you?

Chapter Thirty-one

Laura was getting ready to close the office when the phone rang. Tammy had already gone home, so she picked it up in her office. "Beachside," she said.

A hesitation, then, "Mama, is that you?"

"Sorry, honey, you've got the wrong—" And then something made Laura stop. Slowly, she sank to the desk chair, gripping the side of the desk with her fingers. "Kelly?" she said uncertainly, "is that you?"

"You can come get me now," said the voice. It was a young girl's voice, husky and breathy, but the tone was oddly flat as though she were reading a script. "You can come get me, but you have to come now. Can you do that?"

"Honey, where are you?" Laura's heart was pounding so hard she could barely hear herself speak. "Yes, I'll come, but you've got to tell me where you are."

"Lighthouse Point, at the end of the beach, beyond the rocks. There's an old construction shack there."

"Yes," Laura said breathlessly, "I know it."

"But you've got to come now. Can you come now?"

"I'm on my way, honey, right now."

And suddenly the girl cried, in a much different, more urgent tone, "The tower! It's the—"

And the call disconnected.

Laura spent less than three seconds listening to the dead line, then she grabbed her keys and ran from the office.

After looking over the copies of the newspaper reports on Tanya Little that Guy Dennison had left the night before, Derrick Long spent an hour and a half on the phone with the Gulf County police, who had been in charge up to the point the body was found, and the state police, who had taken over then.

Though the body, like that of Mickie Anderson, had been subjected to predators and natural deterioration before it was found, several things had been determined on autopsy.

The girl had been subjected to torture with a knife. Finger tips and toes had been sliced away and there were cuts on her breasts, thighs, and genitalia.

She had been strangled to death with a narrow leather cord.

She had been killed elsewhere and the body dumped in the cypress swamp. She had been dead less than a week when she was found.

A positive i.d., both visual and dental, had been made. There was no possible way that Tanya Little could have called Carol Dennison two days ago. She had been dead for two years.

There were far too many similarities here between the death of Mickie Anderson two days ago and Tanya

Little two years ago; chilling similarities that all seemed to revolve, somehow, around Kelly Dennison.

It wasn't until he received the case file, which was faxed to him as a simple courtesy from the Gulf County Sheriff's Department, that the most disturbing similarity of all arose. He might not have noticed it right away, if at all, had he not had an opportunity to read Kelly Dennison's file in the past few days.

But just to make sure, he pulled Dennison's file and placed the two photocopied sheets of paper side by side. Kelly's note read: "I am fine. I'm going to Hollywood…"

"… so you won't hear from me for a while. I have money. Watch for me in the movies. Love, Tanya."

Carol looked up from the sheet of lined paper in her hand with a stunned, pinched expression around her eyes and mouth. Yet her hand was steady and her voice calm, as she passed the paper to Guy. "The note we got from Kelly, a little over a week after she disappeared, was worded exactly like this. Exactly."

Henry Little stepped forward and snatched the paper from Guy. "That's absurd. The state police investigated this case thoroughly. They would have known if…" And he trailed off, his skin a sickly color, his eyes filled with confusion and disbelief. "Are you suggesting that the two girls were in collusion?"

Carol glanced at Guy, as though for reassurance against her own rising tide of helplessness and confusion. But he had none to offer.

He said quietly, "You should know that another girl disappeared from St. T. this week. She was found murdered and—tortured—in the same way that your daughter was."

Little frowned. "We've been seeing it on television. You surely can't be thinking there's a connection."

"Before she disappeared, she claimed to have met a man in town who was going to put her in a movie, or a commercial or something. The Hollywood filmmaking connection seems pretty strong. It could be the line he uses to lure girls to come with him."

Sandra Little reached behind her until she felt the support of the arm of a chair, then sat, slowly and gracefully, with stiff back and legs, and folded her hands in her lap. Her expression was locked into composure, frozen.

Carol said hesitantly, "Your daughter was very pretty. So was Kelly, and this—the Anderson girl. They all looked kind of alike, actually. Long dark hair and ... well, girls that age are naturally vain. Even sensible girls can be moved by flattery, tantalized by the possibility of fame..."

Sandra Little nodded slowly.

Henry Little said sharply, "So now you're telling me that the same man who tortured and murdered my daughter two years ago also took your daughter, and this girl who washed up on the beach, and made them all write the same note to their parents—"

"Except for Mickie Anderson," interrupted Guy. "For some reason, he didn't keep her long enough..." The sentence sounded horrible even unfinished, and he let it hang. In a moment, he said simply, "I don't know. I honestly don't know. It's just—a lot of coincidence."

"You seem to be an educated man, Mr. Dennison," said Little sharply. "You should know there's no such thing as coincidence."

"No," said Sandra Little softly. She raised her head slowly to look at them, eyes dark and pained, and she said, "There isn't. And what Mr. Dennison is trying to tell us is that this—monster—who took our Tanya, and their child, and who murdered that girl they found on the beach ... that he may have done it before, many times. And that he's there, in St. Theresa County, walking around free, looking for his next victim. That's what he's telling us." And she looked at Guy. "Isn't it?"

The silence before he answered seemed to go on forever. But Guy didn't flinch, or evade her gaze. In the end, he replied simply, "Yes."

Chapter Thirty-two

Lighthouse Point was the finger-shaped strip of land that had been left jutting out into the ocean when the channel was cut. It was so named because it was here that, if one stood at the end of the jetty, the optical illusion was such that the lighthouse, an easy mile away, looked close enough to swim to. The road ended some five hundred yards away from the Point; there was a narrow dirt-and-gravel turnaround where one could leave one's car and follow the sand path through thorny vines and sandspurs to the rock jetty, but few bothered. The fishing was better on the other side of the Point, and the lighthouse could, after all, be seen from almost anywhere on the beach.

Twilight was falling when Laura got out of her car, and she started thinking of a dozen reasons why she shouldn't have come. She knew she was acting foolish, crazy, she should have at least tried to call the police. But the one reason she should have come—what if it was Kelly?—kept her trudging on down the path, tripping over vines and snagging her clothing on shrubbery, clambering over the spill of granite boulders that reinforced the jetty, stumbling through the undergrowth on the other side.

Sea grasses grew tall around the construction shack, which looked empty and, not surprisingly, somewhat sinister. The sound of the surf crashing against the rocks was loud, and that made her nervous. She started toward the shack, calling loudly, "Kelly?"

She thought about Carol's theory, that Kelly was being held against her will somewhere. Could it be here? No one could hear her scream above the sound of the surf, even if anyone ever did come here, which no one did. But how could she be here? There was no telephone here and she had called....

Laura slipped her hand into her pocket and felt the reassuring weight of her keys, threading her fingers through them tightly. She pushed open the sagging door of the shack. "Kelly?"

The interior was dark and humid, smelling of sea rot and neglect. There were shadowed shapes in the far corner, boxes of rusted and forgotten equipment, but the interior was too dark for Laura to make out much of anything else. She took one careful step inside, worried about snakes and spiders and now all but convinced the place was empty. "Kelly?" she called again, but with less hope this time.

The movement came from behind her so swiftly she didn't sense it coming until it was all over. Something caught around her neck and jerked hard, digging into her skin. She gave a choked cry and, in her confusion, thought she had walked into something—a rope or a length of fishing line—that was tangled around her throat. Instinctively, she stepped back, trying to wrench away even as she brought her hands up to free the cord, and that was when she felt the human body pressing against hers, felt the hands tightening the cord around her neck. All this was no more than a few seconds.

She tried again to scream, but the sound came out as a choked gurgle and lights exploded behind her eyes, there was a rushing sound in her ears. Blindly, she swung her hand up and back, raking down with the keys that were gripped like brass knuckles between her fingers, and her blow met flesh.

She heard something, perhaps a cry of pain; the pressure on her throat gave way as she jerked the cord free and whirled toward the door.

"You're not Carol!"

That was what she heard him say, but she was moving. He grabbed at her hair but caught only a handful of strands. She screamed with the fury of renewed effort as she jerked free and didn't even feel the pain. He had her shoulder by the shirt, but she was almost at the door. She kicked backward, and struck out with the keys and he ducked his head and she had a glimpse of a face, hideously distorted and twisted in on itself, a monster face from a nightmare, a face that would cause her to wake up gasping and sweating in the middle of the night for years to come. And then, with a mighty wrench, the material of her shirt gave way and she was through the door, running, free, sobbing and gasping and running.

She fell once on the thorny path, but didn't look back. She crossed the rocks by sliding on their slippery surface. She was sure he was behind her, she could almost hear him breathing, and when her shoe got caught in a crevice, she tore it off and left it there. She saw her car and only then did she dare to look back. She was alone.

She flung herself into the car and locked all the doors and for a moment, she couldn't do anything except rest her head on the steering wheel, shaking, gasping, trying not to lose consciousness. Then she became aware of the keys in her hand, and of smears of blood on the tips of two of them. His blood. In her other hand, she still clutched the cord with which he had tried to strangle her.

She fumbled until she got the correct key in the ignition. She started the engine and slammed the car in gear, spinning the wheels wildly as she turned away and drove off with a spray of gravel. She did not look back.

Chapter Thirty-three

I always felt real bad about Kelly," John Case said. His tone was quiet and reflective, his pose that of a man who was thinking out loud. "I've known Guy Dennison for fifteen years, we go fishing together, and though I can't say we haven't had our disagreements about what he prints in the paper, I've always known him to be a fair man. A good man. His family, too. That kid, she was bright as a new penny. You could tell just by looking at her she had a future. Then it all started to come apart and I felt bad, real bad. But hell, it's not an unusual story, especially these days. The family breaks up, the kid gets in trouble, ends in tragedy.

"The trouble with this job, especially in a little place like this where you know everybody, is that you start to feel like your neighbor's keeper. You're more of a caretaker than a law officer and I don't know, maybe that's the way it should be. So when Kelly Dennison ran off, I felt responsible somehow, like it was my job, with her daddy living in the capital, to keep a better eye on her and I'd let them all down. I remember thinking, after we interviewed everybody we could interview and nobody had seen her, and when the days went by and she didn't show up, I remember thinking, please, Jesus, don't let anything have happened to that girl, not on my watch. That's what I was thinking. Not on my watch.

"So when her mother got that note saying she was running off to California, I was relieved. Too relieved. Case closed. It was bad, but it wasn't tragic. I could live with that. Maybe if I hadn't been so eager to live with it, maybe if I hadn't been so quick to grab the first out... But that was what he was counting on. That we'd all believe what we wanted to believe in the first place if he just gave us a little push in that direction."

He swiveled his chair from the window with its deep-twilight view of the parking lot and turned to face Long across the desk. "So what we've got here is a genuine, no shit, smarter-than-your-average-bear serial killer. Is that what you're telling me?"

"There's no evidence that Kelly Dennison has been killed," Long was quick to point out. "But"—and he dropped his gaze—"it looks that way, yes."

Case nodded slowly. "I guess you know we're way out of our league."

"The state police will have an investigator down here tomorrow."

"Meanwhile," said Case, leaning back in his chair, "we've got a killer wolf prowling our shores and a thousand or so sheep just waiting to be taken down." He rubbed the bridge of his nose. His voice dropped. "Jesus, I should have called in the state police when we first found out about Saddler."

"By that time," Long said quietly, "Mickie Anderson was probably already dead."

Case gave a brief shake of his head, as though to throw off unproductive thoughts, and drew a breath. "Okay, do me a favor. I know the state boys will check it out if they haven't already, but just for my information. Call the investigator in charge of the Melissa Conroy case—you know that kid from Georgia State who never came back from spring break in Panama City last year. Somebody said she was here in St. T. right before she disappeared. I just want to make sure that's the only similarity between her and Mickie Anderson."

Long made a note, nodding. "I'll start seeing what I can find out about the place Tanya Little worked while she was here that summer, too. Could be there's a connection between her and Kelly Dennison."

"Good thinking. Meantime—" The sheriff's phone rang. He picked it up, listened intently, then said curtly, "Give me the address."

He wrote it down and hung up the phone. "Come on," he said to Long, pushing up from his chair. "It's Laura Capstone. Carol Dennison's partner."

Chapter Thirty-four

C arol said, "I had forgotten how dark these country roads can be." Her voice sounded distant and hollow even to her own ears, as though it were coming from the bottom of a well. "I don't leave the beach much at night anymore."

Guy was driving, and they hadn't spoken much since they had left Panama City. Neither one of them wanted to say what was really on their minds. But even when they didn't speak it, it was there between them.

He answered, "I remember when you first started selling real estate. I used to make myself crazy worrying about you being out at night, showing houses to maniacs."

"In Miami, you were probably right to worry."

"But not here."

A silence. "No," she said softly, turning her face to the window. "Not here."

Guy was silent for a time. Then he said, "I keep thinking about what the prosecutor told me right after Saddler was arrested. That guys like him, habitual offenders and pattern criminals—they rely on the fact that there's so little communication between jurisdictions. That as long as nobody puts it together they can keep getting away with the same crime over and over again. It was just luck that, when I did that story, the broadcast area happened to cover the exact same area he had been operating in. People started coming forward, police departments started putting the pieces together."

"Still," Carol said, "he was only convicted on one count."

"Which, as it turned out, wasn't enough," Guy agreed.

"God, why didn't they figure out what he was really up to back then?" Carol said with quiet anguish in her voice. "If he was this disturbed, this sick and twisted—why didn't they figure it out?"

Guy's tone was subdued. "It kind of makes you wonder how many other unsolved crimes remain that way because the perpetrator went to jail on some other charge, doesn't it?"

"No," Carol said tiredly, leaning her head against the frame of the window. "That's not what it makes me wonder."

She watched her reflection, wan and ghostly, pass across the face of the scrub pines and empty marsh, and listened to the thin whine of tires on the highway. Her throat was tight and achy, and there was a cold emptiness in the pit of her stomach that nothing would ever ease. It was a long time before she spoke again.

"You know what's so strange?" she said, speaking to the closed window. "When we first walked in and saw them—that beaten-up look on their faces, that deadness in their eyes—I thought, from the bottom of my heart I thought, 'Oh, the poor things!' and I really hurt for them. But by the time we left, I realized—we are them, we're the poor things, and that deadness in their eyes, I feel it right here." She pressed a fist to the area just beneath her left breast, her voice growing tight and shaky as she finished softly, "And I want someone to hurt for us, Guy. I want someone to feel how our lives were shattered and I want someone to hurt for us!"

He reached his hand across the seat and covered her fist, pulling it down on the console between them, holding it hard. "Stop it," he said. His eyes were fixed on he road, his voice tense and determined. "I don't want to hear you talk like that."

Carol squeezed her eyes tightly closed. "Don't tell me she's dead, Guy," she said in a low, harsh whisper. "Please don't tell me our little girl ended up just like their daughter. I know it's probably true, but I can't bear to hear it now!" She could feel herself losing control, but she didn't want to give into sobs because she knew if she did, it would be over—all hope, all control, all possibility of denial. So she held her breath and bit back words and pulled her hand away from Guy's, closing both fists into hard, close knots on her thighs.

Guy said, very quietly, "I don't think it's true."

Carol opened her eyes and looked at him. She could see the hard tight profile of his jaw, its familiar stubborn line, the set of his mouth which indicated a decision reached and unarguable. So familiar to her, so predictable, so heartbreakingly dear.

She said, with the greatest difficulty. "Kelly wasn't his first victim. We know she wasn't his last. Why would—she be different?"

"I can't believe you're saying that."

Carol leaned her head against the headrest, her eyes focused on nothing at all. She said softly, "I've been all alone in this for so long. Holding on, believing where nobody else would believe, feeding hope like you'd tend a campfire in the wind. I'm worn out, Guy. I'm out of fuel, and the odds are just too great. I don't know how much longer I can hold on. I need you to make me believe again, or at least ... believe for me, for a little while, until I'm stronger."

Guy said, "The other parents never heard from their daughters again." He took his gaze away from the road long enough to meet her eyes. There was strength there, and conviction; enough to hold on to until she was strong again. He finished, "We did. She called you."

The argument was flawed and she knew it; perhaps, so did he. But because he said it, she believed. Because he believed, it seemed possible.

She smiled faintly in the dark. "Funny. After all this time, our roles are reversed. You trying to convince me while I'm feeling hopeless."

Guy drew in a slow breath, but said nothing for a moment. Then he said, "Maybe I tried to prepare myself for the worst because it was easier than thinking about what she might be going through out there, all alone. But I never believed it, never wanted to believe it—mostly because you didn't, Carol. And nothing has changed. We have no proof of anything, just a lot of pieces to a puzzle that doesn't make sense." He pulled in another breath and glanced at her. "Look," he said, "the time may come to give up. But it's not yet. Okay?"

Carol swallowed hard. "I'm trying," she said unsteadily. "But it's not so easy anymore."

His cell phone rang.

After a moment, Guy fumbled in his pocket and answered it. "Guy Dennison."

Carol knew by the quality of his silence that the call was not an ordinary one. She looked at him sharply, but could discern nothing of his expression in the dark. His voice, however, told her more than his words did.

"Yes, she's with me. Why, what happened?" He listened, then asked, "Is she okay?"

Carol gripped his arm.

Guy said, "We're about twenty minutes away. Should we come there?"

Carol demanded, "What? What's wrong?"

Guy said into the phone, "Right." and disconnected.

He tucked the phone back in his pocket, his expression grim. "That was the sheriff. There's been some kind of incident, they think it was Saddler. He attacked Laura."

Chapter Thirty-five

I'm okay," Laura said as soon as they came in. Carol ran to her and embraced her anyway.

She looked a little surprised when, as soon as Carol released her, Guy put an arm around her shoulders and hugged her, too.

"Jesus, Laura, I'm so sorry," he said.

Laura stepped away, shaking her head as she ran her fingers through her hair. "I was stupid. I can't believe I was so stupid." She turned back into the room. "I guess you know Deputy Long. He's the one who took me to the emergency room and drove me back here. I'm fine," she repeated. "He shouldn't have called you. I just can't believe I was so stupid."

She was wearing a white terry warm-up suit and heavy socks, and even on this mild night she kept hugging her arms as though she was cold. There was a sharp red line on her throat underneath her chin and her voice sounded the slightest bit hoarse, but otherwise she appeared unharmed.

Long said, "They had to be called, Ms. Capstone. It's a matter of safety now."

Carol put her arm around her friend's waist and walked her to the sofa. "What can I get for you? Do you want me to make tea?"

And Guy said, "Tell us what happened."

Laura sat on the sofa, holding on to Carol's hand, and told her story. "It was all so quick," she said, still sounding a little disbelieving of her own ordeal. "I mean, I wasn't in that building ten seconds altogether, even though it seemed like ten hours. I scratched him with my keys and he kind of lost his grip and that's when he said, 'You're not Carol!' " She looked at Carol. "He was expecting you. He must have had whoever it was make that call, and she wouldn't know the difference in our voices. It was after hours, so I just answered the phone 'Hello' and she—or he—must have thought I was you all the time."

Guy's and Carol's eyes met soberly, but neither said anything.

Laura went on, "Anyway, I grabbed the cord he had around my neck—it was a strip of leather, actually, I still had it when I got to the car—and I jerked away and he tried to catch me—almost did a couple of times—but I think he was more afraid of coming out of the shack where I might see him, or he might be seen chasing me, than he was of my getting away. Anyway, I got away." She tried to smile, but a betraying hand wandered to her throat and touched the red mark there. The smile faded.

Carol said, "Did you see him at all?"

Laura shook her head. "Not really. I mean—what I saw was like something out of a horror movie, this awful, distorted face. Then Deputy Long made me realize it was actually a man wearing a stocking over his head. But that was all I saw. Kind of brownish hair, and the side of his neck was bleeding where I scratched him."

"But that's something," Carol said, squeezing her hand. "That's a lot."

Guy said, frowning a little, "This leather strip he used—did it look anything like this?" He pulled from his pocket the bound girl figurine suspended on the leather thong.

Long reached for it. "Where did you get this?"

Guy turned it over to him. "The kid you were interviewing in the Mickie Anderson case said she had given it to him just before she died. He asked me to give it to her parents. I was going to do that, and then I recognized it as the same kind of necklace my daughter used to wear. On a hunch, I showed it to Tanya Little's parents and she had one like it, too. They think she got it here in St. T., at a place she used to work called the Blue Dolphin."

Long scowled at him. "You realize this is evidence in a murder case?"

Guy said deliberately, "Two murder cases."

Carol loved him then, because he didn't say "three."

Laura said, puzzled, "I know the Blue Dolphin—or at least what used to be the Blue Dolphin. They were only in business for a couple of years. They sold nautical knick-knacks—porcelain whales and glass dolphins and mahogany manatees, you know the kind of thing. I used to get a lot of housewarming gifts there, remember, Carol?" She explained to Long, "Whenever we sell a house, particularly an expensive one, we like to give the new owners a personally selected housewarming gift. I never knew the Blue Dolphin to sell jewelry, though. Could I look at that?"

After a moment, Long handed it to her.

She cringed a little as she took it, and glanced at Guy. "It is like the leather cord," she said. "Just exactly like it." Then she turned the figurine over in her hand, examining it. "How odd."

She glanced up. "You know what this is, don't you? That Tarot card—I think it's called the Bound Girl. It means indecision, standing at the crossroads of life, not knowing which way to go, something like that. On the card I think she's on a rock surrounded by water. Pretty gruesome to look at, though."

Long said suspiciously, "How do you know that?

She replied without blinking, "I dated a warlock once."

At Long's expression, Carol quickly explained, "She means Jimmy, the waiter from the Sunrise Terrace in Port St. Joe. He wasn't a warlock, just weird."

"Also ten years younger than me with buns of steel," replied Laura blandly. "I was going through a rebellious stage."

Guy's lips formed a wry smile. "Now I believe you're okay. I was getting worried there for a minute."

"Then my ordeal was worth it."

Carol said, squeezing Laura's arm, "I'm making you some tea."

When Carol was gone, Laura looked back down at the necklace, frowning. "The Tower. That was one of the cards, too. I remember it was an awful-looking thing, with lightning and people falling out of it. Did I tell you about the tower?"

Long replied, "Yes ma'am, you did."

Guy gave him a look that was cautious and questioning, as though he half suspected Laura might be rambling nonsensically.

Long explained, "Apparently, the caller cried out something about a tower just before the connection with

Ms. Capstone was broken. We thought it might be a clue as to the location of the caller."

Guy felt the color slowly drain from his face, even as his heart began to pound hard and fast, with a slow unfolding certainty. He had to stand up and walk a few paces away, forcing a slow deep breath. "The princess in the tower," he said, very quietly, as steadily as he could manage. "That's what I used to call her."

Laura looked at him sharply, and Long said, "Are you suggesting that—"

"It was Kelly," Guy said, and released the breath he was holding. The certainty was quiet and sure and as strong as anything he had ever known. "I'm sure of it."

He could feel both pairs of eyes on him, but whether they held doubt or relief he didn't know and did not care. In a moment, Long said, "I dispatched officers to check the water tower and the airport tower just in case, and we're in the process of examining all the observation towers and platforms on the island. So far, all are negative."

Guy nodded, and turned back to them. Kelly was alive. That was all that mattered.

Laura returned the necklace to the deputy. Her face was strained and her tone reluctant. She said, "If three girls wore this necklace and two of them are dead, and if the man who attacked me used the same kind of necklace, or at least the leather from one—"

Guy said sharply, "It's too soon to jump to conclusions." To Long he said, "You should interview the Littles. Here's their address and phone number."

He produced a slip of paper which Long took with a nod. "I already talked to the sheriff's department over there today. I was going to interview the parents."

"Make it a priority," Guy suggested, and ignored the challenging look Long gave him.

Laura said, "Then I guess we're supposed to think that the man who attacked me tonight was the same one who's been kidnapping and— killing these young girls? And that he's the one who's making these phone calls and threatening Guy? The rapist who just got out of prison?"

Long glanced at her almost apologetically. "It looks that way, ma'am."

Laura frowned a little. "I don't understand why he would have someone pretend to be Kelly, then this Tanya Little person."

"Possibly because he wanted us to find out Tanya Little was dead. Another terrorist tactic."

"But he never used the name Mickie Anderson," Laura pointed out. "If he wanted to make a point, or scare someone, that would be the name to use— everyone knows it today."

"But they didn't know it when all this began," Long pointed out. "And how could he be sure her body would be found so soon—if he meant for it to be found at all?"

"I suppose," Laura said wearily. "It just—well, it just doesn't make sense."

"Criminal behavior rarely does," Long said.

"But he knew Carol," Laura insisted. "The way he said her name—it was as though he knew her."

"He's been stalking her for weeks," Long explained. "He was in her house, who knows for how long, or if that was even the first time. It's not unusual for a stalker to form a personal relationship with his victim, to feel as though he knows her."

Laura rubbed the mark on her neck gingerly. "I thought it was Guy he was after."

Long said, "I don't think there's any reason for you to worry, Ms. Capstone. Your involvement was purely accidental, and the fact that he let you get away tonight proves he's not interested in hurting you."

Laura let her fingers rest on her collarbone, just below the mark of the garrote. "I'm glad to hear that."

Long looked at Guy. "I think it would be better, Mr. Dennison, if you left the investigation of this case to me from now on."

Guy looked as though he was about answer sharply, then tightened his lips and said only, "Just catch the son of a bitch, will you?"

"We're doing our best, Mr. Dennison." He nodded at Laura. "Try not to worry, Ms. Capstone. We'll call you if we need any more information. In the meantime, just—try not to worry."

Laura stood to walk him to the door. "Thanks for your help, Deputy. And like the man said— just catch the s.o.b., will you?"

Carol returned with the tea just as the door was closing behind the deputy. She began setting out cups and saucers with a grim efficacy that was belied by the fact that her hands were shaking so badly that the china was in danger of becoming chipped. Laura came over to her.

"Carol, leave it," she said, laying a hand upon her arm. "It's been a rough day for both of us."

Carol stopped fussing with the cups and straightened up, but she didn't turn around. "You could have been killed," she said in an odd, tight voice. "Just one more on his list."

Guy said, "Carol, don't."

Carol turned to him with a forced tight smile. "Of course. There's a serial killer on the loose with a grudge against you. He's probably taken our daughter and he just tried to strangle my best friend, but that's no reason to upset everyone is it?"

The silence was tense and painful. Carol pressed her fingers against her temples and drew in a long slow breath. "I'm sorry," she whispered. "Laura, I'm sorry. This wouldn't have happened to you if it weren't for me—for us—and I'm sorry."

Laura came over to her, and the two women embraced. It was a singular moment that left Guy feeling awkward and excluded, yet seemed to restore something vital between the two women.

Laura stepped away and took both of Carol's shoulders, looking into her eyes. "I thought it was Kelly," she said. "When I heard the voice—I believed it was Kelly. And maybe Guy's right, what she said about the tower..."

Carol looked quickly at Guy. He said, "The tower, that's what she said just before the connection was broken. Remember what I used to call her?"

He saw the hope dawn in her eyes, just as it had in his. "A signal," she said, half whispering. "It could have been a signal, to let us know it was really her..."

She looked back at Laura, and Laura smiled her encouragement. The two women held the moment, each offering comfort to the other. Then Carol said gently, "You're okay?"

"Scared shitless," said Laura flatly. "But that's a good thing. I won't be so stupid next time."

Carol said, "I'll stay with you tonight. You shouldn't be alone. I know how it feels—"

But before she had finished the first sentence, Laura was shaking her head. Her hands tightened on Carol's shoulders and she pushed her gently away. "No, you're not staying. I don't want you to stay. I want to have a good cry, a cup of that tea, a long hot bath, and one of those sleeping pills they gave me at the emergency room. Don't expect me to be early in the morning."

Carol said reluctantly, "I don't want to leave you."

"I want you to leave me. Besides, I was thinking this might be a good time to call Winston. Damsel in distress, and all that, you know."

Carol looked unhappy. "If you're sure…"

Laura looked at Guy. "Will you take her home?"

Guy came over to her. "Look," he said, "I don't think you're in any danger, but use some sense will you? Lock up when we're gone. And if you really do have a boyfriend you can call, call him."

Laura arched an eyebrow. "I always have a boyfriend."

Guy surprised her for the second time that night by leaning forward and kissing her on the cheek. "Thanks for acting stupid," he said. "But next time—don't."

Laura's smile was stiff. "You can bet on that."

Guy slipped an arm around Carol's shoulders. "Let's go home, sweetie."

Chapter Thirty-six

Guy walked her inside, turning on lights as he went. "I see the locksmith got here," he said, examining the locks on the windows.

She nodded. "They're not very busy this time of year. Actually, they're not very busy on the beach any time of year. Odd, isn't it, all these expensive homes with locks a child could break into?"

"Well, people don't move to the beach to keep themselves locked up like they would in Manhattan. The vacation mentality, I guess."

He sounded tired, as tired as she felt. But they kept talking because it was better than being alone with their thoughts.

"I got an extra key for you," she said. "It's on the kitchen counter by the door."

"Thanks."

They looked at each other for a moment. Then Guy said, "It could have been you tonight."

Carol shifted her gaze, unconsciously rubbing her throat. "The thought occurred to me."

"I keep telling myself Laura's always been the flighty one, that you never would have done anything so stupid, but you would have, wouldn't you?"

Carol smiled faintly. "I would have been the first in line."

Guy nodded. "I guess I would have done the same thing if I had gotten the call. If there was the slightest chance it was Kelly."

"Laura thought it was Kelly's voice," Carol said, and she didn't have to re-emphasize what that meant. Vindication for her own belief, renewed hope ... possibilities, however faint and unlikely, but possibilities nonetheless.

Guy nodded his understanding, and again a small, tired smile touched Carol's lips. "Funny what a difference a near-tragedy can make," she said. "On the way back here I was ready to give up, ready to believe we'd never see Kelly again. Now, just because someone else has heard the voice besides me—even though it's the same voice you and the police heard on the tape, even though there's no more evidence now than there was then that it belongs to Kelly—now I'm convinced that, even if she did fall into the hands of the same killer as those others, she somehow escaped and now she's trying to reach us... It just gets so hard being the only one who believes, sometimes."

Guy slipped his hand around her neck, caressing gently. "It takes courage," he said, "more courage than I had when you needed me. I'm sorry."

"I think you've said those words tonight more times than you have since I've known you."

He dropped his gaze. "Yeah. Something else I should have learned earlier."

He started to remove his hand, but she entwined her fingers through his. "We both let each other down, Guy," she said. "Let's not do that anymore, okay?"

After a moment, he smiled. "You got a deal."

He leaned forward and kissed her on the cheek. Then, hesitating only a moment, tenderly on the lips. When he looked into her eyes, there was no resistance or objection there, just quiet expectation. He moved to her again and they kissed as they used to kiss, with open mouths and mating tongues and pressing hands.

He whispered, "I don't like to leave you alone, sweetie."

And she said, softly, "Then don't."

He held her, his face pressed into her hair. "We can't turn back time, Carol."

He felt her heart beat against his ribs. "Maybe ... for tonight, we could make it stand still."

Hands entwined, they walked upstairs.

Later, wrapped in the embrace of arms and legs and the glow of lovemaking that was as familiar as coming home and just as desperately, heartbreakingly welcome, Guy whispered, "I still love you, you know. I think I always will."

Carol rested her palm against his cheek, tracing familiar contours and textures with the tips of her fingers. "That was always the problem with our divorce. We never fell out of love with each other."

He turned his face to her hair. "Ah, sweetie," he sighed. "What are we going to do?"

She felt his breathing, the heat of his body and the beat of his heart as though they were her own, and there was no surprise to it. There was a part of her that had only been waiting for this moment, that had always known it wouldn't be far away. Understanding that filled up a part of the emptiness that had been aching within her for too long.

"Better," she answered, turning her face to his. "This time ... we're going to do better."

Chapter Thirty-seven

Walt Marshall was working on his boat when he saw the stranger pull up. Walt had six boats, all in various states of repair—except for the new Sea Ray, of course, which he hadn't yet had a chance to take out of the harbor. This particular one was a 1965 mahogany Cris-Craft, with brass trim and all the extras, which he was painstakingly restoring to mint condition. He was in the process of stripping down a previous owner's ill-conceived paint job when the stranger got out of the pickup truck and, closing the door softly, looked around in a way Walt didn't like.

During the busy season Walt didn't have time to keep up with the comings and goings of everyone who cruised by the marina. People tied up, paid their fee, bought their fuel and supplies, sometimes stayed, sometimes didn't, and Walt didn't much care. But right now there were less than a dozen people with business here this time of night, and Walt knew every one of them.

He figured it was some kid looking for mischief. It was after midnight and he wouldn't expect anybody to be around. The way the boathouse was situated, at the end of the pier with a straight-shot view of anybody coming or going, was ideal from Walt's point of view; not so ideal from the stranger's. He could have no idea he was being observed. And from the furtive way he was moving, that appeared to be exactly what he wanted.

Walt put down his stripping rag and wiped his hands on a towel, starting to go out and challenge the young imp. But then he stopped. The stranger moved away from the truck then, and started down the pier toward the docked boats. As he moved, he stepped into the outer circle of one of the mercury-vapor lamps that lined the pier, and then quickly ducked back into the shadows again—but not quickly enough, and Walt caught a glimpse of something he really didn't like.

He turned back toward the shop, where he kept his gun.

Derrick had seen Patsy at the hospital when he brought Laura Capstone in, and he knew she would want to know the whole story. She got in about eleven-thirty, which was, as it happened, only a few minutes after he did. He could tell by the dark circles under her eyes and the stiffness of her movements that she was having a hard day, and he wanted her to go directly to bed. She wouldn't hear of it, of course. He made her sit down and put her feet up while he made popcorn and hot chocolate, and she grilled him about the latest developments in the case.

"Good heavens." Her eyes were wide when he finished. "Derrick, you're dealing with a serial killer. An honest-to-God, headline-making serial killer."

"We hope he doesn't make headlines," Derrick said grimly, "at least not yet. But between Guy Dennison and the Anderson girl's parents, I don't know how much longer we're going to be able to keep a lid on it."

He put the bowl of popcorn in her lap and the two mugs of chocolate on the coffee table on which she rested her feet. He sat down on the sofa beside her and swung her white-stockinged feet into his lap, massaging them gently.

Patsy said soberly, "If there's a serial killer on the loose in a community as small as St. T., I don't think you want to keep it quiet, Derrick. All these young girls here on spring break..." He felt her suppress a shudder. "It's like penning up a hungry coyote with a herd of sheep."

"Yeah." His own voice was heavy. Absently, he reached for the popcorn, thinking out loud. "But we're real close, now, Patsy. And what he did tonight, trying to lure Mrs. Dennison out to Lighthouse Point to kill her, that proves that he's getting desperate. He made a big mistake today, letting Ms. Capstone get away."

Patsy said in alarm, "You don't think he'll come after her, do you?"

Derrick shook his head slowly. "No. She couldn't see his face, he must have known that. All she could tell us was that he had dark hair."

And as soon as he said it, he knew something about that was wrong. Patsy picked up on it immediately. "That mug shot of Saddler," she said alertly. "He had blond hair."

Derrick studied the popcorn in his hand, frowning. "Easy to change the color of your hair. And it was dark in that shack. How well could she see?"

Then she said, "Isn't it kind of unusual for a serial killer to change his M.O.? I mean, if any of what you've put together so far is true, he has a definite pattern—he likes young girls who wear that strange necklace on the leather thong. Laura Capstone—or Carol Dennison for that matter—doesn't fit that profile at all."

"Why," wondered Derrick out loud, uneasily, "would a man who's established a pattern of kidnapping, raping, and killing young girls suddenly take to stalking a middle-aged woman—and man?"

"Well," offered Patsy, though he could tell she was unconvinced, "there's the fact that Guy Dennison put him in jail."

"Shit," Derrick exclaimed suddenly, and sat up straight. "I knew there was something that bothered me about that! That girl who disappeared from here last year, the Conroy girl—we've been assuming that she was part of the pattern. But Saddler was in jail last year. If she does fit the pattern ... damn it, that file won't be here until late tomorrow, earliest. We could have been on the wrong track all along!"

Patsy looked at him with sudden comprehension. "Derrick, you don't think—"

The phone rang. Derrick picked it up on the second ring, still frowning.

It was the night dispatcher. "We got a call from the marina," he said, "about a prowler who matches the description of that guy Saddler. I've dispatched three units and the sheriff said for you to meet them there."

"Son of a bitch," Derrick said, on his feet, "I'm on my way."

He couldn't believe it was all over before he got there. The marina was lit up like a landing strip, blue lights flashing, uniforms everywhere. One of the night deputies was leading away a man in handcuffs, and none too gently either. Long got a good look at his face as he passed: It was Saddler.

And he had blond hair.

Sheriff Case was standing beside a blue pickup truck with two flat tires, talking to a big man with a half-chewed cigar in his mouth. When he saw Long, Case beckoned him over.

"I'll tell you the goddamn truth, Deputy," said the sheriff, "if the public don't stop doing our damn jobs for us, we might just have to go into another line of work. This is Mr. Walt Marshall, proprietor of this fine establishment. I believe you might've been out this way not too long ago, left a flier with a picture of Mr. Saddler on it."

It had been one of the first stops Long had made when he got the mug shots in. Guy Dennison lived here; he wanted to make sure everyone who worked at the marina had a good description of the man who was stalking him. He remembered Marshall well, a big taciturn man who had glared at him over the stump of that cigar and made Long glad he wasn't Saddler, if it meant coming up on the wrong side of this man.

It looked as though his observations on that occasion had been prophetic.

"Recognized him right away," Marshall said matter-of-factly. "Saw him heading toward Guy's boat and knew it couldn't be anybody else. I called you folks, but hell, you're five minutes away at top speed. He would've been long gone by then. So when he came back out and got in his truck, I shot out his tires."

He paused, chewing on the cigar. "Could've shot him, too, I guess, but I figured you'd want to talk to him first."

Long looked at him for a moment, but was unable to determine whether or not the man was serious. He suspected he might not really want to know.

"Our men pulled up about that time," supplied Case, "so no harm done. It was a clean arrest."

"Well," said Long, "I guess that's good news then. And"—he looked at Marshall—"I guess you have a permit for that gun."

Marshall just glared at him. Case chuckled, then turned to accept a slip of paper from a young officer. He glanced at it, then tucked it in his pocket. "Truck is stolen," he said. "So are the plates. Big surprise."

Long looked around. "Where's Dennison?"

Marshall shrugged. "His car's not here. I figured he's not either."

Long glanced at Case. "I'll check out the boat."

Case nodded, then turned back to Marshall. "It'll be Deputy Long who takes your statement, if you'll come down to the office some time in the morning. Do you remember about how long it was from the time you first saw Saddler to the time you called us?"

"Three, four minutes. I thought he was just some kid looking for kicks at first. They do that sometimes, come out here looking for a place to screw or just hang out. Hell, I've caught one or two trying to take one of these babies out for a joy ride. I didn't think it was no more than that 'til I saw where he was heading, and got a look at him."

"Good spotting."

Marshall shrugged. "I figured he'd show up here sooner or later. Say, did you find out what he was carrying?"

Case started to shake his head, then looked at Marshall, frowning. "What do you mean? He was carrying something?"

"Yeah, a knapsack or something." Marshall was frowning, too. "He had it under his arm when he went down the ramp to the boat. But he didn't have it when he came back."

The two men looked at each other as understanding dawned, slowly and horribly. Case turned.

Everything from that moment was in slow motion. Blue lights spinning sickly, slowly, obliquely out of focus. Saddler's face, looking up from behind the window of the squad car. Derrick Long, stepping onto the deck of Guy Dennison's boat, knocking on the cabin door in a perfunctory manner, reaching for the latch...

Case screamed, "Long, no!" and it sounded slowed down, attenuated, dragged across the blue-back sky: "Loonnnggg .... Nooooooo. . . . "

Long turned his head at the sound of the sheriff's voice, very, very slowly, even as his hand turned the handle of the door on the cabin. The door swung open.

And the world exploded in light and flame.

Chapter Thirty-eight

S heriff John Case said quietly, "Thirty years in law enforcement. And for the first time I'm thinking it might be too long."

He stood at the window, hands in the pockets of his rumpled khakis, staring out at the first gray rays of dawn. The door to his office was closed but the clatter came through—phones ringing, doors slamming, voices, both hushed and excited, outraged and anguished: sounds of mourning, sounds of shock, sounds of vengeance.

"His wife is sick, not many people knew that. M.S. She's in remission now. A nurse down at the E.R. You probably know her. Pretty little thing."

Guy felt something twist deep in his throat; he didn't even try to speak.

"I've only had to take that walk one other time in my life. The door I knocked on that time was my captain's wife's. Right after that I left the New Orleans Police Department. Thought, for some damn stupid reason, people don't die as much in small towns. Hell, I guess I was right—most of the time."

Two things would stand out forever and uppermost about that night in Guy's mind: The look in Carol's eyes as she saw the smoldering remains of his boat, and the sight of the coroner wheeling away the body bag that contained the remains of the deputy who had given his life in the line of duty. Guy remembered wondering about that man's wife, and why he wasn't home with her, and feeling angry, so angry he couldn't even think.

It was a long time before he realized what it all meant. Saddler was in custody. Carol was safe. He was safe. Their ordeal was over, and the price they paid was a body bag containing the remains of a man they barely knew. A man who had only been trying to save their lives.

In the confusion and horror, they hadn't talked much. The sheriff, grim mouthed and taciturn, had given them only the barest details. Walt, as visibly shaken as Guy had ever seen him, kept saying, "Man, he had a bomb. I should've known it was a bomb he was carrying, I should've known it." Walt was forgetting that he was, in fact, the hero of the occasion, if such a tragic business could be said to have any heroes.

It was just before dawn when Guy drove Carol back home, and that was when she said in a small, flat voice, "It was supposed to be you. You would have been there. It would have been you." She didn't have to look at him when she said it. He knew what she was thinking, what she was feeling. The night between them was heavy with loss and fearful, guilty triumph and the weight of wrongs, terrible wrongs that could never be righted.

"Let me talk to him," Guy said hoarsely now.

"Take a number." Without turning, Case jerked a thumb over his shoulder to the squad room outside. "You and every one of those uniforms out there, two minutes alone with him ... shit, not that I'm not tempted."

"It's my daughter, damn it!"

Case turned. His shoulders were slumped, his face gray and lined. He said, "He's not talking, Guy. We've got a lawyer on the way."

Guy swore softly and pushed his hands through his hair. He knew that once the lawyer got there, any hope he had of interviewing the prisoner would be over. If he were any kind of lawyer at all, in fact, he would do his best to have his client moved out of this jail, even if it meant putting him in a state facility.

With a distant irony, Guy remembered one of his last encounters with Long had been over just such an issue. That time Guy had been an advocate of the accused.

He was just trying to catch a killer, Guy thought sickly. He was trying to find my daughter and protect my family, and he ended up dying for it.

"You can't question him without his lawyer present," Guy said suddenly, turning on Case, "but that law doesn't apply to reporters."

"Jesus Christ, Guy, you're not a reporter, you're the victim!"

"Let me talk to him, John," Guy said urgently. "It may be our last chance and you know it."

There was no alteration in the sheriff's tired, dull features for a time and Guy thought he would be turned down. Then a slow faint hardness crept into the other man's eyes and he said, "You're a reporter getting a story, that's all."

"I do it all the time," Guy assured him.

Saddler had been put in the last cell in the row, out of sight of the unemployed highway worker who was overdue on his child support, and out of hearing of the DUI who was snoring in the first cell. Saddler was reclining on the bunk when the metal door closed behind them. He got to his feet, a nasty look of recognition sliding onto his face when he saw Guy.

"You've got a visitor," Case said. "I think you know Mr. Dennison. He works for the local paper here. He just wants to ask you a few questions."

Grinning, Saddler walked up to the bars. "I just bet he does." And he looked at the sheriff. "Hey, is this legal, man? I've got my rights, you know."

But he didn't seem very concerned, and the grin returned when Case turned and walked away without a word. "Kind of a cranky old coot, ain't he?" he remarked.

Guy said, "I'm going to do you a favor, Saddler, and tell you something. You're in a backwoods jail in west Florida an hour's drive from nowhere. You're in a cell all by yourself at the end of the row where nobody can see or hear anything, and by the time that fancy lawyer of yours gets here, it could very well be too late, you following me?"

"Hey, are you threatening me?"

"You killed a cop," Guy said sharply, "and they've lynched men in this county for less than that. Believe it or not, Saddler, I might be the best friend you've got right now."

Saddler looked startled. "What the fuck are you talking about? I didn't kill nobody!"

"They didn't tell you? That bomb you planted on my boat. It went off and killed a deputy sheriff."

Saddler looked momentarily confused, then he asserted, "They don't have a thing on me. This is bullshit man. They can't prove nothing."

"You think that matters? Did you get the name of that lawyer from the sheriff? It's probably his brother-in-law. He gets paid whether you live or die."

"Get the fuck out of here, man." But Guy thought there was less cockiness in Saddler's eyes now, maybe even a touch of worry. "There are laws against intimidating a prisoner."

"I'm not intimidating you, Saddler," Guy said softly. "I haven't even started to intimidate you."

Saddler said, "What the hell do you want, man?"

"I want to know what happened to my daughter. I want you to tell me now and I want you to tell me the truth and if you do, I might even testify before the grand jury that your sorry carcass was alive when I left you."

Saddler's scowl was disdainful and dismissing. "You're not scaring me, asshole. And I don't know what you're talking about."

"You'd better be scared. Three girls are dead, raped and tortured, and their fingers are pointing straight at you. You're going to fry this time, Saddler. And I'm going to be there to watch."

"Man, you're out of your fucking mind! Where's my goddamn lawyer?"

"Where is Kelly? Who did you get to make those phone calls to my wife? What did you do to my little girl?"

"Chill the fuck out, man! How the hell am I supposed to know where she is? You can't keep up with your own kid, it ain't my fault."

Guy's hand shot through the bars and grabbed Saddler's shirt and if he could have gotten his fingers around his throat, he would have crushed his windpipe. He jerked him against the bars, hard, and had the satisfaction of seeing Saddler's smirk dissolve into slack-jawed shock as he crashed against the metal.

"You answer me, you piece you shit, you tell me the goddamn truth! What have you done with her, goddamn it!" He pushed him back and jerked him forward again, slamming him against the bars again and again. "Answer me!" He pushed back for one more blow, but the material of the shirt tore and Saddler wrenched away.

"You're crazy, man!" Saddler was screaming at him. "You're fucking crazy!"

And then someone was pulling at Guy's shoulders, demanding, "What's going on here? Are you manhandling my client?"

"He threatened me, man! He tried to fucking kill me!"

Guy jerked away from the middle-aged lawyer, shrugging off his touch, straightening his shoulders. "Sue me," he told Saddler, and walked out.

At the door that separated the cells from the interrogation room, he met Case coming down the hall with strong measured strides, a dark cold light in his eyes and a grim set to his mouth. "Now," he said, "it's my turn."

Chapter Thirty-nine

I would have killed him," Guy said. "If I could have gotten my hands on his throat, I would have killed him and I wouldn't have been sorry. I never knew that about myself before."

They were on the deck in the late morning sunshine, a pot of coffee on the table between them, the Gulf pristine and sparkling below. It was a morning like so many others in the life they had shared, and unlike any other they would ever know.

Carol said, "Do you know what I keep thinking? I keep thinking about that poor man's wife, and how it could be me who's picking out a coffin now and reserving the chapel and God, I hate myself, but I'm so glad, so glad it's not me."

Stress and sleeplessness were evident on her face in the clear morning light; her hair was tousled and her eyes were haunted. Guy reached across the table for her hand. She squeezed his fingers lightly, then pulled gently away.

She lowered her eyes and cleared her throat slightly. She said, "Everything—happened so quickly, didn't it?"

It was not the kind of question that required an answer, so Guy said nothing.

Then she looked at him, her eyes troubled and uncertain. "Guy," she said, "I want you to know that being with you again the other night was wonderful. It was exactly what I needed—"

"What we both needed," he corrected quietly, watching her.

Her smile was faint and transitory. "But everything has been so sudden, so intense, and now, this." She swallowed, and shifted her gaze. "It would be unfair of us to expect promises from each other right now, and I'm not asking them. Just—help me get through this, okay? Whatever we're going to do, let's not do it now."

Guy said, "Keeping promises was never one of my problems, Carol."

She still wouldn't look at him. "I know that."

"The ones I make, I keep."

Her eyes were pained when she looked at him. He almost preferred no eye contact at all. "When you can."

"Do you want a promise from me?"

Her eyes darkened, and her voice broke on the next words. "I don't know."

Guy got up and knelt behind her, encircling her shoulders with his arms, pressing his cheek briefly against her hair. She was fresh from the shower, smelling of warmth and soap, and he could feel her gentle nakedness beneath the terrycloth robe. He said, "We're going to get each other through this, sweetie. We can talk about promises afterward if you want to. But right now I'm not going anywhere unless you ask me to."

Carol reached up and took his hand. Her voice sounded husky, though he saw the curve of her smile. "I'm not going to ask you to. Not anytime soon, anyway."

"Good." He kissed her fingers, and stood up.

Carol took her coffee over to the rail and looked down in silence for a time. She said, "I keep telling myself the worst is over. But it's not, is it? Because by the time the investigation is over, we'll know what happened to Kelly. And all of a sudden I realize it was easier not to know."

Guy said, "I think she's alive, Carol. If Saddler wanted to hurt me, the quickest way to do that would have been to let me know he'd killed my daughter. If he was going to taunt me with anything, that would have been it—not those phone calls from a living girl. I think he might have had her, but she got away somehow—and I think he's holding that as his trump card."

Carol rubbed her forehead wearily. "I don't understand why none of this came out at his first trial. Why the phone calls, who the girl was ... why he won't tell us anything."

"It hasn't even been forty-eight hours of interrogation," Guy said. "It could take weeks."

Carol drew a slow, careful breath. "I'm not sure I can take it that long."

He came forward and put a hand on her shoulder. "Yes," he said, "you can."

Then he said, "I have to go into the office this morning. Ed called and said the TV stations had gotten wind of developments down here and we can expect a zoo. I don't think they'll track you down, but if they do, try to stay out of the line of fire, okay?"

"They won't find me. I'm supposed to go with Ken Carlton to see some property today—by boat, no less. God, it all seems so bizarre. Life goes on."

He kissed her hair. "It always has."

Then she turned around. "When is the memorial service for Deputy Long?"

"I'll call his wife today. I should—anyway."

Carol nodded, and started to go back inside to finish dressing. Then she looked back. "There haven't been any more phone calls since he was arrested."

"It's only been a day," Guy reminded her.

She nodded and tried to look reassured. But she wasn't, and neither was he.

"Why are you coming at me with them murdered kids again? I'm telling you, I didn't have anything to do with any disappearing girls and I don't know nothing about it, so just leave me the fuck alone will you?"

Saddler was putting up an angry show, but he looked haggard and worried. Sleeping conditions had not been the best in the county jail since Saddler had been in residence, and the only times Saddler had been allowed out of the interrogation room during daylight hours were for meals and bathroom breaks. It was unlikely that a big-city, civil-rights lawyer would have allowed John Case to get away with as much as he was doing, but William Soffit, whose name had rotated up on the court-appointed attorney list, was more comfortable defending DUI and teenage breaking and entering than he was murder cases, and he had not yet figured out that he just might be handling the case of the decade as far as the state of Florida was concerned.

It had been thirty-two hours since Saddler's arrest. The state police were already sending a team of investigators to try to make a case in the deaths of Mickie Anderson and Tanya Little, and the D.A. had assigned two prosecutors to the case. The sheriff figured he had until noon, tops, before his authority in this case all but disappeared.

He could hear the clock ticking like a time bomb in the back of his head.

Soffit said, "Sheriff, I've asked you repeatedly to confine your questions to the charges against my client." He didn't bother to keep the boredom out of his tone. "Mr. Saddler, do you wish to take a break?"

"What for?" Saddler shot back irritably. "All they do is leave me sit in this goddamn room. It takes two goddamn hours to get a deputy in here to take me back to my cell so I can take a goddamn leak. Can't you do something about that, for christsakes?"

Case replied equitably, "As I've explained to you, Mr. Saddler, we're a little shorthanded, right now. All my deputies are tied up investigating the disappearances of several young girls, two of whom have turned up dead. We don't have a lot of time left over for escorting prisoners back and forth from their cells. Now, if you'd like to tell us anything that might make our investigation easier, I'm sure it would free up enough personnel to make sure you get your meals and your potty breaks on time."

Saddler said, "Jesus, man, I keep telling you, you got the wrong goddamn guy! I don't know nothing—"

"We've got the right guy, all right," Case said, smiling genially. "We've got your fingerprints on the fireplace poker that you used to assault Guy Dennison. We've got ignition wire and explosive powder in that rat's nest of a trailer you've been squatting in that matches the wire and explosive used in the bomb that killed my deputy. We've got an eyewitness who saw you place the bomb. What we've got, Mr. Richard Saddler, is a cop killer who's going back into the Florida prison system and as an ex-con I'm sure you probably know how much fun that's going to be."

Saddler gave an angry hiss and started to turn away, but Case went on mildly, "And let me tell you what else we've got. We've got a convicted rapist, a pathetic little dickhead who likes to play with little girls, prowling our shores and making threatening phone calls just about the time one of those young girls washes in with the tide, dead, raped, and a victim of some pretty weird games. Then we got a whole collection of newspaper articles and fliers and photographs of Kelly Dennison in your trailer. That disturbs me, Mr. Saddler. That disturbs me a whole lot."

There had also been clippings on Carol Dennison, pictures of that big house of hers torn from some magazine, some miscellaneous scraps of newspaper with Guy Dennison's byline on them. Case had not told the Dennisons about this yet, and he hoped he didn't have to—not until he had answers to the questions he knew Dennison would ask.

Saddler was stony faced. Soffit glanced at his watch. Tick, tick...

"Now as you can see, you don't have a whole lot of bargaining room here. I'm counting three solid counts of murder one, two of kidnapping and sexual assault, one of assault with a deadly weapon, two of stalking, one breaking and entering, one illegal possession of an incendiary device, and we haven't even gotten to parole violations yet. In short, Mr. Saddler, you are in deep, deep shit. But I'll tell you what I'm going to do for you."

Case paused for a moment, letting Saddler mull over his situation and anticipate what was to come. Then he said, "You help me find Kelly Dennison and I'll make sure the judge knows you cooperated. It might mean the difference between life in prison and eight to fifteen years waiting for Old Sparky."

That was bullshit, of course, but it was amazing what a man would believe when he was desperate. And if Saddler wasn't desperate by now, he soon would be.

Saddler said, "How the hell am I supposed to do that man? I'm telling you I don't—"

"Who'd you get to make those phone calls to Carol Dennison, Saddler? Was it Kelly? Is she still alive? Who've you got working with you?"

"What phone calls? Man, I don't have to listen to this bullshit!" He turned to his lawyer. "Are you going to let him harass me like this? I done told him—"

"Because that's your trump card, Saddler, that's your chance to come out of this with a nice cozy prison cell instead of a one-way ticket to Death Row, if that girl is still alive. But you'd better tell me quick because this is a limited time offer and it expires"—Case looked at his watch—"in just about an hour."

Saddler pushed up angrily from the table. "This is bullshit."

And Soffit said, glancing at his own watch, "Are we about done here?"

At a tap on the door, Case turned with a frown of irritation. A deputy came in with a folded slip of paper, which he handed to Case, and a murmured, two-part message. The first part was good news: They had tracked down the shop in town that sold the bound-girl necklaces, and the name of the shop owner and the address were on the paper Case had been handed. The second part was not so good: The D.A. himself was waiting in Case's office for a full briefing. His time was almost up.

When the deputy was gone, Case said coldly, "Sit down, Saddler."

Saddler glared at him.

"You know that deadline I mentioned?" Case said. "It just got a lot shorter. You see, we've found the place where you bought those necklaces. All we've got to do is get the shop owner to i.d. you and we've got an unbroken chain of evidence. So if you've got anything on your mind that might save me some trouble, the time to say it is now."

Saddler was frowning. "Necklaces? What the hell are you talking about now? I ain't no damn jeweler." He gave a half-hearted laugh in the direction of his lawyer. "This is going to be the easiest case you ever tried, man. These assholes are fucking crazy."

"You're telling me you've never seen this before?"

Case removed the bound-girl necklace from his pocket and swung it in front of Saddler's face, counting on the element of surprise. He was rewarded with a scowl of disdain and then a slight narrowing of Saddler's eyes as he looked closer—a definite flicker of recognition.

"This is how you did them isn't it, Saddler?" Case demanded softly, swinging the little figure on the end of its leather thong. "You gave them this little toy, made them feel special, like a part of the club, and then, while you were raping them, to make it that much more exciting, you took the leather cord and tightened it around their necks until they were dead. Isn't that about what happened, Mr. Saddler?"

He saw Saddler swallow, and he thought, Gotcha, you son of a bitch.

But all Saddler said was, casually, "You get that off the Dennison girl?"

Case snatched the swinging pendant out of the air with his fist and returned the necklace to his pocket. To

Soffit, he said, "This interview is over. The district attorney is waiting for us in my office."

"Hey," Saddler objected as they started for the door, "don't you just leave me here! I want to go back to my cell! Don't you just walk the fuck out and—"

"I'll see what I can do," said Case.

He closed the door as soon as the attorney was through it, leaving a guard outside and Saddler alone to kick the wooden table like a child having a tantrum.

Chapter Forty

P atsy Long said, "It's good of you to come, Mr. Dennison."

"I should have come earlier. I'm sorry I didn't."

She smiled wanly and gestured for him to be seated on a sun-faded tropical print sofa.

She wasn't alone. Her mother had answered the door, and he had been vaguely introduced to sisters and sisters-in-law and cousins. They all had swollen eyes and stunned expressions, and Guy wished he had asked Carol to come with him. She was good at these things, the way women always were and men were not, and Patsy Long would have liked her. And then Guy felt a sharp stab of gratitude and wonder that seemed distinctly out of place here, because he could ask Carol, because she was safe and he was alive, and in the midst of tragedy they had found each other again; they would always have that.

But Patsy Long had nothing.

There was a pitcher of iced tea on the coffee table and Patsy offered to pour him a glass. He refused. The others withdrew to another part of the house, and he could hear the low murmur of voices, the occasional sniff or muffled sob.

Guy sat on the edge of the sofa with his hands linked between his knees, and he said, "I don't know how to tell you how sorry I am. How responsible I feel."

"Derrick was a police officer, and proud of his work. He knew the risks and so did I. I think … he would have wanted it this way. Death on the field of honor. At least, that's what I keep telling myself."

She dropped her gaze and Guy was silent. After a moment, he said quietly, "My wife and I would like to attend the service, if you don't mind."

Once again she searched for a smile. "So many people have been to pay their respects. I don't think I ever realized how many friends he had. The service is tomorrow at four, at Daltry's Funeral Home. I'd be honored to have you and your wife come."

Guy said, "I wanted to tell you that the media has picked up on the story. There were television crews at the newspaper when I left and it won't be long before they're knocking on your door. It might be a good idea for you to ask someone—a neighbor or a friend—to deal with them until you feel up to it."

"Yes. I'll do that. Thank you." Then she looked uncertain. "Are you printing the whole story in the paper tonight?"

"I don't know the whole story yet," Guy admitted. "All we can report is a follow-up on yesterday's story— that your husband died while investigating a stalking— mine."

"I couldn't read the feature on the accident," Patsy admitted, "but my mother read it out loud to me—most of it, anyway. I thought it was … dignified. Thank you."

"I didn't write it," Guy said. "But I'll pass your thanks on to the reporter."

She nodded. "Maybe that explains it then. I didn't understand why there was no mention of your daughter, and Mickie Anderson. That was what Derrick was really investigating."

He must have looked surprised, because she explained, "It probably won't sound very professional to you, but Derrick and I always discussed his cases. I was his sounding board, I guess—or at least he used to pretend that talking to me about them was helpful. Sometimes I think he really just did it because he knew that feeling like I was involved in his work gave me more of a sense of control, and made me less afraid. Of course, in the end, it really didn't matter, did it?"

Guy was silent for a moment. Then he said, "We're trying not to print any speculation about this case, especially since the other local media are looking to us for leads. The truth is, even though everyone involved— your husband included—thought Saddler was connected with the death of Mickie Anderson, and possibly the kidnapping of my daughter, there's still not any proof."

She nodded slowly, frowning. "There was something … something I meant to tell John. Something Derrick was thinking." She pressed her fingers to one temple. "Everything is so confused. Sometimes—most of the time it doesn't even seem real, you know?"

Guy said, "I've felt that way since the whole thing started. And even now that Saddler's in custody, it doesn't feel over."

"That was it," Patsy said suddenly. "Derrick was talking about patterns, and how that other girl who disappeared from here last year was probably part of the pattern—only Saddler was in jail then. He thought..."

She looked at Guy. "I think he thought Saddler was innocent."

Guy stared at her for a moment, not knowing how to respond. Then he said gently, "Mrs. Long, it was Saddler's fingerprints on the poker that knocked me out. He was seen planting the bomb on my boat. I don't see how—"

"You said it yourself," she pointed out simply. "There's evidence to connect him to everything—except the murders of those girls ... and the attack on Laura Capstone."

Now Guy was confused. "What?"

"She said the attacker had dark hair. Saddler has blond. That was what was bothering Derrick."

"She could have been mistaken," Guy said uneasily.

"But if she wasn't, Saddler didn't make the phone call that lured her to Lighthouse Point—or any of the other phone calls that were attributed to your daughter—and he didn't try to strangle her with the leather thong that was like the one Mickie Anderson or Tanya Little or your daughter Kelly had."

"And that was the only thing that tied all the girls together," Guy said slowly. "I never realized how fragile the chain of evidence was before. It all seemed so— logical."

And then he looked at her with a new and difficult understanding. "But—if your husband was right, if it wasn't Saddler who made the phone calls and attacked Laura ... that means there's a murderer still running around loose out there. And he has my daughter."

Chapter Forty-one

Nah, these here are custom-made," said Leon Beker, owner and manager of Brother Sun, Sister Moon, the new age jewelry and bookstore which had been the second one the deputies had checked in connection with the pendants. It was located on Pacific, next door to an ice cream shop which had once been the location of the Blue Dolphin where, one summer three years ago, Tanya Little had worked.

"See that craftsmanship?" Beker went on, his obvious pride in the notice his work was attracting outweighing—momentarily at least— his curiosity over why. "You don't get that off an assembly line. Each one of these babies is hand cast from a mold I created myself in the back room there. I don't offer 'em retail—you wouldn't believe the shoplifting that goes on in a place like this. These are solid pewter, you know. I hang 'em out front with the rest of the merchandise and I'm out one-fifty a pop."

Sheriff Case thought he had rarely heard such good news in his life. A limited clientele, an exclusive, handmade product—breaks like this only came along once in a career, and he was damn due for one.

"So who do you sell them to?" he asked impatiently. "If not to retail customers—"

"Well I have a catalogue. I sell a lot of jewelry to retailers across the country, I'm pretty well known in my field—"

"This piece," insisted Case, shaking the little figurine before him tightly. "This one piece, that's all I'm interested in."

"You mind if I ask why?"

"Yes."

The way he said it must have given Beker a hint as to just how far Case could be pushed, and that he was very close to that line now. A certain wariness came into his eyes. It could have been the normal uneasiness ordinary citizens are prone to feeling when being questioned by the police. It could have been something more. Case couldn't help thinking about how many kids must come through a shop like this in the course of a year, and how easy it would be to suck them in with this new age crap. He decided to run a check on Beker when he got back to the office, just in case.

In a moment, Beker said, with a forced casualness that didn't quite ring true, "Fact of the matter is, I started doing a series about five, six years back on the Tarot. I figured it would go over real big with my kind of clientele, but only a couple of pieces took off. The Devil—a lot of them go to Satanists, stands to reason, and the Hanged Man, God only knows why, and the knight of swords. This little girl, she's the eight of swords, and I never would have done another firing of her if I'd had my way. All that hair, it's got to be detailed by hand, and—"

"Why did you?" interrupted Case. "Why did you keep making them?"

"Because I had a customer," reported Beker smugly. "Walked in off the street one day, bought every one I had. He really bought that line about them being limited-edition collector's items. Didn't even blink when I told him one-fifty each. Comes back every now and then, and picks up three or four more, a hundred and fifty dollars each and every one. Hell, for that, sure it's worth running a little detail work."

Case asked, "How many have you sold him?"

"Over the years? Oh, a dozen, maybe two."

Case felt sick. "He give you a name?"

"Sure. Jack Smith. Says he's a dealer, but I don't believe it. A dealer buys in bulk and what kind of profit is he going to make once he's paid one-fifty a pop for these things? There's just not that kind of money in novelty jewelry, I'm telling you. Besides, I never see him at any of the shows. You want to know the truth? I think he's giving them to his girlfriends, probably into kinky sex." He gave the pendant on the end of the thong a nudge with his fingertip and set it swinging. "Tell the truth, it does kind of put you in mind of that, doesn't it? Is that what you guys are sniffing out? Some kind of porno ring?"

Case took out a folded flier with the mug shot of Saddler on it and thrust it toward Beker roughly. "Is this your Jack Smith?"

Beker barely glanced at it. "Not even close."

Case stared at him. "What?" Then, "Look again. Are you sure?"

"Not him." Beker shoved the paper back across the counter. "Come on, the dude was in here just last week. I ought to know what he looks like."

Case felt his blood start to run cold. "Describe him," he commanded hoarsely.

Laura said, "I had Tammy do a little research, and our man Carlton is definitely ready to deal. His investment group, Main Street Enterprises, closed the sale of Little Horse Island last week. Here's the file if you want to see it." She passed a manila folder across her desk and gave a sad shake of her head. "Forty three million dollars. And we never had a clue."

Carol took the folder absently, opening it, but only pretending to read. "That's the way the rich folks play. And we're not even close to their league."

"We might be, after today."

"Do you think so?"

"And why not, I ask you? Haven't I batted my big blue eyes at him every chance I got? Haven't you driven him all over this island, given up your free time, practically become his best friend? Aren't we due for a break, for God's sake?" And she smiled, sympathetic to Carol's weariness and cynicism. "Yes, I think this is our big chance, and yes, I think Carlton is the key—and yes, I think he would understand if you asked to postpone the meeting."

Carol shook her head. "No way. Major players like Ken Carlton don't understand excuses. Besides, I've already put him off more than once. I'm not taking the chance."

"Then let me go. It's not as though you don't have other things on your mind."

"Like you don't?" Carol closed the file and returned it with a wry smile. "Thanks for doing this. You didn't have to."

"It gave me something to do."

Carol said, "We didn't get to talk much yesterday. How are you doing?"

Laura shrugged a little uncomfortably. "Okay. Scared sometimes. Most of the time. But Winston has stayed over the last two nights, so all that lost sleep wasn't entirely wasted, if you know what I mean."

Carol's smile was more relaxed this time. "Good for you. Try not to blow it again, okay?"

Laura regarded her steadily. "I should say the same for you."

Again, Carol shook her head. "No, I think it's best to stay busy, to try to pretend everything's normal. The waiting is the worst part. I know I've been waiting for two and a half years but now…"

"Do you really think Saddler will confess?"

"I can't let myself think about that. The only thing I can think is that he knows where she is and he'll tell as part of the plea bargain."

Laura's eyes were full of sympathy and understanding. "It was Kelly's voice on the phone, Carol, I could swear it. Her voice, only deeper."

"That's what I thought at first," Carol said, "kind of husky, like she had a sore throat…"

Unconsciously, Laura's hand went to her own throat, where the narrow bruise had darkened to a sharp blue-violet. "Like mine," Laura whispered, and the two women's eyes met in horrified comprehension.

"God," Carol said, turning away. "God, I can't think about this."

Laura got up from the desk. "Go home," she said. "Go find Guy, go hold a vigil at the jail, go do what you've got to do. I'll take care of Carlton."

Carol shook her head. "No, that would leave the office without an agent. Besides, if I go to Guy's office or the jail, I'll only end up fighting my way through cameras and microphones. I don't know why I'm so jumpy anyway. I mean, the worst is over, right? Saddler's in custody and…"

"And you don't want to be here if he says something you don't want to hear," Laura said with sudden understanding.

After a moment, Carol nodded, dropping her gaze. "I know it's silly, but I feel if I'm not here to hear it, maybe he won't say it. Oh, I don't know. But right now—it's just been so much so fast and I need to be away from it, just for a little while." She hesitated. "Are you going to be okay here alone?"

"I'm not alone, Tammy's here, and Winston's picking me up at five. I won't be working late, so be back before dark."

"You can bet on that. If Guy calls…" And she shook her head. "He won't. I told him I would be out. But if…" She drew in a sharp breath and finished, "If he does, I have my cell phone."

Laura nodded in what she hoped was a reassuring way. "I'll tell him. But it's going to be okay, kid. I have one of my famous feelings."

Carol didn't point out that her famous feelings were famous for being wrong.

Chapter Forty-two

Derrick Long's official mail had been quietly and routinely forwarded to Case's desk. He found the padded envelope from the Gulf County Sheriffs Department at the bottom of a rather thin stack. He had never doubted it would be there; Long was too efficient an investigator not to have followed through on the last order he received before going off duty. Case had asked him to find out if there were any similarities between Melissa Conroy and Mickie Anderson. The file inside the envelope was the result.

Case skimmed it quickly, but didn't find anything he didn't already know. He dialed the detective in charge of the case and found him at his desk.

"Listen," he said, after introducing himself and explaining his interest in the case, "what I want to know is if anyone you talked to ever mentioned this girl wearing a necklace, real unusual, a leather thong with a pewter figurine of a girl with her hands tied behind her back and a blindfold over her eyes."

The detective sounded puzzled, and asked him to repeat the description. A little impatiently, Case did.

"No," allowed the detective slowly, "I can't say I recall anything like that. You've got a description of what she was wearing there in the file. But if you want, I'll check with the parents."

"And her friends," suggested Case. "It's the kind of thing she might show off to her friends but not her parents. It's real important."

"I'll do what I can."

"Will it take long?"

"Sheriff Case, those parents haven't let a day go by that they haven't been on the phone to me three or four times. I don't think they'll put off returning my call if they don't happen to be in."

"All right, thanks. I'll wait to hear." He hung up the phone, frustrated that he couldn't do more.

"Where the hell have you been?" demanded a voice at his door and when he looked up, Fred Lindy, the district attorney for St. Theresa County was standing there scowling at him.

"Investigating a case. Last I heard that was my job."

Generally, Case liked Lindy. He was sometimes a little too political for the sheriff's taste—the seersucker suits and straw hats, for example, looked better in a newspaper photo than they did in real life—but for the most part the two men thought alike and worked well together. The past couple of days and the promise of a sensational case had brought out the worst in Lindy, however, and he was beginning to get on the sheriff's nerves.

"Well, let somebody know where you're going next time. I've been buzzing your office for the past two hours."

"I don't work for you, Lindy."

"You're right about that." Lindy dropped his attitude and came inside, closing the door behind him. "We both work for the people of this county, which is something we might not do much longer if we blow this one, but I guess you know that. How sure are you that this pervert Saddler murdered those two girls?"

A treacherous little voice muttered in his head: *Less sure than I was four hours ago.* But out loud he answered brusquely, "You know what I've got, Lindy, and you know what I don't have. You can either go with it or not."

Lindy hooked his toe around a hard chair in front of the desk, pulling it out, and he sat down. This time of year he abandoned seersucker in favor of blue chambray shirts and narrow red suspenders, every inch the country lawyer. He wore round steel-frame glasses and beneath them, the expression on his face was a mixture of anxiety and satisfaction. It was a look Case knew well, and it meant good news, because Lindy only worried when things were going his way.

He said, "I used the time while you were gone to talk to our prisoner a little bit."

Lindy was a hell of an interrogator. He had a flat, dry voice and unwavering gaze that had been known to put the fear of God into men stronger than Saddler. When he spoke, you listened. What he said, you believed for a fact. Case could threaten and manipulate and fire off two-sided questions, but when Fred Lindy said, "We're going to trial," and walked out of a room, the accused started to quake. He had that way about him.

"He doesn't like me, for some reason," Lindy went on. "He's ready to talk, but he won't talk to anybody but you. He's scared, Case. We've got him now."

Case pushed up from the desk and started down the corridor with the D.A. keeping in step. "He wants his lawyer there. I figure he's going to try to make some kind of deal. No deals, you got that?"

Case gestured for the deputy to open the door.

"Case, did you hear me? You are not authorized to make any deals!"

The door closed on his voice and Saddler and Soffit got up from the table at which they had been conferring. "I've tried to explain to Mr. Saddler," said Soffit, "that it does no good for me to be here unless the prosecutor is, too. If you'd just ask Mr. Lindy to step in—"

"I'm here," Case said, glaring at Saddler. "Talk."

Saddler licked his lips nervously and sat down again. "Look, I ain't taking no murder rap. What happened on that boat—it was an accident and you know it. You were there, goddamn it. You saw. The other son of a bitch, he's crazy, man. He's trying to pin these girls on me, and this goddamn state is so screwed up, he might just get away with it. What chance has an ex-con got, I ask you that? I ain't taking the rap for something I didn't do. I'm not going to be your goddamn scapegoat!"

Case turned toward the door.

"Wait! Listen, you said something about a deal. You still interested?"

Case turned. "What kind of deal?"

Soffit said. "I really must advise you, Mr. Saddler not to say anything further until I can—"

Saddler turned on him. "Shut up, you little prick! They're trying to turn me into a goddamn serial killer and I ain't copping to that, do you hear me?"

He turned back to Case. "Look, I messed with Dennison's head a little, made a few phone calls, no harm done. And so maybe I watched his wife sometimes from the beach, but hey, she leaves her curtains open, what does she expect?"

Case said, "And did you call her up, pretending to be her daughter? Or did you have somebody else do it?"

Saddler shook his head impatiently. "Man, that's what I'm trying to tell you, I ain't never called that woman in my life and I don't fucking know anybody I could get to do it, either. What's the big goddamn deal, anyway?"

Once again Case turned for the door.

"Hey, wait, now listen to me! Look, okay, I was in her house that night, but I don't know nothing about any phone calls to her, you got that? And when Dennison walked in on me, I might've beaned him with the poker, but no permanent damage done, so what are we talking here? B&E, three years, six months served? I can deal with that."

Case looked at him coldly. "What about Laura Capstone? Did you lure her to the beach and try to strangle her to death?"

"Who the hell is she? What are you doing, trying to charge me with every crime that's been committed in this crappy little county since I got out? Jesus Christ!"

For the first time he shot a nervous glance at his lawyer, but saw no help forthcoming from that quarter. He folded his arms on the table and leaned forward, addressing Case with all the sincerity he could muster. "That bomb, man, you know I didn't mean to hurt no one. That boat was empty, man!"

"You're not telling me anything I don't already know. I'm real busy here so if that's all——"

"That necklace," Saddler said quickly. "You seemed mighty interested in it. You think it's got something to do with that Dennison girl and you'd be right."

Case said carefully, "Go on."

"Mr. Saddler, as your attorney—"

"When I first got here, I spent some time casing the Dennison place. Them houses down on the beach, they're so easy to get into, a three-year-old could do it. So sometimes I'd just go into one and have myself a look around. Never stole nothing, never did no harm. But I saw some mighty interesting things."

Case said, "I'm getting bored."

"Like one of them houses, great big fancy place right down the beach in front of the Dennisons'. In a drawer in the upstairs bedroom, all kinds of shit, child porn shit, weird stuff, man. And that necklace, that's where I saw it. There were a bunch of them all hung on hooks in a row, like neckties or something. And photos. Snapshots of real live girls, stripped down and trussed up just like the girl on that necklace. Some of them looked pretty bad, man."

Case heard his voice from a very great distance. "Can you tell me exactly where this house was?"

"They've all got names on little plaques at the end of the boardwalk, and I remember this one real well. Hell, man, I can give you the address."

His private phone was ringing when Case walked back to his office with Lindy dogging his heels demanding to know what Saddler had said. Case ignored him and snatched up the receiver, speaking into it brusquely.

"Yeah, Sheriff, this is Detective Rickman over in Gulf County. I talked to the Conroy girl's kid sister, and she recognized that necklace you described. Said she got it from a boyfriend a few days before she disappeared.

Only I don't think it was a regular boyfriend, if you know what I mean. This guy sounded older, and Melissa was going to an awful lot of trouble to keep him secret from her folks. We always thought he had something to do with her disappearance, but we never could track him down—or even be sure he existed. Is any of this helping?"

"Yes," Case said hoarsely, "it is."

"If any of it pans out, you'll send it on over, won't you?"

"Yes. Thanks, Detective."

He hung up the phone and Lindy demanded, "What? What's going on?"

It was a moment before Case could trust himself to pick up the phone, another to trust that his voice would work. He had to consciously steady his breathing as he spoke into the mouthpiece. "Get me Judge Wagner," he said. "And do it quick."

Then he turned around, and told Lindy what was going on.

Chapter Forty-three

How're you holding up, sweet thing?" Walt Marshall spoke around a mouthful of unlit cigar, squinting into the sun as Carol came down the pier toward him.

"Holding up, Walt," she answered with a tired smile and embraced him. "Thank you for what you did the other night," she told him sincerely as she stepped away.

He shook his head sadly. "Not enough, baby doll, not enough. This whole mess, it's shook me up real bad, I don't mind telling you."

Carol replied, "It's shaken a lot of us, Walt."

She had parked on the side of the marina that was opposite that on which the larger boats were docked so that she would not have to pass the charred rubble with its police-tape barrier that was all that remained of Guy's boat. Now she could not even look in that direction.

And Walt, trying to lighten her mood, said, "Well, hell, baby, I guess it ain't every day a man gets to be a bigshot, anyway. How'd you like that picture of me in the paper?"

Carol smiled. "It didn't show off your best side."

He chuckled. "I didn't know I had one, sweetheart. But I got to speak my piece for two television stations and I reckon that's about as much fame as I ever want to see. What are they getting out of that son of a bitch, anyway? Anything helpful?"

Carol hesitated. "Not really. Not yet."

He nodded, understanding, and did not question further.

Carol said, glancing around. "I'm supposed to meet a client here. Ken Carlton, do you know him?"

Walt nodded. "Sure, he's got that hot-looking Donzi over there." He nodded toward the gleaming blue-and-white speedboat bobbing between two smaller recreational boats at the end of the pier. "Takes it out just about every day, rain, shine, or small craft advisory. That is some mean vehicle. If I didn't know better, I'd say he was running drugs in that thing, as much time as he spends on it."

Carol managed a laugh. "I think we can eliminate that possibility, Walt."

"Yeah, I guess. Not too many drug runners dock their yachts in a little place like St. T. every year, and he has got one gorgeous-looking sleeper for serious travel."

"The advantages of being independently wealthy, Walt," Carol replied, and then saw Ken come up from below decks of the Donzi. Ken spotted her and lifted an arm in greeting. She waved back.

Walt said, scanning the horizon, "Ya'll aren't thinking of taking her out today, are you? Looks to be blowing up a squall."

The sun poked through dark-blue-lined clouds in brilliant intermittent spikes, and the darkening water line in the distance did suggest rough seas. Carol found herself half-hoping a storm would force them to turn back, and then she thought with sudden intensity, *This is stupid. I should be with my husband at a time like this. I should be with Guy.*

Ken waved to her again, and sensibility reasserted itself. A couple of hours and her obligation would be fulfilled. There were twelve other realtors on this island who would have fought her for the chance to take a ride in Ken Carlton's Donzi and she owed it to Laura—and herself—to see it through.

She said, "We're just taking a quick run over to Little Horse. We'll be back before the rain falls."

Walt nodded. "Well, I wouldn't take her any further than that. You watch out for snakes now."

Carol grinned and waved at him as she started down the pier.

"I was beginning to think you might not make it," Ken greeted her when she came within speaking distance. "It looks like we'll be heading into a little chop."

"As long as the rain holds off." Carol extended her hand and he helped her onboard. "Beautiful boat. I can see why you'd want to bring it down for the summer."

"It was a necessity as much time as I've been spending over at Little Horse," Ken admitted. "Not to mention the fact that I'm never really comfortable unless I know I've got access to the water. Of course, I was beginning to think I'd picked the wrong marina when that boat blew up the other night. Did you hear about that?"

Carol had that strange feeling of having walked into another world—a world where other people actually walked and talked and lived their lives, where the center of the universe was not Carol Dennison and her struggles and adversities.

She said, "That was my husband's boat."

He looked stunned. "My God. I guess I should have known that, but I haven't listened to any local news the past couple of days. I only knew about the boat because I asked about the damage to the pier. Was anyone hurt?"

Carol wondered vaguely how anyone, even a tourist, could have failed to hear what had been going on here the past few days. And yet, in a way, the innocence of ignorance was restorative, and she did not want to drag up too many details.

She swallowed hard and said, "A deputy sheriff was killed, actually. My husband wasn't on board at the time."

He said, "Thank God for that." She saw the question in his eyes, but was grateful that he did not push for more information. He said, "I'm sorry for all your troubles. I have a feeling I'm imposing on you at a bad time. Has there been any word on your daughter?"

Carol shook her head, mustering a grateful smile. "Thank you for your concern. But please, don't think of yourself as imposing. Actually, the one thing I needed most was to get away for a little while."

"Then maybe this afternoon will work out to the benefit of both of us," he said, and started the engine.

Laura looked up when Guy came in. "You just missed her," she said. Then noticing the distracted look in his eyes, she added anxiously, "Is there news?"

"Laura," he said abruptly, "how sure are you about the color of your attacker's hair?"

"Well, it was dark, and the stocking over his head, and I wasn't taking notes ... under the circumstances, as sure as anyone could be I guess. Has something happened?"

"So it was definitely brown?"

"Brownish, as far as I could tell."

"Like mine?"

"Maybe not that dark."

"So it could have been blond."

"No, not blond. Why, what's happening?"

"Saddler's hair is blond," Guy said.

Laura stared at him. "Kind of dirty blond? Brownish blond?"

"White blond, going gray. Noticeably blond, Laura."

She swallowed hard. "Maybe he dyed it."

"You're that sure? You couldn't have been mistaken about the color?"

"It was too dark to tell the difference between brown and red and black, maybe, but between blond and brown—I think I would have noticed, Guy. I think I would have remembered. He must have dyed it."

Her intercom buzzed. When she picked it up, Tammy said, "Sheriff Case is on line one."

"Is he looking for Mr. Dennison?"

Guy stepped forward curiously.

"No. He asked for either you or Carol."

"Thanks, Tammy." She pushed the button. "This is Laura Capstone, Sheriff."

She could feel Guy listening attentively.

The sheriff said abruptly, "I have your office on my emergency contact list for the address 'Sea Dunes' in Gulf View Acres. Are you the owners or just the managers?"

"We own it, but it's rented now. What—"

"Who to?"

"Um, Sheriff, I'm not sure I'm supposed to—"

"Who's living there now, Miss Capstone, and how long has he been there?"

"It's rented to a man from Tallahassee by the name of Ken Carlton. He moved in at the first of the month, but I happen to know he's not at home now. Could you please tell me——"

"I'm on my way over there with a search warrant. If you want to meet me there with a key, it would save some trouble."

"I—yes, all right. I'm five minutes away."

She hung up the phone and looked at Guy in stunned disbelief. "A search warrant," she said. "This place just gets crazier and crazier."

"Ken Carlton," Guy said. "Why does that name sound familiar to me?"

"Because that's Carol's client—the one she's showing property to today. And now the police want to search his house."

Guy said, "I'm following you over there."

Chapter Forty-four

Carol let herself be hypnotized by the flash of sun and shadow on her face, the rhythmic bounce and slap of the waves, the roar of engines that precluded conversation and even thought. It was not until they had left the channel cut and started to circle around the back side of Lighthouse Island that she realized they were headed in the wrong direction.

She leaned forward and tapped Ken on the shoulder. As she did, the wind caught the hood of his windbreaker, tossing it away from his neck, and she noticed for the first time the jagged abrasions on the back of his neck.

He turned to her and she shouted, "We're going the wrong way!"

He eased back on the throttle to make conversation easier. "Just a little detour," he shouted back. "You said you needed to get away. I thought you might enjoy a tour of the lighthouse."

Carol pointed to the sky, and the deep indigo clouds from which the sun had only momentarily escaped. The water beneath the boat was a fascinating gradation from deep purple to gold-touched aqua, but the chop was growing stronger.

"We're going to get caught in the rain," she called back. "Besides, there's no place to dock there. You can't bring a boat in."

He just smiled. "There've been a few improvements since you were there last."

"You've been there before?"

"Once or twice. You see, I own it, actually."

Carol was merely confused.

"You—own it?"

"Oh, yes. I'm the second owner, in fact. It went on the auction block shortly after the lighthouse was condemned, and a development company bought it with the thought of building a resort much like the one I described to you. It was completely unfeasible, of course, and my company bought it after they went bankrupt. I can't believe you didn't know all this."

"I might have. Seems I heard something about the first sale."

"It was never brokered," he said, by way of an explanation. "That's probably why you didn't know about it."

She raised her voice to be heard above the pitch of the motor, still struggling with her confusion. "Will Lighthouse Island be part of your development, too?"

He turned his attention to the wheel for a moment, turning the boat against the wake and toward the leeward side of the little island. Then he answered, "No, it's an utterly impractical investment. The state refused to grant permission for a causeway to be built and there's no ground water. The cost of development would be astronomical and it would never pay for itself. But it's perfect for my purposes."

"Which are?"

He looked back at her and answered simply, "Privacy."

That was the first time she suspected something might be wrong.

The sheriff and three deputies were waiting when Laura and Guy parked their cars in the street before the sand-colored Mediterranean-style house known as Sea Dunes. Fred Lindy, the district attorney, was with them. Guy nodded at him curiously, and Lindy groaned.

"Jesus, Dennison, there's no story here. Go home."

Laura regarded the entire group nervously, but proceeded up the steps with authority. The group followed, with Sheriff Case in the lead.

"You are making a huge mistake," Laura said as she unlocked the door. "Do you have any idea who this guy is? He could bankrupt the whole county if he decides to sue you for false—whatever."

"Then we'll just have to be real careful not to piss him off."

She stepped back from the door and the law officers entered, with Lindy staying close to the sheriff. Case called over his shoulder to the deputies who followed him in, "Ledbetter, Harly, take the downstairs. Humphries, you're with me. Keep it neat, boys, you're not at home."

Guy caught Laura's arm as she started to go in. "What is Carol doing with this man?" he demanded quietly.

"Jesus, Guy, he's a client." She twisted her arm away irritably. "Now let me go before these goons break something I have to pay for."

Guy caught up with Case and Lindy at the bottom of the stairs. Lindy said, "You don't belong in here, Dennison."

"I'm part owner."

Case grunted, "Yeah, in what divorce court?"

Guy said, "Carol is with him right now."

The two men's eyes met for a moment, and nothing else was said.

Laura followed them up the stairs anxiously. "Sheriff, this is making me really nervous. I know you've got a warrant but—"

The sheriff said, "This Carlton fellow. Is he about five-ten, auburn hair, gray eyes, thirty-five or so?"

Laura's footsteps slowed as they reached the landing. "Well, yes ... I've only seen him once but... yes."

"How many bedrooms?"

"What? Um, three. This is the master." She gestured toward the first open door.

The sheriff nodded to Humphries. "You take the one next door."

Lindy went with Humphries, and Guy and Laura followed the sheriff into the bedroom, which was unnaturally neat for a bachelor. "How come a single man would want three bedrooms?" asked Case, sweeping the room with a cataloging glance.

"Three bedroom units are the smallest houses we have. This is a luxury market, Sheriff. If you would just tell me what you're looking for—"

"It might be best if you waited outside, Ms. Capstone."

Laura, it was obvious, had no intention of doing anything of the sort, and she stood by impatiently while he slid open drawers and removed neat stacks of shirts and underwear, then took the drawers off their runners one by one, turning them upside down, his expression tightening as the procedure repeatedly yielded nothing.

"Drugs?" Laura said. Her voice held a mixture of incredulity and indignation. "Is that what this is about? Drugs?"

"Son of a bitch," Case muttered, scowling. "My own damn fault for listening to that lying piece of scum…"

Guy said, "You talked to Patsy Long, didn't you?"

The sheriff didn't respond.

Guy's heart started to pound. He repeated, "You talked to her and you found something else to back up Long's theory."

The sheriff slammed closed a closet door.

Guy looked at Laura. "You said you couldn't have told the difference between brown hair and red hair in the dark."

Laura's face reflected an utter lack of comprehension.

"Sheriff." They all turned to see Humphries standing in he doorway. "They were hanging in the closet in the other room," the deputy said, "a dozen of them or so. Like—trophies."

He held out his hand and all eyes focused on what he held. From his outspread fingers dangled a leather thong with a silver-colored figurine on the end.

Carol said, "You never mentioned to me that you come here every year."

He had dark glasses on, even though the sun had been swallowed by darkening clouds and showed no sign of returning any time soon. He looked at her, and she saw nothing but her own dim reflection in the black lenses. "Who said I did?"

"Walt Marshall, back at the marina. He said you dock your yacht there every spring."

Ken turned his attention to the wheel. "He must be mistaken."

Carol knew that Walt never made a mistake about a boat or a paying customer, but there was no way to point that out without sounding argumentative. Why would Ken lie?

A gust of wind kicked spray over the deck and tore wildly at Carol's hair. She fumbled with the scarf she wore about her neck, bringing it up and over her hair, and that was when she noticed the scrapes on Ken's neck again.

"What happened to your neck?" she inquired, but the wind and the engine noise must have drowned her out because he didn't respond.

She leaned forward and tapped him on the shoulder. "How did you hurt your neck?" she repeated, louder.

He turned and looked at her, his expression as opaque as the concealing lenses of his glasses. Then the sun reappeared, briefly, from behind the clouds, and he smiled.

"Looks like we're going to miss the rain after all," he said.

"Damn it, I can't remember her number." Guy stared at the telephone receiver in his hand in helpless frustration, his lips white and compressed tightly together.

"Here, give it to me." Laura snatched it from him and began to punch out numbers. "We won't alarm her, just tell her to come home, that there's been an emergency."

"She'll be alarmed," Guy said. "But it's better than—"

He didn't finish.

Laura's knuckles were white on the receiver as she held it to her ear. "We don't know anything. This doesn't prove anything. It could be a coincidence. I'll just tell her to come home. It's ringing."

Guy waited impatiently. They were using the phone in the hallway outside the master suite. Uniformed deputies moved past them up and down the stairs, in and out of rooms. They were no longer bothering to be neat. They were tearing the place apart.

"Come on, Carol," Guy muttered. "Answer the damn phone."

Laura looked worried. "Maybe she left it in the car."

"She wouldn't do that."

"She could have. She was distracted."

"Could she be out of range? You said they were going to Little Horse—"

"No, there's a service message when you get out of range. It's just ringing."

Guy became aware, in that slow, cold blood-draining way one sometimes has on the brink of crisis, that a quiet had come over the upper hallway. Guy had had that feeling twice before. The first time was when Carol told him she wanted a divorce, and he looked in her eyes and saw that she meant it. The second time was when he learned that Kelly was missing.

He turned and he knew from the look in John Case's eyes that what he was about to hear was worse than either of those things.

"Guy," Case said quietly, and then he dropped his gaze. He cleared his throat. "I need you to identify this," he said.

And he handed him a photograph.

Chapter Forty-five

Whan Carol's phone started to ring, she was absurdly grateful. She quickly pulled open her purse and fumbled for it.

"Don't answer that, Carol," Ken said pleasantly.

She tried to laugh. "Don't be silly, Ken. I'm a working girl, remember, and I'm on duty."

She got the phone in her hand, out of the purse; she started to flip it open. And in a single smooth motion so swift she never saw it coming, Ken swooped forward and snatched it out of her hand and dropped it into the ocean.

Her cry of angry protest came out choked and outraged, and he laughed. "Technology," he commented conversationally. "Damned nuisance. That's how this whole thing started, don't you know that? The little nowhere town of St. Theresa-by-the-Sea gets a cell tower and the timing couldn't be worse."

He looked straight at her and he said, "Didn't you ever wonder why she never called you before?"

"She's alive, Guy," John Case said quietly. "The others ... some of them weren't."

The girl in the photograph was standing against a white wall in a bra and panties that hung on her thin frame. A white cloth bound her eyes and her hands were behind her back, presumably tied. There were bruises on her ribs, her cheek was blackened and misshapen, and there was a thin dark line around her throat. There was a necklace or heavy cord around her neck, from which was suspended a small pewter figurine. Her hair was lank and tangled. But the photograph was of Kelly, Guy's daughter.

He heard Laura's soft sound of horror as she looked over his shoulder at the snapshot. But he didn't feel her touch his arm. He was not aware that the snapshot was crumpling in his hand until the sheriff seized his wrist and tightened the grip hard enough to hurt. Guy's fingers slowly opened, and the sheriff removed the photograph.

His face was cold and bathed with sweat. It hurt to breathe. The world narrowed to a single pinpoint of focus that was that photograph of his daughter, burned indelibly on his mind.

Someone said his name, but he threw up both hands to ward the speaker off. He started to walk away, but his legs were rubbery, he stumbled. He sat in the nearest chair and rested his elbows on his knees, staring straight ahead, breathing slow and deep. And then the twisting pain in his chest seemed to explode and he bowed his head and covered his face with his hands as his shoulders began to shake.

"Damn cell phones," Ken continued easily. "The trouble with them is that after a while they become like furniture, like clothing—you forget they're there. You forget to watch out for them. Now on the boat, it was easy to keep her away from the radio, not that she could have figured out how to work it if she tried. But phones … I never predicted it. It was totally my fault."

Carol was breathing fast and light. The sun sparkling on the water looked like slivers of broken glass, and every time the boat bounced over a wave, another shard of dizziness stabbed into her brain. It made sense. It would never make sense. Kelly. He was talking about Kelly…

She managed, barely above a whisper, "You know where she is. All this time … you've had her. You … you've got my daughter!" The small nebulous cloud of horror and disbelief that had settled just below her solar plexus suddenly hardened into a knot of fury, of certain truth, of blind unthinking hysteria, and she leapt to her feet, launching herself at him, screaming, "You've got Kelly! Where is she? What have you done with my daughter!"

There was a moment of quick surprise on his face, as though he didn't understand why she should be angry, but it was ephemeral. Almost in the same motion as she stood, he swung out an arm to block her attack, catching her in the stomach, pushing her backward. He didn't use much force and the blow didn't hurt, but Carol stumbled back and for a moment struggled with her balance in the pitching sea. He watched with idle interest as she flailed her arms and twisted around, catching the back of her seat just before going over.

He smiled. "Good. I'd hate to lose you after all this trouble. Now settle down, for God's sake, before you get us both killed. This baby can handle just about anything, but the sea is getting rough."

Listening to him, Carol could almost believe she had imagined the previous conversation. Imagined it, or misinterpreted it. No, he hadn't kidnapped Kelly. No, he hadn't kept her prisoner for two and a half years. He hadn't been the one she was so frightened of. The one who hurt her, the one from whom she couldn't get away. No, the person who had done that was insane, a madman, a conscienceless psychopath. Ken Carlton wasn't insane. He was a billionaire, a genius, a highly successful man, and he was just as reasonable when he spoke to her now as he had ever been when they discussed real estate.

Carol said hoarsely, irrationally, "But—we checked you out. You're Ken Carlton, you've won all those awards, you just closed that development deal... we checked you out."

He laughed, seeming genuinely amused. "Just because a man has a successful career doesn't mean he can't have outside interests, now does it?" He moved the throttle up. "Hold on, darling, I'm taking her around."

Sheriff Case said in a low voice, "Ms. Capstone, where did Mrs. Dennison say they were going?"

Laura pressed her hand to her chest, as though she was finding it hard to breathe. Her face was paper white and lipstick clung to her cracked lips; she stared at the sheriff as though she hadn't heard him.

He started to repeat the question when she said, "It was—they were going to Little Horse Island. He owns it, he's going to develop it. It's just a routine property tour. You don't understand—"

Sheriff Case turned around and barked out, "Ledbetter, Humphries, Little Horse Island. Get a description of his boat from the marina. Notify the Coast Guard. Tell them we're on our way." He started down the stairs.

Laura cried, "But he wouldn't hurt Carol!"

"We hope not, Ms. Capstone."

"It couldn't be him," Laura whispered, and her hand went to her throat, rubbing. "It couldn't be." But her eyes were dark with fear and the truth.

They came around the back side of the island, and the chop grew more severe. He cut the engine and let the little boat ride the waves that tossed them toward shore. The only sound was the slap of water, loud and foamy, and the screech of gulls. He turned away from the outboard, resting both elbows on his bare knees, and smiled at her as he said, "There, that's better. We can hear each other. And I think we should have a talk before I take you in."

Carol gripped the bottom of the seat with both hands, holding on to a balance that was precarious both mentally and physically. The cockpit of the Donzi was neither wide nor deep and she realized suddenly neither of them was wearing a life vest. But it wasn't the surging dark water below that terrified her most; it wasn't even the man before her who now held her captive as effectively as he had held Kelly for the past two and a half years. What frightened her more than either of those things was not knowing.

"Where is she?" Carol demanded tightly, very carefully. "What have you done with her?"

"All in good time," he assured her. "That's why I brought you here, after all. She wanted her mother, so I brought her mother. What could be more accommodating?

"I want you to know," he added, and his expression grew serious as he said it, "That I adore Kelly. The others..." he made a snapping motion with his wrist. "They were trash, flotsam, and I did them a favor by giving them what they deserved. Hell, they were runaways, dropouts. Nobody'd miss them or even notice when they were gone. I gave them one moment of glory in their sorry, pathetic little lives, one moment of believing there was someone who cared about them, and I like to think that on some level they were grateful for that.

"But Kelly was different, and now that I've met her mother, I understand why. She had class. She had potential. She didn't belong with those others. So I kept her. And whenever I'd grow discouraged, I'd look at her and think there is hope, after all, for mankind. I might have kept her forever, a symbol of what perfection could be. But she wasn't perfect after all. She betrayed me."

Carol saw his face darken with the words and something clenched and twisted inside her. She didn't think she could bear to hear the next words and she thought if he said them, if after all this, he said them, she would launch herself at him and claw out his eyes, kick in his ribcage, tear out his throat with her bare hands.

He said, "She stole my telephone and she called you not once, but over and over again. Even after I gave her a chance to earn my trust, she continued to disobey me. She made me so angry. I always make mistakes when I'm angry. Mickie Anderson was a mistake, obviously, but after what she did ... She was the one who called you that day I was in the car with you, wasn't she? Jesus, can you imagine how I felt? I trusted those girls, both of them, left the telephone there just to prove how much I trusted them, and they betrayed me."

He hesitated, then added with a hint of surprise, "So did Tanya Little. The only two bodies that have ever been found, and both of them done while I was angry. Tanya was a great disappointment to me, much like Kelly in a lot of ways. She wasn't as refined as Kelly, of course, but she was amusing—had a wicked mouth on her, and she never got tired of standing up to me. I should have known that would lead to trouble. I kept her too long, even after I had Kelly. I was selfish. I should have been satisfied with one. And then Tanya, the little bitch, tried to escape when we were docked in Mexico Beach, can you believe that? I had to track her down. I was angry and I was careless and it could have been all over." He shook his head slowly, remembering. "I've been a lot more careful since then."

Carol said, "Kelly…"

"Ah, yes, Kelly." He came back to the present. "You see what can be accomplished when one keeps one's composure and thinks things through? From near-tragedy was born the kernel of an idea. Mother and daughter, a vignette. Something I'd never attempted before. Of course, from a merely practical standpoint, it all worked out well, too. I could keep an eye on you while staying close to my, er, hobby, and being in the midst of spring break—well, as I've said, it's amazing how the universe will work for you, sometimes, if you just keep your head."

Her hands tightened on the seat. Something metal dug into her fingers and she realized vaguely it was one of the clips that held the fire extinguisher in place beneath the seat. She held on more tightly as the boat rode a wave. "You could have taken me at any time," she said. "That morning on the beach, the day we looked at property..."

He nodded. "Of course. That was my plan, both times. The day you got the phone call from Mickie—"

"It wasn't Mickie," Carol said automatically. "She called herself Tanya."

Ken frowned. "She did? I'll be damned." And then his face made a wry, unconcerned expression. "It was Kelly then, too. Sometimes she calls herself Tanya. It's a game we play. And poor little Mickie died for nothing." He shrugged. "Not that she would have lived much longer anyway. But she made a nice object lesson on obedience and I hated to get rid of her so soon."

Carol's fingers sought the clips beneath her seat and held firm.

Carlton shrugged. "At any rate, I had no intention of driving you home that night, and I wouldn't have let you leave if you hadn't gotten that second call—from your husband, was it? Bad timing once again. Fortunately, I'm a patient man."

"You were watching my house, you broke in..." But then she stopped, and shook her head. "It couldn't have been you who attacked Guy. We were together when it happened."

"Of course, it wasn't me. I had no interest in your husband. It was you I wanted."

"Why—did you wait so long?"

He smiled. "I could have taken you by force, but I don't do that. They always come willingly, my girls. Why should you be any different? Although, I must say, I was beginning to get a little anxious, after all the times I tried to get you out on the water and you refused. Even Kelly wasn't this much trouble."

"Laura," Carol said. "You called her, lured her to the beach——"

"It was Kelly, I told you that. I'm afraid I had to get rather severe with her before she'd make the call, and then she almost blew it at the end. But I think she honestly thought the woman who answered the phone was you, and how could I know? The thing is, after they found the Anderson girl's body, I was getting a little nervous. Foolish I know, but I panicked. Then you turned me down when I tried to get you out here, so what else was I to do? Some people might say, of course, that it was a mistake to let her get away, but I like to think of it as merely generous. And no harm was done."

"No," whispered Carol. "No harm."

"Surrounded by water." Laura said softly, staring out the window. "On the card they were bound and blindfolded and surrounded by water. Oh, my God." She gripped Guy's arm. "Guy, you don't think he's keeping Kelly on that island..."

The sheriff was rushing down the stairs. The Coast Guard had already been notified, his men dispatched. Guy lunged to his feet. "I'm going with them," he said, pushing past Laura.

"Guy, no!" Once again she clutched at his arm.

Guy looked back impatiently. Her eyes were big and focused on something beyond him. He started to pull away.

Slowly she turned her eyes to Guy. "Kelly—when she called, that's what she said. The tower. The tower, Guy," she repeated with forced intensity.

She was staring, dark eyed, over his shoulder. Guy turned around.

Framed in the picture window behind him, close enough to touch, was the lighthouse.

Chapter Forty-six

Carol's hands were gripping the seat with painful force, partly for balance as the boat rose and sank with the waves, partly out of sheer terror. She could see a small dock ahead, the narrowest of approaches between two rock jetties. The boat was riding the waves at an oblique angle toward the rocks; it would take engine power to dock safely.

She said, "Are you going to let Kelly go now? Is that why you brought me here, for an exchange? Because I'll stay, of course, I'll stay, and I won't be half the trouble she's been. Just let her go home."

He smiled. "You are naive. Of course I'm not going to let her go home, or you either. I have something very special planned for both of you. But first there are rituals to be observed."

He reached into the pocket of his windbreaker and brought out a necklace. Carol recognized it immediately: the leather thong, the pewter figurine.

"It's not the same, of course," he acknowledged. "It means nothing to you. But humor me." He held it out to her. "Put it on."

"No." Carol said.

He looked surprised.

"If you're going to kill me with it, I'm not going to make it easy for you."

He sat back, a thoughtful set to his mouth. "So. You are clever."

"Clever enough to know you won't get away with this, whatever it is. Everyone knows I'm with you—my partner, my husband, the police."

"Of course, they do." He said it dismissingly. "Do you really think they worry me?"

"They know about the necklace. They know about Tanya Little and Mickie Anderson and Laura, for God's sake. Do you really think they won't be able to put the rest of it together?"

He smiled benignly. "My dear girl, they haven't been able to put it together in half a dozen years. Why should I think they could do so now?"

Carol inched forward on her seat, pretending to seek balance against the waves while her fingers worked the clips on the fire extinguisher. The rocks loomed closer. He would have to start the engine soon. "The necklace. Tell me about it."

He shrugged. "It's a conceit, really, not much more than that. It attracts the girls, makes them feel special, sometimes for the first time in their life. Makes them feel they have a friend when they need one most, someone who understands when their parents and their friends have deserted them. I've never taken a girl against her will. They always come to me."

"Do you always use that phony line about being a movie director?"

He was amused. "Not always. You'd be surprised how often it's effective though. For the most part I'm simply a friend who manages to be there when they need me. In Kelly's case, because I know that's why you're asking, I knew she wanted to go to that concert. I offered to give her a ride. I told her to keep our friendship a secret, and she did. They always do."

"And then later, you make them write a note so their parents won't keep looking for them."

"Only if I think it's necessary. Some parents never look at all."

"You took an awful chance, using the same pickup line every time, writing the same note ... using a place as small as St. T. to take the girls from."

"Don't be absurd, it wasn't just St. T. Daytona, Panama City, Miami—wherever the girls in trouble are, that's where I would be. But St. T. did have the added convenience of being off the beaten track, and during spring break there was just enough confusion to make anything possible. And the deep water dock, of course, so that I could bring in whatever kind of boat I needed. That was important."

Carol felt ill. Determinedly, she concentrated on the task at hand, inching her fingers back until she felt the slim neck and hooked nozzle of the fire extinguisher. "And you kept them on your boat?"

"My yacht, yes, most of the time. Always docking in a different port, no one ever notices much or asks questions. With Tanya, then with Kelly, it became something of an inconvenience. But I have a safe room in my house in Tallahassee, which made it a little easier. Until I found this place."

He turned toward the lighthouse, smiling. "Do you know what it reminds me of? A castle keep. That's what I thought the first time I saw it. It will become my own little fortress on my own island kingdom."

He turned back to her and made a move as though he was going to reach for her. Desperation shot through Carol, and she said quickly, "But why? Why Kelly, why any of them? Why do you do this?"

"Power, of course," he answered easily. "That's the why of everything, isn't it? To take unstructured, undisciplined young flesh and mold it, shape it, control it, turn it into what I want it to be. To capture the runaways and the rebels and break their spirits, to take the bad girls and show them what bad really means—it's a rush, I won't deny that. To have a living, breathing human being to do with whatever I want—to dress as I want, treat as I want, play with if I want, hurt if I want, even mutilate and dismember if I want."

The horror Carol was feeling must have been reflected on her face because he smiled, seeming to enjoy her reaction. And he finished simply, "Because I want to, that's why. And that's what power is all about. Because I can. Now, don't ask any more stupid questions. Put the necklace on." He held it out to her.

Carol lifted her chin. Her fingers closed around the neck of fire extinguisher; with her other hand, she tried to loosen the base. "No." she said.

He stood up with a grimace of impatience and swung toward her, his hands lifted to drop the necklace over her head.

With all the strength she possessed, Carol lunged to her feet, wrenching the fire extinguisher out of its bracket. In the same motion, she pivoted on the balls of her feet and swung it toward him hard, as hard as she could.

In her mind's eye she saw it all very clearly, in stark slow motion and three-dimensional detail. She saw his auburn head framed against a darkening sky. She saw spray slap the side of the boat and leave shiny beads on the gleaming trim. She saw the surprise on his face as he turned his head to follow her motion; surprise that was already fading to amusement as he ducked one shoulder in a half turn and reached out to grab the weapon from her. She felt the impact as he blocked her forward motion and sent her reeling backward, the backs of her legs crashing against the cockpit. She felt herself losing balance, saw the grim glee in his eyes as he wrenched the fire extinguisher from her and she began to fall backward into the icy water.

But that was not what happened. That was what she expected to happen, that was what she knew would happen the moment she shot to her feet and, in retrospect, that was what should have happened. She did see the surprise on his face and that was what saved her. He was accustomed to dealing with uncertain teenage girls, easily controlled, easily predictable. He had not been prepared when Laura fought back, and he was not prepared now for a mother's rage.

She swung the fire extinguisher with all her might and felt the staggering impact as it struck him across the middle. A wrenching pain tore through the muscles of her back and she cried out, stumbling backward, even as she saw him do the same. Only it was Carlton who lurched back against the cockpit, Carlton who flailed for balance, Carlton who, with a cry that registered nothing more than stark disbelief, plunged into the dark, tumbling water.

There was a part of Carol that wanted to collapse on the floor of the boat and cover her head with her hands and scream and scream. There was a part that wanted to search the waves for signs of life, and a part of her that hoped grimly and coldly that there were none. But the only part that mattered was the part that saw the rocks, throwing back foam in angry gusts, lurching ever closer. And beyond the rocks, the lighthouse.

Pain stabbed from her hip to her lung as Carol threw herself toward the control panel. She grabbed the wheel, planting her feet for balance and gritting her teeth against the pain as she fumbled for the ignition. A moment of panic shot through her as she thought Ken might have removed the key, but no, it was there. She turned the key frantically and was rewarded with a shuddering cough from the engine, then nothing.

The boat turned broadside against a wave just then and the crash sounded like cannon fire. Flames stabbed through the muscles of Carol's back as she struggled to remain upright. A sheet of water lapped over the deck and soaked her canvas shoes.

Carol grabbed the key again, then forced herself to stop, to think, to push back panic. She was not an expert seawoman by any means, but she had been in and around boats all of her married life. She knew enough to cope with an emergency in just about anything that was seaworthy, from a wave-runner to a sailboat. She had never been at the controls of anything this powerful, it was true, but one inboard was very much like another. She could manage this, if only she didn't panic.

She thought briefly about life vests, and a radio, both of which were no doubt located below if they were onboard at all. She dared not let go of the wheel long enough to search for them. When the boat crested the next wave, it did a half-turn and she saw the rock jetty was less than thirty yards away. The boat was caught in the undertow and being sucked in.

She found the gearshift and levered it into what she hoped was the neutral position. She turned the key again.

Nothing happened. Was the battery dead? Had that last wave gotten into the engine? She turned it again, frantically. "Start, damn you. Start…"

The powerful twin inboards roared to life, drowning out the sounds of the surf and wind. With a sob of relief, Carol turned the wheel hard to port, away from the rocks, and forced the engine into gear.

The boat shot forward with a force that threw Carol against the wheel and she almost blacked out with the pain. The deck tilted beneath her, a fan of water slapped hard against her face and for a terrifying moment she thought the boat had capsized.

Sobbing for breath, she wrestled the wheel against the power of the tide, easing up on the throttle experimentally. The sun was lost behind a cloud just then and the air was abruptly cold against her face.

Carol looked back over her shoulder. The water was a dark, undulating sheet of purple and indigo, and the sky had lost its color. Just across the channel, less than twenty minutes away, was St. T., safety, the promise of help.

Carol did not even consider turning the boat in that direction.

Chapter Forty-seven

I need a boat," Guy demanded as he burst through the door. A sheet of rain and wind followed him into Walt's office.

"Yeah, I just bet you do——" Then Walt looked up and saw the sheriff standing beside Guy and he removed the cigar from his mouth. "What the hell's going on? Your office just called wanting the description of Ken Carlton's boat." He looked at Guy. "Say, is Carol——"

"No time to explain," Case said. "We need something that'll get us to Lighthouse Island fast."

"He's got Carol!" Guy pushed around the counter and searched the pegboard for a familiar set of keys.

"Hold on there, pardner, nobody's got Carol. I saw her myself leave with——" And understanding darkened his face. "Holy shit," he said softly.

Guy said, "He killed all those girls, Walt. And he had a picture of Kelly."

"We've got to move, Walt," Case said urgently.

Moving with startling speed for a man his size, Walt snatched up a key and pushed it across the counter. "The

Sea Ray," he said. "It's the only thing that has a chance of catching them in this weather. Go on, git!"

Guy snatched up the keys before the sheriff could take them and Case did not waste time arguing. They ran out into the rain.

By the time the makeshift pier came into view, a fine cold needlelike rain was driving into her face and the sea had taken on a blue-green ferocity that was typical of brief, angry storms offshore. It took two tries, and when she finally got close enough to the stanchion to drop anchor, a surging wave tossed the boat against the pier with a grinding, crashing sound on the hull.

She had never been good at docking procedures, and Guy's patience had generally not endured her attempts. But today, there was no one to take over, no one to cast the line for her, no one to hold the wheel steady in the tossing sea. The pain in her back had transformed into an odd, tingling numbness, but she was beginning to lose sensation in her left hand. A lifetime passed while she cast the line, missed, reeled it in, cast again.

Finally the loop caught and held, and she drew it tight, pulling with all her strength to bring the boat close enough to allow her to climb out onto the pier. The boat rose and fell beneath her and her feet almost slipped on the slippery deck, but she grabbed on to the pier and pulled herself up.

The lighthouse loomed like a giant, prehistoric monolith before her. Its huge, scarred white base took up her entire field of vision, blocking out the sea and the sky, filling the whole world.

The last time Carol had been here, there had been a small sandy beach, tall sea grasses, and twisted pines.

Pink and white flowers had bloomed in the spring, and deep orange ones in the fall. Now all that remained of the land upon which the lighthouse sat was covered with broken rocks from the dredging. It was ugly, barren, deserted.

Carol drew an arm across her face to clear her vision of sea spray and rain, and it was only then that she realized the distant wheezing sound in her ears was not the wind at all but her own desperate, chopping sobs.

The rain turned into a dampening mist as she scrambled over the rocks, slipping and sometimes falling hard on her hands and knees. Her hair clung limply to her scalp, and rainwater mixed with the sea spray and tears that trickled down her face and into her mouth. She could no longer feel the fingers of her left hand, and when she tried to move that arm, the response was slow and clumsy.

She reached the lighthouse in a state of shock and exhaustion, and for a moment, simply pressed against the rough tabby with both hands, unable to understand why she couldn't get inside. Then she realized that she had come upon the lighthouse from the backside, and she followed the circular wall around until she came upon a boarded-up entrance.

The barricaded doorway was mere yards from the ocean. Surf splashed against the boulders below and spray blew through Carol's clothes and hair. She pounded a fist against the barricade in a gesture of helplessness and frustration, and then stepped back, gasping for breath, to examine the situation.

The entrance was covered with a thick sheet of plywood reinforced by several crossed two-by- fours. She didn't see any opening or weakness in the barricade and she wondered for a moment— just a moment—

whether Carlton had been lying after all, whether anyone had been here in years, whether it was all some trick.

Furiously, she pounded the door again with her closed fist. "Kelly!" she screamed.

She heard nothing in reply, but she hadn't expected to. The rumble and crash of the surf drowned out everything except her own gasping breath. She tugged at one of the two-by-fours, knowing it was useless, and met nothing but resistance. Carlton was lying—no one had been here since the Coast Guard had boarded up the place.

And then she noticed one of the nails in the topmost board was protruding a little. It was still new looking, not rust-covered like the others that had been driven, deeper. In fact, the wood itself had not yet weathered to gray, and if it had remained undisturbed since the Coast Guard closed down the lighthouse, the entire barricade would have rotted away by now.

Frantically, Carol looked around for something with which to pry away the boards. What would Carlton have used? He had to have a way of getting in and out.

The boat. He had planned on bringing her here; of course, he would have whatever tools he needed in the boat.

Half running, half crawling, Carol made her way back to the boat. All the while she was expecting that when she reached the pier, the boat would have disappeared, pulled loose from its moorings or swallowed up by the sea and she would be stranded, helpless to find Kelly, powerless to save even herself.

But the boat was there. She climbed over the rocking, swaying deck and half leapt, half tumbled into the cockpit. She threw open the hatch that led below decks and left it open to the meager light that seeped in from outside. She stood for a moment, bracing herself against the bulkhead as she tried to get her bearings, gasping with exertion and desperation. She could see nothing but shadows. Shadowed bunks, shadowed lockers...

She dropped to her knees and jerked on the handle of the locker beneath the nearest bunk, expecting it to be locked. But why should it be? There was no law against carrying ordinary marine tools.

And that was exactly what she found, in a gray watertight pouch in the second locker—a neat and organized assortment of hand tools. Two screwdrivers, a plastic box of heavyduty nails and screws, a sharp-pointed awl, a set of wrenches, pliers, a hammer.

She zipped the pouch closed when she saw the hammer and spun to her feet. "Thank you," she whispered, and lurched toward the square of light that was the open door.

Then the light disappeared and at first she didn't understand why. Slowly a figure straightened in the doorway, moving toward her, filling up the space, blocking out the light.

Ken Carlton was dripping seawater and rivulets of blood from half a dozen small injuries. His hair was slick against his scalp and his clothes molded to his body. His smile was stiff and cold.

"Well now," he said, "this is going to be more interesting than I thought."

Chapter Forty-eight

arol's hands were tied behind her back with a length of marine rope, and the position turned her spinal column into a pillar of fire. Carlton had to drag her the last few dozen yards over the rocks because her knees kept buckling with the pain. She couldn't have escaped from him, even if he had not taken the keys to the boat.

He used the hammer to pry out the nails on one side of the barricade, creating an opening large enough to crawl through. He pushed Carol through first and, unbalanced, she fell facedown onto the hard floor. He was close behind her, jerking her upright, but not before she noticed the dark, splattered stains on the floor in front of her eyes. She refused to look at the floor again, but she couldn't get the stains out of her mind.

The narrow windows that climbed the height of the structure had not been boarded up, and they admitted enough light to dispel most of the shadows and give substance to shapes. Carol saw some concrete blocks and cardboard boxes, a couple of five-gallon buckets, and a tray and trowel encrusted with mortar. In the center of the room, where the metal spiral staircase climbed to the top of the lighthouse, an enclosure had been built of concrete blocks. It had a narrow wooden door with a brass padlock. Carol's heart began to pound when she saw it, seeming to shake her ribcage.

Noticing the direction of her gaze, Ken said in a tone that was almost conversational, "It was a stroke of luck, really. Most of the supplies I needed—the wood and the concrete blocks and a lot of the hardware—were mine for the taking with what was left of the old lighthouse keeper's cabin. It would have been a perfect setup." He looked around almost wistfully. "Almost inaccessible, completely sound proof ... but you've spoiled all that, haven't you?"

He did not sound angry over the fact, however, merely stressed and distracted. He glanced at Carol as he thrust a hand into his pocket. He brought out the ring that contained the boat keys and separated one of them from the others. "Now that you've gone to all this trouble," he said, "you may as well see what you've come for."

He went over to the concrete-block room and unlocked the padlock on the door. She heard sounds inside, scraping metal and his low voice, and in another moment he came out.

The girl was wearing a soiled white dress that came to her ankles, and a pewter figurine on a leather thong around her neck. Her feet were bare and manacled with a heavy chain no more than eighteen inches long. One wrist was enclosed in a handcuff that was attached to another, slightly longer chain that ended in a second handcuff. Carlton held the chain in the middle as he led her out of the room, although he did so almost casually, as though knowing she had long since passed the point of resistance.

Her dark hair was tangled and her face was pale and pinched. There was a discolored line around her throat where the leather thong of the necklace had been drawn tight so often it had created an almost permanent bruise. Her arms and shoulders were tiny, birdlike, painfully thin. Her eyes were sunken and dull. But it was Kelly.

Carol sobbed her name and took a stumbling step toward her. Needles of ice twisted through her spine and shot down her leg. She fell to her knees, sobbing, struggling against the rope that bound her hands. "Kelly! Oh, God, what has he done to you? Kelly, honey, it's all right. It's Mama. Kelly!"

Nothing registered in the girl's eyes.

Ken came over to her, jerking on the chain to which Kelly was handcuffed so that she was forced to follow. She did so with dragging, uncertain steps. He said, "A touching scene. But ineffective without the embrace, I think."

He knelt behind her and Carol felt the sawing, slicing motions of a blade against her ropes. The ropes fell away, but before Carol could free herself, he grabbed her right wrist and fastened the other handcuff at the end of the chain around it. At that moment, Carol didn't care. She flung her arm around Kelly and held her tightly, weeping, caressing her hair, kissing her cold cheek.

"Kelly, sweetheart, oh, baby, I'm here, I'm here..." Words of joy, words of relief, words of welcome and comfort—nonsense words. "Kelly, I'm sorry, I'm so sorry, I love you. Thank God, I found you, thank God..."

Nonsense words.

Carol lifted a shaking hand to Kelly's face, smoothing back the tangled hair, greedily examining the adored familiar face with all its ravages, the face she had feared she would never see again, Kelly's face. "Kelly," she whispered, searching those eyes in love and fear, hoping and daring not to hope that, having found Kelly alive, she might also find her sane and sound. "Kelly, it's Mama. I'm here. Baby, talk to me."

She said, quite clearly, "I'm not Kelly. My name is Tanya. Kelly is dead."

Carol's heart stopped.

For those few intense moments since she had flung herself against Kelly, the world had ceased its forward motion. This cold and ugly tower with its terrifying stains on the floor, the chains on their wrists and the madman who had put them there—all of it had faded beneath the joy of finding her daughter again. But now it all came tumbling back.

Carol twisted around to look at Carlton. He was smiling. "Tanya and Kelly were companions, you know, for almost a year," he explained. "They became quite close, which worked out well for all of us. The girls had someone to keep them company, I had someone to use to keep the other one in line when it was necessary. I wanted a matched set, and they were perfect—until, of course...." And his face darkened with the memory. "Well, you know what happened. Kelly took it quite badly, I'm afraid. Sometimes she becomes a little deranged on the subject, pretending to be Tanya, as though that might bring her back or some such nonsense." He shrugged. "I really don't mind. We all have our little games, don't we, lover?"

He bent as though to reach for Kelly and Carol flung herself between them, drawing Kelly's face against her shoulder and holding her tightly. "Get away from her, you bastard!"

Ken Carlton laughed. "Like mother, like daughter. Looks as though I have my matched set after all. Too bad it can't last."

Carol ignored him, stroking her daughter's hair. "Kelly, honey, it's okay, don't be afraid. I'm here, I'll take care of you now."

And this time when she held Kelly's face, and looked into her eyes, she saw confusion there, and uncertainty. Kelly said in a small voice, "Mama?"

Hot tears scalded Carol's eyes, tightened her chest. "Yes!"

She clasped Kelly to her, and in a moment Kelly's arms went hesitantly, slowly around Carol's neck. Carol sobbed with joy, and the tentative embrace tightened, became more certain.

"Don't cry, Mama," Kelly said. Her voice was husky and tremulous. "It wasn't so bad."

But then Carol couldn't stop crying. She held her daughter and she felt those small strong arms tighten around her, and tears soaked her face and choked off her breath and once again the world stopped. She was holding her daughter, and the moment was complete unto itself.

Ken's hand came down hard on her shoulder, pulling her away. "All right, that's enough. The storm's passing and we've got to get moving."

Kelly clutched at Carol when Ken tried to pull her to her feet, and Carol grasped her hand. "Ken, listen to me," she said, gasping on the last of her tears, "this isn't going to work. You know it isn't. My husband and my partner both know I'm with you. Walt Marshall saw me leave with you! They know we wouldn't stay out in the storm. They probably have the Coast Guard looking for us now. You're not going to get away with this one, Ken. In your heart you know that. I don't care what you've done in the past, it's over now. Just let us go. There's no point in going further."

Ken just smiled. "You still don't get it, do you? The beauty of being me is that I can get away with anything. I have a passport, I have a boat, I have bank accounts in ports all around the world. Do you think I'm afraid of your husband or the Coast Guard or the police? I'll be out of their jurisdiction long before they find your body, and you'd be surprised how many countries do not have extradition treaties with the U.S."

He walked across the room and picked up his tool pouch, bringing it back to where they huddled together. He leaned down again, but this time it was not to reach for Kelly. He took Carol's chin in his hand and tilted her face upward toward his. He said, in a soft and pleasant tone, "Have you figured it out yet, Carol? Why it was so important for me to bring you here? I'm going to kill you, yes, but only because I have to. Perhaps it will comfort you to know that you will be a better mother to Kelly in death than you ever were in life. You will teach her her finest lesson, as she watches you die."

He unzipped the pouch and reached inside, bringing out another pewter necklace on a leather thong. He dropped it over Carol's head.

Carol's right hand was handcuffed and held tightly by Kelly's. Her left arm, as desperately as she tried to lift it, would move only a few inches. She couldn't have wrenched away from Ken, even if she had known what he was about to do, and she didn't.

He took hold of her blouse with both hands and ripped it open. Kelly screamed. Carol was too shocked to make a sound.

Carlton said, in a tone that was most polite, "You belong to me now, and clothes are not allowed unless I say so. I don't say so."

He reached for her again, hands pulling roughly at her bra, and suddenly the small, breathless sounds Kelly had been making at her mother's side became a roar. The roar was a word and it reverberated throughout the enclosure: "NOOO!"

She lunged to her feet, swinging upward with her chained hand. Carol was flung backward but carried by the momentum, both emotional and physical, and she scrambled to her feet as the chain tightened between them. Startled, Ken stepped back. The tool pouch fell and scattered its contents at their feet. In a single motion, Carol and Kelly swung forward. Ken threw up his hands to stop them but too late. The chain caught him across the throat and the three of them tumbled to the floor in a heap.

Ken was stunned, groaning and gasping for breath, as Carol and Kelly scrambled quickly away from him. Carol gasped, "Kelly! Hurry, baby, we've got to——"

But Kelly was scrambling on the ground for something and she didn't turn when Carol cried out. Carol was on one side of Ken; the three-foot chain stretched across him to Kelly. Any moment now he would regain enough consciousness to grab that chain and bring them both down. Carol screamed, "Kelly!" and pulled on the chain.

Kelly spun around on her knees. She had the awl in both hands.

Carol cried, "Kelly, no!"

Kelly raised the awl in the air above Carlton's throat. Her eyes were fastened on the soft tissue below that was her goal. She said breathlessly, "I'm going to kill him. I have to kill him. You know I do, so he won't hurt anyone else. You know I have to, Mama, I have to!"

Carol knew that if she jerked on the chain Kelly would drop the awl. She would drop the awl, but she might not move fast enough and Ken would have them both. Awareness was beginning to congeal in his eyes. Kelly was the only defense they had, and even that might not be enough.

Ken's eyes moved from the ice-pick-sharp tool poised just inches above his throat to the eyes of the girl who held it. Carol saw him swallow. Carol dared not speak, or even breathe. Her eyes were riveted on Kelly.

Kelly's knuckles were white on the handle of the awl. The set to her jaw was sharp and square, like her father's. Her eyes were enormous and dark and on fire, but it was a cold fire, the fire of a long dark dream finally brought to life, the fire of justice served, of grim and desperate certainty. Carol thought she had known heartbreak. But until she saw that look in her daughter's eyes, she had not begun to understand what heartbreak was.

Carlton met that look in Kelly's eyes without fear. He said quietly, "You're not going to hurt me, precious. Put it down."

Kelly's hands tightened on the handle of the awl. "I'm going to kill you," she said, with equal quietness, equal certainty.

"No, you won't. You need me. You depend on me. You can't hurt me."

For a moment, Kelly seemed to falter. Carol thought desperately, No, Kelly, don't, but she did not know whether she meant *don't kill him* or *don't back away*.

And in the next moment it didn't matter because Kelly arched her back and raised the awl for its downward plunge before Carol could react, before she could stop her, even if she had wanted to, had intended to.

"Kelly!"

The voice was male, and it came from behind them, and it was as dear to Carol as her own life. She knew it, her breath caught in her chest for the love of it, but she dared not take her eyes off Kelly. Kelly stopped her motion in midair, a confused hesitation crossing her face.

Carlton saw his chance and tensed to take it, but the next sound from the doorway was equally as identifiable, though less familiar. It was the sound of a round being loaded into a chamber, ready to fire. The low rough drawl commanded, "Freeze, you son of a bitch." John Case's footsteps, slow and measured, approached.

Sweat began to bead on Ken Carlton's upper lip. His eyes were locked on Kelly's. Kelly's eyes were locked on his. The muscles in her small arms trembled with the effort to hold the deadly weapon steady—or perhaps to prevent herself from driving it home.

Behind her, Guy's voice said, "It's okay, honey. Daddy's here. I'll take care of you now."

Kelly dropped her head, and then her arms. A sob broke from her throat.

In two swift steps, Guy was upon them, sweeping them both out of the path of danger and into his arms.

Epilogue

They wore cable knit sweaters and jeans, for although the sun was bright, the late November wind had a bite to it as it swept across the deck of the big gothic gray house on the beach. Faraway someone tossed a stick for a black dog and watched it trudge into the breaking surf to retrieve it; closer in, a man and a woman tossed a Frisbee against the wind, laughing and chasing when it went awry. Other than that, the beach was deserted.

"This is my favorite time of year," Carol said, cupping her hands around a mug of hot brandied coffee and smiling at the antics of the Frisbee players.

"Thanksgiving is just around the corner," Laura said.

"You're invited. We're having turkey."

"Thanks." She swung one foot onto the cedar picnic table and sipped her own coffee. "I'm going to New York for Christmas," she announced.

Carol stared at her, and Laura looked embarrassed.

"Winston has a buying trip," she explained. "And I thought—Rockefeller Center, Saks Fifth Avenue, all expenses paid—why not? Could be kind of—I don't know, romantic."

Carol smiled. "Good for you. Bring him for Thanksgiving. And don't worry about the office. I'm closing the whole place down for the holidays."

Laura chuckled, and then let the amusement fade into a smile of quiet contentment. Her eyes, too, went to the Frisbee players on the beach.

After a time she said, "She looks so good, Carol. Sometimes it's eerie. Almost as though she'd never been away."

Carol nodded. "For us, too. Sometimes she forgets, you know. She wakes up in the morning and she's fourteen years old again and none of it ever happened and, God, I want to keep it that way. But I know I can't."

"What do her doctors say?"

Carol smiled. "She's doing good. Better than they expected. She'll make a full recovery." And now a quiet determination came into her voice. "I know she will."

Laura reached across the space between their chairs and squeezed her hand. "I know she will, too."

Another moment passed in sun and wind and comfortable silence. Then Laura said, "Is it true Carlton is pleading insanity?"

Carol nodded. "He'll get life in a mental hospital. I don't know whether to be furious or relieved. It spares Kelly, but..."

She didn't finish. She kept thinking about that moment when Kelly held the awl above Carlton's throat, when Carol could have stopped her but she hadn't. These days, however, she thought about it with less and less guilt.

Laura said nothing, and didn't have to. Carol knew her friend understood what she had left unsaid.

"There are parts of it," Carol said in a moment, "that the doctors don't think Kelly will ever remember. I'm glad."

Laura agreed quietly, "Me, too." Then, "Will she be able to start school next year?"

"We're bringing in a tutor after the holidays and we think she'll be ready for classes by next fall. She'll probably only be a year behind. She's so bright, Laura. And she picked up her music right where she left off." Carol gave a throaty chuckle. "I never thought I'd be glad to hear that CD player going again. And you should see the sound system Guy's getting her for Christmas. Never mind, you don't have to see it; you'll hear it. No matter where you are on the island, you'll hear it."

Laura chuckled. "I consider myself forewarned."

Carol's smile was wistful as she looked down the beach. "Sometimes," she said, "it's almost as though we turned back time."

Laura looked at her across the brim of her coffee cup. "If anyone deserves to do that," she said, "you three do."

Carol smiled gratefully, and they were silent for a time, watching the beach.

The Laura asked, "So how are you doing? Are you going to be up for cooking a turkey?"

Carol had spent most of the summer recovering from surgery for a pinched nerve in her back, and she winced at the memory. "You better believe it. I might not be able to lift it out of the oven," she admitted, "but that's what husbands are for."

Laura gave her a thumbs-up, then cocked her head toward the sliding glass door that was open to the faint sound of a buzzer from within. "That must be the lasagna. Do you want me to go down and call in the troops?"

Carol hesitated. "Do you mind setting the table instead? I'd like to do it."

Laura smiled. "Be my guest."

Carol put aside her coffee cup and went down the stairs to the beach. But she didn't call to them right away. She stood on the boardwalk watching them play, the dark-haired girl and the tall slim man, loving them with all her might, and listening to the sound of their laughter on the wind.

More spine-chilling suspense by Donna Ball

NIGHT FLIGHT

She's an innocent woman who knows too much. Now she's fleeing through the night without a weapon and without a phone, and her only hope for survival is a cop who's willing to risk his badge—and his life—to save her.

SANCTUARY

They came to the peaceful, untouched mountain wilderness of Eastern Tennessee seeking an escape from the madness of modern life. But when they built their luxury homes in the heart of virgin forest they did not realize that something was there before them... something ancient and horrible; something that will make them believe that monsters are real.

EXPOSURE

Everyone has secrets, but when talk show host Jessamine's Cray's stalker begins to use her past to terrorize her, no one is safe ... not her family, her friends, her coworkers, and especially not Jess herself.

RENEGADE by Donna Boyd

Enter a world of dark mystery and intense passion, where human destiny is controlled by a species of powerful, exotic creatures. Once they ruled the Tundra, now they rule Wall Street. Once they fought with teeth and claws, now they fight with wealth and power. And only one man can stop them... if he dares.

Also by Donna Ball

The Raine Stockton Dog Mystery Series

SMOKY MOUNTAIN TRACKS

A child has been kidnapped and abandoned in the mountain wilderness. Her only hope is Raine Stockton and her young, untried tracking dog Cisco...

RAPID FIRE

Raine and Cisco are brought in by the FBI to track a terrorist ...a terrorist who just happens to be Raine's old boyfriend.

GUN SHY

Raine rescues a traumatized service dog, and soon begins to suspect he is the only witness to a murder.

BONE YARD

Cisco digs up human remains in Raine's back yard, and mayhem ensues. Could this be evidence of a serial killer, a long-unsolved mass murder, or something even more sinister... and closer to home?

SILENT NIGHT

It's Christmastime in Hansonville, N.C., and Raine and Cisco are on the trail of a missing teenager. But when a newborn is abandoned in the manger of the town's living nativity and Raine walks in on what appears to be the scene of a murder, the holidays take a very dark turn for everyone concerned.

THE DEAD SEASON

Raine and Cisco lead a group of troubled youth on a winter wilderness hike that turns deadly.

The Ladybug Farm series by Donna Ball
For every woman who ever had a dream... or a friend
A Year on Ladybug Farm
At Home on Ladybug Farm
Love Letters from Ladybug Farm
Christmas on Ladybug Farm
Recipes from Ladybug Farm

Romance Revisited by Donna Ball

MATCHMAKER, MATCHMAKER

He was a cowboy looking for a wife. She was a lady specializing in brides. They were made for each other... They just didn't know it yet.

A MAN AROUND THE HOUSE

He was the answer to a busy working woman's dreams. But was he too good to be true?

FOR KEEPS

He's an animal trainer who lives by one rule: never get attached. She's a social worker who knows all too well the price of getting involved. It may take an entire menagerie to bring them together, but eventually they both must learn that sometimes it's for keeps.

STEALING SAVANNAH

He was a reformed jewel thief now turned security expert and her job depended on his expertise. But could he be trusted not to steal the most valuable jewel of all-- her heart?

UNDER COVER

She's working on the biggest case of her life, and her cover has already been blown-- by the very man she's investigating. Now they must work together to solve an even bigger mystery-- their future together.

THE STORMRIDERS

They were thunder and lightning when they were married, and their divorce has been no less turbulent. But trapped together during a deadly blizzard with the lives of an entire community depending on them, they discover what's really important, and that some storms are worth riding out.

INTERLUDE

Sometimes a chance encounter is over in a moment, and sometimes it can last a lifetime.

CAST ADRIFT

She was a marine biologist on short deadline to find a very important dolphin, with no time to waste on romance. He was a sailor who knew there could only be one captain on his ship-- himself. But two weeks at sea together could change everything...

ABOUT THE AUTHOR....

Donna Ball is the author of over a hundred novels under several different pseudonyms in a variety of genres that include romance, mystery, suspense, paranormal, western adventure, historical and women's fiction. Recent popular series include the Ladybug Farm series by Berkley Books and the Raine Stockton Dog Mystery series. Donna is an avid dog lover and her dogs have won numerous titles for agility, obedience and canine musical freestyle. She lives in a restored Victorian Barn in the heart of the Blue Ridge mountains with a variety of four-footed companions. You can contact her at www.donnaball.net

25159057R00205

Made in the USA
Middletown, DE
19 October 2015